LENA ANDERSSON

Acts of Infidelity

Translated from the Swedish by Saskia Vogel

PICADOR

First published 2018 by Picador
an imprint of Pan Macmillan
20 New Wharf Road, London N1 9RR
Associated companies throughout the world
www.panmacmillan.com

ISBN 978-1-5098-4112-7

The author and publisher gratefully acknowledge The Swedish Arts Council
as sponsor of the translation costs.

Typeset by Palimpsest Book Production Limited, Falkirk, Stirlingshire
Printed and bound by CPI Group (UK) Ltd, Croydon, CR0 4YY

Visit www.picador.com to read more about all our books
and to buy them. You will also find features, author interviews and
news of any author events, and you can sign up for e-newsletters
so that you're always first to hear about our new releases.

Prologue

Around lunchtime one day in late April, a flower shop in Karlstad received an unusual request. An order for a single gerbera was phoned in by someone who asked for a name other than their own to be signed on the accompanying card. The flower was to be delivered at six p.m. to the Scala Theatre on Västra Torggatan 1. The instructions were thorough and detailed, and they conveyed the fear that there'd be a hitch, that the task would not be carried out to perfection. It all seemed to be of the utmost importance to the caller.

At ten to six, the florist walked through the cold spring night to the Scala with a wrapped gerbera and a card that read:

> *Remember me? How could we possibly forget . . .*
> *Meet me on the main square here in Karlstad at 10 p.m.*
> *I'll be wearing an oxeye daisy in my buttonhole. Ilse.*

The flower was left at the ticket window, and the florist explained who was to receive it and that it should be handed over during the curtain call. She too gave thorough and detailed instructions to ensure nothing could go wrong. Then she went home to her husband, and over dinner they speculated about the sort of relationship that might include a game like this.

'She must love him very much,' the florist said with a dreamy tone, perhaps unfamiliar to her husband, for it rattled and piqued him as he sat in his place at the table, the one he'd always had.

'A woman like that doesn't love,' he said.

'Do you think he's already spoken for?'

'You don't get up to that sort of nonsense for a husband.'

'Perhaps one should.'

'If women went after available men, then they wouldn't have to prance about coming up with these tricks. Anyway, I suppose actors are known for having this effect on women.'

The florist put down her knife and fork and said:

'She was so anxious. You know, she called several times to ask if we'd got the card right, and reminded us not to sign it with her real name, but with "Ilse". She spelled it three times, and at five thirty she called to ensure I was on my way. She was self-conscious but firm – quite a handful – all the while saying how sorry she was for making extra work for us. It was touching, somehow. But it makes you wonder.'

Ester Nilsson had arrived at that point in her life when each birthday leaves its mark. It had happened, she determined, when she had turned thirty-seven. In the past five years, she'd published four more slim but densely written volumes, two of anti-lyrical poetry and two philosophical examinations. As for love, she had been in full and continuous operation and hadn't taken on board any lessons she considered inhibiting; to be precise, she thought that such lessons must always be weighed against the risk of tedium and tristesse, of a passive life ruled by the fear of rejection and failure.

You could also say that she hadn't yielded to cynicism. She suffered from a certain naive open-mindedness: each situation, each person was new and had to be judged independently and on their own merits, they had to be given the chance to defy the dictates of nature and do the right thing.

In the past few months at home in Stockholm, she'd written her first play, which was to be performed the coming autumn at the country theatre in Västerås. The play would send her life in a new direction, but of this she knew nothing yet. The production was called *Threesome* and was a melancholy reflection on the agonies of love. Ester Nilsson had striven for psychological realism, and that's exactly what she thought she'd achieved, but the critics would call it absurdist.

It was during the first read-through in August that she met Olof Sten, one of the actors in the play. Ester hadn't heard of him and neither did she recognize him, but after the first day-long meeting she experienced a familiar fluttering inside that she had no intention of quelling. It had something to do with how his gaze lingered in hers – pure, vulnerable and naked – and with his deep melodic voice, what it did and did not say, and how nothing bromidic ever spilled from his lips; rather, he displayed a sober restraint that Ester greatly appreciated. The rest came down to a sense of recognition, chemistry, encountering and corresponding, all of which would be pointless to question or ponder. There are neither words nor syntax for falling in love, however many attempts have been made to parade it through the alphabet.

Olof Sten wore a thick oxblood-coloured shirt too hot for the season, but in it he looked cool. The first question Ester asked him was how he spelled his name.

'With an f and one e,' he said, giving her a second glance, as if he understood.

Threesome was about a man trapped in an unhappy marriage who meets another woman but can't bring himself to leave his wife. The play was not prophetic. Nothing is prophetic. What may look like a prediction is really just a heightened awareness of what has previously come to pass. What has happened will happen again sooner or later, somewhere, sometime. And it's likely that it will happen again to the same person because people have their patterns.

When the ensemble broke for the afternoon and scattered in their various directions, Ester sought out Olof Sten in order to ask him an irrelevant question that had taken her some minutes to think up. She thought his behaviour towards her made it clear he didn't belong to anyone in particular. On the train home from Västerås that evening, longing ravaged her cells, nerves and veins. Walking up Flemminggatan from Central Station, she was deep in thoughts of embraces and courses of action.

The next day she posted her latest poetry collection to his home address in Stockholm with an inscription she had worked on for a good while to make sure it seemed insouciant and casual. Not one week later, when Olof had been home over the weekend, a handwritten thank-you note arrived. It said that he would read it with great interest. Ester wrote back and asked if they couldn't go for a coffee sometime during a break in the rehearsal schedule. Another weekend and a few weekdays went by, after which he called from Västerås to say that he'd read her book and liked it. As for the coffee, he said nothing. Nothing Ester heard, anyway. Only much later did she realize that he'd accepted her invitation, but in a manner so cryptic and covert it had passed her by: a while into their conversation he'd mentioned walking past a lovely cafe on Skånegatan at the weekend, one he'd never seen before and that looked cosy. Had she ever been there?

When she didn't immediately reply, he added that he wasn't wild about coffee or about sitting in cafes, but of course one could make an exception when a new spot opened up in the area. Perhaps.

It was too early in their entanglement for Ester to know that this was Olof's way of saying he'd very much like to go for a coffee with her. It was subtle, and that was the point. Ester would eventually get used to Olof Sten's negative affirmations and would become their most experienced exegete.

When Ester didn't think her invitation to coffee had been accepted, she retreated with an unpleasant feeling of having misread the signals, downcast that no ecstatic encounter was to materialize from their obvious chemistry.

Her silence caused Olof to ring her a week later, asking if they could meet up to discuss the interpretation of his role in the play, the one she'd written. He said he had a dentist's appointment in Stockholm on Wednesday. They met at Pelikan over creamy macaroni and Falun sausage, and there a conversation began.

Olof and Ester were like two cogs. Cogs don't merge or intertwine. They don't lose their sense of where one begins and the other ends; they presuppose each other, propel each other forward, are in perfect calibration. That's how it seemed to Ester. On its own, a cog is but a toothed unmoving artefact without function or direction. Which is fine, but it takes two to create movement and to realize a cog's intrinsic potential and purpose. Unfortunately this is also true with three cogs; mechanically speaking, three can be downright excellent.

Olof Sten, as it turned out, had been married for a decade or so. The wife's name was Ebba Silfversköld and she was the daughter of the late painter Gustaf Silfversköld, a prominent figure in the country's cultural history, albeit from sepia-tinged times. She was a doctor whose weekly commute meant she travelled between the general hospital in Borlänge and the home they shared in Stockholm's Södermalm. As such, they had a sort of long-distance relationship but cohabited at the weekend and in the summer. Both had children from previous marriages who no longer lived at home.

This came as a severe blow to Ester. Olof had neither hidden nor highlighted his marriage, they simply hadn't touched on the subject, but Ester thought that, really, he could have mentioned the wife and not have exclusively used the first person singular when discussing his life. And yet as soon as the disappointment abated, she began to realize that this conduct, combined with the exceptional connection she and Olof had so quickly established, must suggest that the marriage was in decline. It made no sense otherwise.

Friends always told Ester that men don't leave their wives, but things had to change for her at some point. No two people were identical. If she kept trying, one fine day the course of events would align with her view of how the world should be.

A month after their first rendezvous, Ester, quaking on every level with yearning, called Olof one Friday night when she knew he was home alone. They spoke for a while. About halfway through their conversation, she mentioned that Olof was always on her mind. His reply was immediate, and it filled Ester Nilsson with a sensation not unlike laughing gas and which launched her skyward even as she lay on the bed in her dwelling on Sankt Göransgatan.

'The feeling's mutual,' he said and added something about the wife being on call and not returning until the following day, whereupon the line fell silent. Then he asked:

'So what do we do now?'

Thoughts lose their density at high altitudes, so Ester didn't notice that she'd been asked this question before, verbatim, by another man with the same intention. The consequences on that occasion had been regrettable.

What do we do? she thought. I'll waste away with longing and you'll start planning your divorce, that's what we'll do.

'Let's get a drink next time you're home,' she said.

'Yes, let's.'

'I've been thinking about what you said last time.'

'What did I say?'

'That you were a "nomadic soul" and wished to remain one always. And that "actors are people who don't have an identity", who "lack a core". I want to hear more about that. I think it's good for the Self to be nimble, if that's what you mean, and to not believe you are and for ever will be one and indivisible. It keeps you from becoming too rigid, because there's no holy ego to preserve.'

She would get to see and hear more of this subject and would even come to revise her views on it. His ability to make precise observations made Ester happy but that's not what had drawn her in, for infatuation is primitive, not sophisticated. You love those who give free rein to the parts of you with which you are comfortable and feel at home, whether or not those parts are rotten or healthy, scuffed or polished to a shine.

'I don't think anyone's ever wanted to hear more of what I have to say,' Olof said.

And so Ester lay on her bed, emanating until long after midnight. His marriage was disintegrating; there was no doubt about that. All she had to do was wait.

Threesome premiered in Västerås. The audience grew and grew each week because people were talking to each other about what they'd seen and experienced in the theatre. When Ester came to see the performance, the actor who played the mistress told her that you could tell by the breathing, sighs, and other sounds if the house was chiefly comprised of wives or mistresses.

Halfway through October, Olof called out of the blue one Monday when the theatre was dark and asked if Ester wanted to go to a gallery on Karlavägen with him to see an exhibition of Gustaf Silfversköld's art on the occasion of his recent death at the age of one hundred and two. He'd had his heyday in the late 1930s, and it had lasted some years.

Olof needed to speak to the gallerist on Ebba's behalf. Ester didn't like the wife being mentioned so casually, but of course, it was promising that he wanted to take Ester with him.

When they left, Olof asked for her opinion on Gustaf Silfversköld's work. Ester said that it felt heavy, reactionary and old-fashioned.

'Just like the man himself,' Olof said with a lilting chuckle.

It was the middle of autumn, and the pavements were carpeted with yellow leaves. Olof and Ester followed their feet wherever they led them and ended up at Jensen's Bøfhus on Sveavägen. It was four o'clock. At six Ester was to take part in a seminar at the Workers' Educational Association, a few hundred metres from there. Olof had a steak; Ester only drank a cup of green tea because she'd arranged to have dinner with one of the other participants after the seminar.

Wrapped in the shadowless sterility of the family-friendly restaurant chain, the rumble of the soft-ice-cream machine in the background, Ester Nilsson said to Olof Sten that he was the one with whom she wanted to share her life. As they'd been sitting there idly chatting, she'd begun to fear that the time would slip away without her having completed this important task she'd set for herself today. And these were her very words:

'I want to share my life with you.'

This time around, she was determined to be clear from the start. Ambiguity would not prevail.

Olof flinched:

'But you don't know me!'

His objection embarrassed Ester because what he was saying was true, but she decided not to back down.

'I know you well enough to know this. And it won't be long until I know you even better.'

Olof began shredding a napkin with a keyring he'd

nervously fished out of his pocket. Ester said nothing more. She was aware her actions had not been strategic and went against all sound advice, but she was tired of waiting for the indecisive to make up their minds and wanted to quash the possibility of Olof wriggling out of their relationship later by saying that her intentions had been nebulous and she should've known where they stood because he was otherwise involved. She wanted to force a response from him at this early stage so she could know whether to persist or walk away.

Olof hadn't said no, that was the important thing, he had not said no. He glanced at the table, the napkin in shreds, gave her a serious look and said:

'It's not every day someone tells you they want to share their life with you. Of course it makes an impression.'

In the month that followed, they weren't in contact, but they did run into each other once: when Ester travelled to Västerås to attend a performance of her play. The encounter was stilted and he kept her at a distance, and so with great anguish she decided to walk away, whereupon Olof, just as she was about to leave, murmured in her ear:

'Let's be sure to see each other when the run is finished and I'm back in Stockholm.'

After this, the autumn flew by on wings of hope and desire, and her heart suffered a severe enlargement.

—

Olof called a few days after the run had ended and suggested lunch at Blå Porten on Djurgården Island. The choice of location implied time for togetherness and immersion, the start of a new phase and a reorientation from old to new; it implied that Ester had been correct in her calculations, particularly because he wanted them to take the ferry instead of reaching Djurgården by bridge.

The day when everything would begin was upon her. They'd decided to meet at noon at the Djurgård ferry. Anticipation made it difficult for Ester to swallow. In her apartment, which she'd lived in for five years yet still hadn't furnished properly because she'd always been about to leave, hindered only by the fact that she didn't have anywhere to go, she spent the morning putting fresh sheets on the bed and, on the kitchen table, an oilcloth from the Ten Swedish Designers group which she'd bought the day before on Götgatan. Further down the hill, she'd found three beautiful art deco lamps which were now on the windowsills. It was late November and forever dark. Ester counted on being able to light them for Olof in the afternoon.

At the stroke of twelve she was on the quay, waiting in the grey mist. It was one of those days when nothing seemed to be moving, all was still. Olof was fifteen minutes late. Ester was determined not to mention the delay, but saw that his movements were tinged with unease. Perhaps he was gripped by the thought of all that lay before him; this was a big step to take.

Upon arrival the first thing he said was that they didn't have to go all the way to Blå Porten, they could go to a simpler lunch spot nearby in Old Town so it wouldn't take as long. Faced with Ester's silent but apparent dismay, he changed his mind and they bought their ferry tickets. They were practically alone on the crossing to Djurgården and during those few minutes Olof mentioned his wife several times. When he noticed it was getting Ester down and causing her to disengage, he stopped calling the wife by name, but it continued to weigh on her during the short walk from the ferry to the restaurant through drifts of maple leaves.

It was a Thursday and the wait at Blå Porten was unusually short. They ordered fried herring with mashed potatoes and lingonberries and sat at a table in the middle of the restaurant, where they couldn't be overheard. Olof was holding his cutlery straight up, ready to tuck in, but not quite, not before he said what he had to say. He looked at her. Their food had a greasy shine. He seemed to be gearing up for something. And as he did, Ester had the time to think that the way he was holding his cutlery was childlike and charming. Then all thoughts of charm ceased. He was speaking with a confidence that stemmed from practised courage:

'I think you've pulled a Pygmalion.'

Ester didn't understand, but knew it was a dig. She went numb, silent, still and cold. This compelled Olof to clarify:

'You've fallen in love with a character of your own creation.'

She was deeply disheartened by the suggestion that she was unable to keep track of herself and her feelings.

'You wrote that play and liked what I did with the role. Most of all you liked the role. You fell in love with your own character.'

From inside her vacuum Ester noted that it took a not altogether attractive arrogance to suggest she liked what he'd done with the role. Although she'd often praised his performance that autumn, it didn't mean that praise was based in fact and should be repeated as fact. There were reasons unrelated to fact for praise and criticism.

'Why would I do something as strange as falling for a character I wrote? The role you played wasn't even particularly sympathetic.'

'You know "Pygmalion"?' Olof asked.

'I've read Shaw's play, yes.'

'I mean the Pygmalion myth. The Greek one. About the man who made a sculpture and fell in love with the sculpture.'

'So you don't think my feelings have anything to do with you?'

'They have very little to do with me.'

Olof began eating with delight unbefitting the situation. He had fulfilled his task and was now in better spirits. His lateness and the frequent mentions of his wife during the crossing, as well as his discordant arrival, were thereby explained. The weight had been lifted from Olof's shoulders and placed on Ester's.

'Is it good?' he asked her.

'Not especially.'

'No?'

'No. I've lost my appetite.'

'My, what a shame.'

Olof thought for a moment and said:

'I'm thinking we should meet up now and again in the future and see what happens. Decisions don't always have to be made right away.'

Not again, Ester thought, never again, I'm going to get right up and go.

She stayed put and finished her meal. Soon they were walking from Djurgården towards the city along Strandvägen, arm-in-arm on Olof's initiative. In line with Grevgatan, Ester stopped and embraced him, and he reciprocated, while saying he shouldn't be doing this. They were approaching Dramaten National Theatre, their bodies close, when Olof stated:

'Leaving my wife isn't on the cards.'

This was exactly what married people said when someone else had shaken their foundations, Ester thought. When people felt an intense desire, they might insist otherwise. The trick was knowing when they meant what they were saying and were saying it to be clear and honourable, and when they meant the opposite. The question demanded a far-reaching and risky act of interpretation, work to which Ester was always willing to subject herself.

If Ester had taken him at his word here, she would have been spared considerable time and effort, likewise she would have missed out on many wondrous moments. Ester had a girlfriend called Lotta who often asserted that one should 'Take people at their word. It's simpler and more practical. Don't interpret. Assume they mean what they say.' Lotta was cautious and clever, but Ester believed that hardly anything would come of a budding romance if you were cautious, clever, and took people at their word because it was then that language was used deceptively in order to avoid making difficult decisions and to evade love. People feared love, as she'd read in the works of the great bards, because it bears the germ of supreme delight and so too the germ of the gravest losses.

Olof and Ester crossed Raoul Wallenberg Square with its scattered sculpture group. Ester said she liked it and spoke of the controversy the choice of work had caused in the 1990s. They agreed on the life-affirming quality of a work that is able to offend through form alone, and that this often happened when the form, as here, was its content.

'The artist must have thought Wallenberg had become a monument in himself,' Ester said, 'and so he didn't want the monument for him to be monumental.'

Olof asked how she had the energy to have ideas about everything all the time. She could tell that the question wasn't a question at all, but a poison dart, if shot with a smile. She didn't like that he wanted to shoot such things at her and answered dryly that it came naturally to her and was how she earned her living, she had to have the energy. It wasn't any more unusual than him making a living by becoming someone else and having to summon the energy for that time and time again, night after night.

'Which is a rather strange occupation,' he said.

'What's strange?'

'Acting: such a strange profession. It's not really for me. For long stretches in my life, I've done other things, had respectable jobs, and actually, I've always wanted to get away from it.'

He gripped her arm a little tighter so she would move even closer to him. She was of a mind to ask if he should really be taking her arm, for there was a risk she would begin to perceive a chasm between his words and his actions and would place her trust in actions. But because she wanted him to hold her arm, she held her tongue.

They walked along Arsenalsgatan towards Kungsträdgården Park. Plenty of people, most in suits and dresses, were on the move. When they'd made it over the crossing at Kungsträdgårdsgatan Olof said that conversing with Ester was remarkably fun and stimulating, it was like talking to a man. Ester searched his face for something that would dignify such cruel words. Olof's world couldn't possibly be so banal as to have been entirely lacking in interesting conversations with women. It attested to something deficient in his relations with his wife, which was good, but also to a deficiency in perspective.

'Is this some sort of Aristotelian deduction?'

'What's that?'

'Everyone with whom you can have an exciting conversation is a man. I can have an exciting conversation with Ester Nilsson, therefore Ester Nilsson is a man.'

Olof grimaced.

'I'm afraid that's how I've been conditioned, even though it sounds skewed when put so plainly.'

'You need to do something about that. With me, you could have the whole package.'

This bold act of courtship seemed to delight him. It was two thirty. Olof had made sure to be otherwise engaged at three. The first thing he'd said when they'd met at quarter past twelve was:

'I don't have all day.'

Ester had thought they had all day as well as the rest of their lives now that they'd finally had the chance to see each other properly, and this is precisely what he sensed and wished to stave off, that much was clear. The boundary to intimacy is asserted by industry. Scheduling an appointment after a date was the best fortification against the person who always wanted more.

But when they'd reached Tegelbacken, he was more relaxed about this scheduled meeting. Rolling in from the town hall, the bus was under the viaduct when he took Ester's hand and said:

'Should I catch the next one instead?'

'I don't know. Should you?'

Ester just wanted to go home and get on with dying. Today's conversation had to mean farewell. She had no interest in meeting up 'now and again in the future' and seeing 'what happens'. The bus came and went. Olof stayed at the bus stop and ran his stubble across her cheek, his lips searched for her closed mouth.

'Talking to you is so much fun.'

As their 'talking' had just been defined in opposition to erotic love, these words did not sit well with Ester. He gave her a peck on the lips and took the next bus to Södermalm.

Walking home along Vasagatan, Kungsbron and Fleminggatan up towards Fridhemsplan, Ester felt weary. It wasn't the scenic route. Though it would have been shorter from Tegelbacken, she didn't take the picturesque walk along the Karlberg Canal or Hantverkargatan. She didn't want to see anything beautiful today, not even beauty nestled in a sodden-grey November.

As she walked, she thought her problem was that she always pawned her life's meaning for the man she'd chosen. As long as he existed, everything else was cast in shadow. It was never a question of a diffuse and tempered searchlight, no, she directed her slim, harsh light beam with appalling precision only to burn a hole in the object with the full destructive power of her longing.

Now the light had to be put out. Olof didn't want the same thing she did. Deliberating by the bus and pressing

21

his lips to hers in parting were nothing to cling to. She must not let herself begin the process of interpretation. This was only fleeting lust and a result of his fear of losing the attention of a lover. That which disappears can't help but seem a little attractive once it has loosed its grip on you.

Olof had given her a clear answer. Ester accepted it.

She came home, got under a blanket, and stared at the ceiling. After a while she started to call around in an attempt to stem the flood of pain. All her girlfriends were at the ready to hear the results of that day's encounter. Ester told the story from beginning to end and they shared their opinions.

'Run, Ester, run!' said Lotta. 'And do it now while there's still time.'

'He's married,' said Fatima, 'and as a married man, he's far too willing to see you again and again and not tell his wife. Be happy you found out now before you got too involved. It won't be that hard; in a month or so you'll be free.'

'Chill,' said Elin. 'Ask yourself what you want out of this, not what he wants. Then do what you want no matter what the rest of us say – and that includes Olof.'

'He'll get in touch again,' said Lotta, 'but make sure you tie yourself to the mast and cover your ears.'

'If he had said that he was ready for a divorce, but that it was a lot to take in right now,' said Fatima, 'then I would've said "hold on". But this, sneaking around with you when he knows how you feel, putting the brakes on your hopes while being open to *maybe* starting something in secret soon. No way. Leave him right now if you can and leave yourself open for someone who can't live without you.'

'He wanted to catch the next bus?' Vera mused. 'He kissed you at the bus stop and didn't really feel like going home? This'll take time, but it's not over. It's all about how long you can hold on.'

'Is it?' Ester asked. In her chest, hope bloomed like a rose.

'You need to be patient, but one day he'll be yours.'

'You think?' Ester gasped. 'Do you really think so, Vera?'

'He's a slow one.'

Elin said:

'This doesn't sound good, but you were the one who was there and you're the only one who can know how much you can take. What are you hoping I'll say most?'

'The truth about what he's really feeling.'

'Unfortunately that's a mystery to us all.'

'Do you think *he* knows it himself?'

'That depends on who he is.'

After a day of considering the girlfriend chorus's opinions, Ester made a decision. She deleted his number and decided to never expect to hear from or see him again. She wasn't about to wade back into the bog of uncertainty. She emptied herself of hope and longing and reconciled the idea of a new order. She hadn't got anything sensible done since she'd returned from their date, and it was high time she put Olof behind her and got a grip on her own life.

And right then, a text message arrived:

> *I think I've been unclear and caused you to believe something I didn't mean. Of course I'm flattered by your feelings for me but I can only reciprocate with friendship. I like you! Your wicked sense of humour. Your slightly misbuttoned self. Your thoughts entice me. You're great! Let's leave it at that. Otherwise it'll get too complicated. At least it will for me. Olof.*

With that, her equilibrium and the foundation for all wise decisions were dashed, for it did not escape Ester's philological mind that his message was not in the text itself, but rather in the action of sending it. If it had been about the content, he wouldn't have needed to text her because everything had already been said.

She could tell he'd taken great care with the text. He wasn't a man of words, and it must have cost him dearly to formulate the message. There were four parts to it. The first was about her (great, funny, slightly misbuttoned). The second was about how he still couldn't reciprocate her love but that in truth, he was tempted; only the consequences were stopping him ('too complicated'), that is, there was no lack of lust or desire. That was enough for Ester, the loam was there and Olof was writing to let her know it was. The third part was apparently an excuse ('I've been unclear'). But the writing underscored that he wanted to, but shouldn't, because he'd been unclear for a reason, namely the forbidden temptation she presented to him.

The fourth was the most important part. The act of sending the message could not be read as anything other than a wish to stay in contact, with all that this implied.

Ester understood that he wasn't finished and hadn't arrived at a decision. A spinnaker of love was hoisted inside her. His clumsy effort to let her know he wanted to see her without him having to come right out and say it made her heart swell and pulse with tenderness.

Vera said that Ester's interpretation of the text message came from an overheated brain. What he was writing, she said, was that he wanted to keep her as a friend, not fall in love with her. This also explained why he sent the message even though everything had been said.

But their connection, Ester protested, never had anything to do with friendship; right from the start it had been something else. You didn't get that kind of thing wrong and Olof was old enough and experienced enough to know you can't be friends with a person you've just met who's said they want to share their life with you.

Ester was quite sure she hadn't misjudged this series of events but needed an active sign to be certain. And on the Monday night on her way home from the grocer's shop she saw Olof from afar at the entrance to her building, his face pressed to the entryphone. The lighting was dim but more than bright enough for her to discern his silhouette. She stopped, unsure if she should make herself known. And then he hurried off, disappearing around the corner. It didn't occur to her to call out to him. Up in her apartment, her telephone showed that someone had buzzed for her.

Forty-five minutes later, Olof called her from his land-line. It corresponded with the time it took to wait for the bus, travel the five kilometres to his and gather himself for a call. He spoke with a devout, pleading tone that she hadn't heard before. He asked how she was doing and if she'd received his text on Friday. He mentioned that he'd visited the mall in her neighbourhood in the afternoon and had been hoping to run into her.

Ester's heart stopped and turned. They decided to meet the following day, take in a matinée and then go for dinner.

Olof could be quite a sensible man at times. He wasn't espe-cially interested in the cinema, but he understood that he needed to oblige Ester because he was running out of capi-tal with her. And yet, having to make these large withdrawals from his account for her benefit – sending long text mes-sages, calling her, standing at her door and admitting to his doings in the mall – necessitated one minor act of resist-ance: arriving at the cinema slightly after the agreed time. After all, one can't let on just how eager one is.

Ester on the other hand was punctual and waited for Olof at Söderhallarna. The film was about to start. She worried he might not turn up or arrive so late they'd miss the beginning. She'd rather skip the film than miss the first few minutes.

Medborgarplatsen was covered in banks of slush and preparations for the Christmas festivities were in full swing. The usual addicts and alcoholics were hanging about. She breathed a sigh of relief when she saw Olof strolling across the square, again nearly fifteen minutes late. They bought tickets.

During the film, Ester was acutely aware of his body next to hers and wanted to pounce on him. Judging by his deep breathing, the feeling was mutual. From her cinema seat, she slipped inside his mind and gathered that he was focusing not on the film, but on erotic self-restraint. Afterwards, he said he couldn't remember anything about the film and asked what it had been about. What this meant for the future made Ester a little dizzy.

They went straight from the cinema to a bar at the top of Götgatsbacken. On this evening, Olof didn't have anywhere else to be; he was attentive and present and they parted at two in the morning. They'd ended up wandering from one place to the next and had spent eleven hours together. The staff had already started putting chairs on tables by the time they managed to get rid of the pair of would-be lovers furtively holding hands. Out on the street, Olof said he was insulted that they'd been shooed off, but the way he said it gave Ester her first fleeting sense, both obvious and odd, that he didn't in fact feel offended but thought he should because that's what people felt in these situations. He seemed to be conjuring a well-considered emotion. She let it slide. It had been a fantastic evening, and she was as good as happy.

During the evening Olof had introduced her to the Italian drink Strega, a yellow liqueur in which three coffee beans are placed. The waiter had told them that once upon a time in Sicily, the coffee beans were used to signal if there were enemies in the venue. Three beans meant all was well, two meant head for the back door and one meant run for it. According to another story, the waiter said, the three beans represented faith, hope and love.

Ester said it sounded like one and the same story.

When Olof announced at Blå Porten that Ester shouldn't harbour any expectations, it had freed him up to be with her. Because he'd so clearly articulated his intentions, he thought she should understand the deal, no matter what they'd go on to do. And Ester thought that because she had so clearly articulated her feelings and desires, he should understand that everything they'd go on to do would impact her on-going interpretation of the encounter's trajectory.

They started seeing each other regularly and always for many hours, spending most of the night sitting in some pub. They talked and talked but they didn't make it to bed even though that was where they seemed to be heading. Olof was holding on. And like any party-in-pursuit throughout history has responded to coquetry and ambiguous restraint,

Ester assumed the answer was a 'no' only until it became a 'yes'.

On the eve of St Lucy's Day they met again, also at Söderhallarna, where Olof bought a piece of beef from a counter just before the market hall closed. The meat was for the following night, when the wife would be back after the week's work and another couple was coming over for dinner. At the counter, they ran into the director of a museum, and he and Olof chatted. The museum head asked after Ebba and her father's retrospective. Olof said that the reception had been brilliant, they'd sold well and all in all Ebba and her siblings were very pleased. He added that Gustaf was a singular talent, not to mention unique.

For Ester, who in a practised way was standing at a discreet distance so the acquaintance wouldn't connect her with Olof, their conversation hurt as much as the impending couples' soirée. When the museum director left, Olof didn't comment on the encounter, he talked about the dish he was planning to make and how it would take up most of tomorrow afternoon. Upon noticing Ester's dejection, Olof said he didn't feel at all like having dinner guests and should really serve up something quick and simple, macaroni with frozen meatballs at best. The inclusive look he gave her and the sensitive deprecation of his dinner plans pleased her so much that the worry in her heart over how she would go on to free him from his marriage was temporarily mitigated.

They stayed in the market hall a little longer, walking

around, smelling and looking at all the delicious things laid out for Christmas. A St Lucy's procession* passed by. Right in front of Olof and Ester – and to the other children's delight – one of the star-bearers blew out a candle held by one of St Lucy's attendants. Ester's empathy was heightened by all that was straining and incomplete inside her, as well as the thought of the Sten–Silfverskölds' upcoming meal. She said:

'How nice it is to never have to be a child again.'

'Maybe he has a crush on her.'

'That's a sorry way to show it.'

'But isn't that exactly how people show it?'

They went down to Zum Franziskaner on Skeppsbron where they ate *pyttipanna* hash and drank beer. Ester had given up her usual diet, which had been mostly plant-based. The quantity of food you had to gnaw your way through each mealtime was too large, the consistency monotonous, and it led to social complications.

Olof reached across the table and took her hands in order to warm them up and said:

'We're not in a relationship, you and I.'

'No, we're just sitting here.'

'And it's very nice.'

'Because you're in a relationship with another woman, we're not in a relationship.'

---

* St Lucy's Day is celebrated on 13 December, and involves solemn processions of children with candles in their hair and hands.

'Precisely.'

They listened to their surroundings.

'But aren't we in the preliminary stages of a relationship?' Ester asked. 'Embryonic.'

Olof laughed mildly. Ester said:

'As we know, it can go one of two ways with an embryo.'

'As you know, I'm married.'

'When people have what you and I have, this potential, one doesn't have the right to throw it away. One has an obligation to care for it.'

He rubbed his thumb over Ester's.

'An obligation to whom?'

'Life itself.'

Ester was carefully balancing elation and reserve, but the situation and her eager love were making Olof puckish.

'Can't you just enjoy the fact that we're sitting here?'

'I am enjoying it. But I'm being left hanging, which means I'm enjoying it less.'

'You always want clarity and definition. Life isn't clear and defined. It's blurry and chaotic, messy and confused. Can't it be allowed to just be that?'

Ester wanted to say that statements on 'how life is' don't tell us anything about how to act, but didn't want to seem finicky. It lay in the nature of having the upper hand to resist definition and justification, that much she knew, to neither argue nor account for. Greedily, he helped himself to the upper hand in love and offered her ambiguity in reply.

She withdrew her hands and said:

'I've figured out what our problem is, the root of our imbalance.'

'We have a problem?'

'Well, I do. We live in the worst of two worlds, hiding and keeping secrets even though we aren't even doing anything.'

'No, that's the best of both worlds! Being the only one who knows, so no one else can meddle in what you're feeling, thinking and doing is the most fantastic aspect of a person's life, an indispensable construction.'

Ester ignored this comment. She shouldn't have. Of all that Olof would go on to say, this is the assertion she should have taken seriously. But she couldn't believe that a person would seek obscurity while wanting to be close, for the two were irreconcilable.

'If this was an innocent friendship,' said Ester, 'you'd tell your wife that you're seeing me at the pub and going to the movies with me.'

'We've only been to the movies once.'

'But you didn't tell her about it, did you? And if she calls you later to ask where you've been all night, you're not going to say that you've been out with me.'

'OK, so what do you think is our problem?'

'You're a fatalist and I'm an existentialist,' Ester said. 'That's our problem.'

'I've got to go home and look that up.'

'Existentialists act as though will were free and choice defines a person. Fatalists let the world choose for them.

Inaction is their action, not-choosing is their choice until they are swept away by others' choices, others' actions.'

Olof straightened up in his seat and said:

'Will is only as free as waves are free to decide when they roll in and out. There are higher powers at work.'

'And this attitude of yours is what's going to keep us from getting anywhere, ensuring nothing will happen in spite of your obvious interest.'

'I'm not sure we *are* going anywhere,' said Olof, though the lusty sparkle in his eyes contradicted his words.

'The question of free will isn't something we're going to be able to clear up,' Ester said, 'but you get more done if you assume there is free will and choice is real. Free will is a metaphysical concept, sure, but one that to the highest degree impacts material fact and how a chain of events will unfold. If you live by the idea that will is free, you're less passive than if you assume the opposite.'

Olof listened carefully and Ester continued:

'For us, it would've been much better if I was the fatalist and you the existentialist. Then you would've cut ties with your former life and we'd be spending all day in bed.'

His laughter was tinged with a clucking rumble of pleasure.

'I'm going home to look up what "fatalist" means.'

'It means what I just said it did.'

'Yeah, but I'm going to go home to look up the neutral, objective definition.'

Their plates were whisked away by a speedy waitress,

34

and Olof ordered a glass of red, which to Ester's delight meant they'd be there for a while. Ester ordered another beer. Olof took in the venue and said:

'Has it occurred to you that this might be the case: I'm making a choice. But it's not the one you want me to make.'

Again, his harsh words were contradicted by the casual vanity at play in his face, the desire for the game and the hunt.

'Why do you keep wanting to see me?'

Olof squeezed her hand. He looked open and soft, winsome.

'You know why.'

'No. I don't.'

'Aren't we having a good time?'

'Yes, very.'

'Isn't that enough?'

'So you can have twice as much and I get half? No thank you.'

Olof's next line was notable in that he either misspoke or was offering a sharp self-analysis. He reflected:

'I'm probably quite a heterogeneous person.'

'Heterogeneous?'

'No. No, not heterogeneous. What's it called?'

'Monogamous?'

'Monogamous, yes. Right.'

Ester thought this was good. A monogamous person was exactly what she wanted, a person who would choose her and only her and be happy with that.

It was three days before Christmas and Ester was lounging on her bed reading a recently published book on the relationship between post-structuralism and the sophists of antiquity. Bathed in the glow of a carefully chosen accent light that Olof had yet to see, she received a text message.

Olof wrote: 'Let's lie low with the texting over the holidays, shall we?'

The message came out of nowhere, neither an answer to something she had written or said, and they hadn't been in touch for a couple of days. The expression 'lie low' made his request sound like a confession or an acknowledgement of their association. Ester could tell the break-up was just around the corner. After the holidays, he'd leave his wife. Being so open about deceiving his wife as to put words to the deception could only mean the wife was on her way out of the picture.

Ester answered immediately, texting that over these Christmas weeks she intended to be the definition of lying low, becoming one with the silence, becoming its very synonym.

Their familiarity struck her deeply and with this feeling

impressed upon her, Ester lived through Christmas, the first with-Olof-without-Olof. Her flesh burned, her brain was in flames, her entire being was nigh on charred, but it was a happy charring. She went to Christmas parties and Boxing Day dinners, played party games and conversed, but she was only fully present in her daydreams. In the mornings she embraced Olof's body in bed and caressed the contours of his silhouette. Soon he would be there with her, very soon, and life could begin. Only in longing was she alive – not in her everyday with its insignificant little goings-on.

And yet the worry that it wouldn't turn out as she hoped was constant. It crept and crawled in her, hollowing her out, resting, rising again. She feared something would happen over the holidays that would cause him to alter his plans for a new life. They were in a fragile state and there was a great risk that he, on New Year's Eve when all resolutions are made, would decide to disengage from Ester before it was too late and before the gravest betrayal had yet to occur.

New Year's Eve was spent alone so she could yearn in peace. She took care preparing her dinner: prawn cocktail with fresh coriander as a starter, then entrecôte, potatoes au gratin, baked tomatoes and haricots verts, and a chocolate cake with cream and berries to finish. With this, she drank a glass of red wine and watched a rented movie.

She both hoped and feared that Olof would send a New Year's greeting at the stroke of midnight. A sign of life would have been wonderful, but it could also be read as a foreboding attempt at neutralization. On the other hand, not sending a message would suggest that what they had was so serious that it left no room for the banal.

No message arrived. Something big was on its way. Olof's break-up. Ester and Olof's union.

Three days into the new year, she decided 'the holidays' were over and sent a text message. 'Am being c-c-c-on-sumed by d-d-desire. We m-m-must m-m-meet up to stop my t-t-eeth from chatt-tt-ttering. /Est-t-t-ter'

The reply came within five minutes:

'Tom-m-m-orrow f-f-five o'c-c-clock?'

A man who sent a reply like this couldn't not be loved. Ester exploded with joy and channelled her surplus energy into thirty sets of press-ups.

At five o'clock the next day they converged by the doors to Slussen's metro station. He said he'd found a pub on Gåsgränd in Old Town that he wanted the two of them to try. They headed in that direction through an inky winter darkness broken only by the snowbanks that had escaped the new year's thaw. The chairs at the Gåsgränd pub were rickety and the food bizarre, and the waiter bore a striking resemblance to a former culture editor at *Svenska Dagbladet*. When Ester enquired, he denied any relation. She told Olof that she'd asked a similar question once before in Vienna at a pub where the waiter looked like Robert de Niro. Unsmiling and with lightning speed – clearly he was used to the question – he'd replied: *leider nicht*, unfortunately not. Olof laughed out loud and then they ate. When they were finished with Gåsgränd, they wanted to keep going and found themselves at Gyldene Freden, where they stayed for a number of hours. They spoke generally and with not a word about what they'd done over Christmas or why they were where they were. And so it was a tad unexpected when Olof said:

'I need you, Ester. I can talk to you about anything. Sports, literature, art, politics, ideas, theatre. With Ebba, it's completely mute.'

Ester grabbed the bar and held her breath.

'I'm yours if you want me. I'm here and you know what I want.'

His follow-up to the comment he'd just made seemed oddly misplaced to her. It was as though he'd got hold of two conflicting scripts and was cross-reading from them.

'We have to be careful,' he said. 'You can't call or text. Ebba's keeping her eye on me.'

Over Christmas, she'd even gone through his wallet, found a key and 'made a scene and asked a lot of difficult questions'.

Ester was trying to understand why they'd have to be careful when he was about to leave Ebba, which was reasonable to assume based on his words and actions.

'What did Ebba think the key was for?'

'Your place, I assume.'

'My place?! Does she know we're seeing each other?'

'No. But after the premiere party in Västerås she asked me if I had a crush on you.'

'She did?'

'She must've seen my eyes wandering every time you came near. Ebba is observant. She noticed a change in me right after the read-through.'

Though many strange things were being said, this was nonetheless a significant disclosure.

'What did you say?'

'That you're not my type.'

'You said that?'

'What was I supposed to say?'

Olof took out his snus and tucked in a fresh portion, then he sucked the wine through the snus, as was his habit.

'I should stop with the snus. Be healthier.'

'Isn't it just as well that Ebba finds out what's going on sooner rather than later?'

In the old dusky venue, its pleasing buzz meant there was little risk of overhearing other parties, Olof changed tack:

'She could tell you were very interested in me.'

The arrogant cruelty in this distancing wasn't lost on Ester, the lash across the mouth that it was.

'*I* was interested?'

'Well, you were.'

'But didn't you just say that *you* had changed and *your* eyes were wandering when I was nearby?'

She had experienced this before, this manoeuvring, the subtle shift that looked exactly the same each time. It was the kind of thing that made her wish she had a witness, someone who could hear what she hearing, thus rendering impossible any evasion or distortion of what had been said and done.

'We have to be careful,' Olof repeated. 'Ebba's keeping an eye on me.'

'But you can't live like that.'

In the new year, Olof had started rehearsing a short play he'd been in the previous year and that was about to tour through Sweden. Until then they would continue to spend their evenings together at their usual pubs and bars. Ester went around in a fever of expectation conjured by their kisses and caresses. During the day she worked on a difficult but interesting commission, the translation of a short book by the mathematician and philosopher Gottlob Frege. She was getting into the material and had ordered secondary literature.

At the end of January when they'd met up in the evening and stayed together long into the night as usual, Olof suggested she visit him whilst he was on tour.

'But that'll be the end of it,' he said, 'if we start a sexual relationship, that'll be end of it.'

The end of what? Ester wondered to herself, hoping he meant his marriage, but certainty evaded her for this was yet another strange thing to say. If they began a sexual relationship, it was because it was already the end, not the other way around.

Olof was to perform in Arvidsjaur one weekend in the middle of February. Taking out his diary, he suggested that she visit him there, so they could go cross-country skiing together, he said. He'd continue to refer to it like this: going skiing together one weekend. Clearly, he had to take baby steps in order to transport this big thing he was shouldering; not only did he have to displace their physical encounter, but also conceive of it as fitness. His conscience was counting kilometres and it was a long way to Arvidsjaur. Olof's conscience was constantly counting everything, Ester would later think, but it also seemed broken.

Having reached a decision about consummating their relationship – even if they were calling it 'going skiing' – made Ester shiver and quake. This was heading in the right direction, there was no turning back.

Outside, the wind was harsh and the temperature had dropped to minus ten. Ester's head was bare, the only reason being that she didn't want her hair to get flat. Normally, she'd never leave the house without a hat if it was colder than five degrees, but tonight she wanted to at least try to maintain some sort of hairstyle. They walked towards

Slussen. The decision had been made. Olof lifted his arms to warm her frozen head and said:

'Wear a hat next time.'

'I'll wear two hats in Arvidsjaur.'

'Going skiing with you will be fun.'

There were three weeks to go. Desire ravaged Ester day and night, but not for cross-country skiing. When the trip was close she got her equipment out of the attic, covered the floor in newspaper and rubbed easy-glide wax into her skis' well-worn bases.

On the way from Stockholm to Arvidsjaur, her plane touched down in Lycksele to drop off some of the passengers and pick up others. The flights cost five thousand kronor, as much as a ticket to New York. On top of that, she'd bought a pair of warm winter boots, a jacket and a blouse for another few thousand. Their first lovers' weekend cost her dearly, but what did money matter when you were buying bliss?

She travelled on Friday morning. When she walked home from Central Station two and a half days later on Sunday night, one of her new boots was pushing so hard against her Achilles tendon she thought it might snap. The pain lasted for four days, whereupon she put the boots in a cupboard, never to be used again.

The Arvidsjaur airport consisted of a landing strip and a low corrugated metal building out in the middle of nowhere. The ecstatic lust that would finally be given an outlet after six months' waiting made her knees weak, and it was on these shaky legs that she hailed the area's only taxi, which transported her soundlessly through the primeval forest.

When she stepped inside the lobby of the Hotel Laponia, Olof was sitting there, waiting. To her surprise, he was all muffled up. For days and weeks she had pictured him receiving her in his room, unreserved and exuberant. They would slip between freshly ironed sheets, dive into each other's bodies, sticky with love's fluids, and have no desire to go back out all weekend.

But there he sat, clad in a jacket, scarf and gloves.

They went to the room with her bag and skis. Olof seemed rushed and hunted, saying that he wanted to go into the village and have a look around.

What were they supposed to be doing in the village? Hadn't they been waiting months for this?

'Let's get out of here,' Olof said, and proceeded to take a seat in an armchair.

Since they'd set a date for this tryst, his voice on the phone had had a civilized veneer stretched over wild arousal. And now: this play at nonchalance. It was comically transparent, so Ester sat in his lap and caressed his forehead, hair, cheeks, took off his jacket and boots, touched his chest and thighs.

Their lips met. They lay naked in bed. The act was hurried and hot.

Olof seemed to want to get it over with, and his gaze was absent. It seemed absurd to her that he'd want to appear ambivalent even though he'd asked her to fly to Lapland and had months to prepare himself, not to mention the three weeks since he'd invited her, during which he could've changed his mind. There was something unintelligent about this discrepancy, or perhaps it was a constitutional ambivalence and beyond his control. But these thoughts caused nothing to wane. If she was in love with a dimwit, then so be it. If she loved a constitutional hopelessness, then so be it. More than anything, Ester wanted to love Olof and to be received by him.

Before they went out to 'look at the village' they visited the hotel's dining room where a small buffet had been laid out, ample but hardly delicious. Ester helped herself to a passionless mix of blood dumplings and vegetables au gratin. Her portion was large, for she sensed a vacuum had formed between them and she wanted to fill it with food. Or perhaps she had become aware of a vacuum that had been there all along but that she'd thought their corporeal meeting would oxygenate. She recalled with horror how losing touch with a former lover, the artist Hugo Rask, had coincided with them having had physical contact.

But things have to change eventually. No two people are the same. Nothing is predestined.

In the middle of the meal, with half of the blood dumpling stuck to the roof of Ester's mouth, Olof gave her a look that flickered between mischief and fear.

'I couldn't believe how hot we were for each other up there.'

His perception of the world was becoming increasingly inexplicable to her. The only reason they were here in this place was because they were hot for each other. It was the only reason she had flown to upper Norrland to meet him. How could he, then, comment on their heat as if it were news to him? Was he still pretending they'd met up to go skiing and just happened to fall into bed together?

'I mean, we couldn't hold ourselves back!' he added when he saw her confusion thickening with each utterance.

Why should they hold back when the whole point of the trip was to not have to?

Ester knew words and actions were never accidental and spent a minute wondering if she should indeed give more weight to this constant friction with reality that his words communicated, these two scripts he was shuttling between. Was he trying to tell her something that should already be clear to her?

He was indeed, but Ester couldn't see that, during this tryst in which they'd gained carnal knowledge of each other, Olof Sten's every statement was made so that he and an imagined audience would find it plausible that what had happened between him and Ester Nilsson was an accident in which he was barely involved. It eased the blame. People like this have never done anything, they've been done to. Olof Sten was one of these people. He also believed that reality was created through statements. He'd studied neither Wittgenstein's language-games, Austin's performative utterances nor Butler's development of these, and it wasn't necessary. It was enough that they'd studied him, so to speak, that the philosophers of language were hot on the heels of the human psyche's patterns.

Ester had cleared her palate of the dumpling and pushed her plate away when she said:

'You asked me to come here. Why should we have held back?'

'We did make the decision together, didn't we?' he replied quickly with a hint of indignation.

'Yes. Together.'

After lunch they finally made their way to the village. They began with the old church. It was empty, beautiful in the way that old churches are. In it hung a painting by Hugo Simberg that Ester knew well. It had been a source of inspiration for Hugo Rask and he'd shown her reproductions and an essay he'd written on its composition and historical background. She said this to Olof in the church. He listened somewhat absently and seemed confused as to why she thought he'd want to know this.

They stayed in the church for only a few minutes and then Olof wanted to press on. He got it into his head that they should borrow the theatre's car and go away somewhere, but after five kilometres he realized that the road was just going to keep winding endlessly through the subarctic Lappish wilds. They turned around and drove back the way they came. Ester couldn't tell if Olof felt distant or plagued by a far too strong sense of being present. They parked the car and walked to a log cabin selling Lapland kitsch; Olof rummaged restlessly through the items – butter knives made of birch branded with curlicues, knitted sweaters in bright Sami colours, birch bark trinkets, ceremonial drums in miniature – and said he wanted to buy something, anything, to commemorate the day.

Commemorate the day? Was the day important to him? Was this why he was so out of sorts? Her devotion to him rose to its old heights.

Empty-handed, they went to a tall, vast market tent nearby. Homemade cinnamon buns and cheap jeans with wide seats, shaggy sweaters and warm slippers were on offer. Ester's gaze landed on a display of simple cotton reels in every possible colour. They cost fifteen kronor, would last a lifetime and had a colour for every imaginable garment she would ever buy. She picked up one packet. Olof decided he had to have the same, but once at the register found he had no cash and asked Ester to cover the fifteen kronor.

Each holding their packet of cotton reels, they went on their way and the devotion that had flared extinguished itself just as quickly. Olof buying the cotton reels was an awful sign. He should have thought of the cotton reels as belonging to her, to be placed in a sewing kit that they soon would share. He was displaying no natural inclination to start a life with Ester. This pained her.

Or was it the other way around? Was he trying to keep how close he was to starting a life with Ester at bay, and because change was difficult for him, he had bought his own set of cotton reels to ward off the pain of the break-up? This would explain the twisting worry that seemed to have been tormenting him from the first moment in Arvidsjaur.

They were at the crossing on the main road, trying to decide whether or not to go back to the hotel, when out of the blue, Olof wrapped his arms around Ester and said:

'How I've been longing for you.'

'Have you?'

'So, so much. Just to be able to push myself inside you. I've been rock-hard for three weeks.'

They went back to the hotel. This time it was exactly as Ester had pictured it, except the sheets were wrinkled, not freshly ironed. After their lusts were satisfied, Olof wanted to rest. He rolled over and Ester snuggled against him. He asked her to keep a little distance, to stay on her side of the bed.

'I'm not used to having someone so close when I sleep.'

Outside the hotel windows, you couldn't see where the shore ended and the forest lake began, everything was the same shade of white. White but dark. Ester read while Olof rested. She reached for the nape of his neck, but didn't dare touch him, her hand hovered a centimetre from his skin, close enough to feel his heat.

Not used to it, she thought. Doesn't sound like a particularly sensual relationship.

———

At the edge of town lay a modest ski hut. They drove there the next day. They waxed their skis and strapped them on.

They skied the first hundred metres together, Ester behind Olof. This didn't sit well with her, she was at once uncomfortable and irritated. In her youth, Ester Nilsson had competed in orienteering and in the wintertime she'd kept in shape with cross-country skiing, though she had never really liked it, it was too monotonous. Even twenty years on, her skiing technique was unassailable. That made it easy for her to reach speeds she simply couldn't maintain.

She deliberated: 'Going skiing together' could mean you were out in the forest at the same time; it didn't have to mean you were doing it side by side. And if she was going to spend time doing something as unnecessary as skiing when they'd finally coupled she might as well get in a work-out. Besides, Olof wouldn't want her on his tail scrutinizing his technique, she thought.

So she chose a different track and skied away from Olof. Really going for it.

After just a few kilometres, her lungs were about to burst. She'd been on a steep incline, and at the crown of the hill she stopped and slumped on her poles, exhausted, heart racing.

The scene embedded itself in her senses and everywhere else memories are stored: the taste of blood that comes with exertion, the dry creaking snow, the tall pines, the shards of cold in her lungs, the forest's mighty silence, the scentless freeze, the desolate trail, the pointlessness of the endeavour.

What was she doing here – worn out on this five-kilometre trail in Arvidsjaur that resembled any other five-kilometre trail she'd ever been on – when she could have been gliding forth in peace and quiet with the person she would do anything to be near? What was going on with her?

After forty-five minutes and two dutiful laps, she was back at the waxing hut. There was Olof, putting on a dry undershirt. They didn't say much. He didn't comment on Ester having zipped off, but she sensed suppressed resentment. They got into the car and drove to the hotel.

Ester showered first. When she came out of the bathroom, Olof's phone rang.

'It's Ebba,' he said tensely. 'What should I do?'

'I suppose you should answer it.'

'But I can't talk to her while you're in the room.'

He let it ring and went out into the corridor. One minute later, hardly more, he returned, relaxed and happy. After a moment of hotel-silence Ester asked what Olof had in store for them. The day before, he'd casually introduced her to his young colleagues in the ensemble when they ran into them in the hallway. The colleagues were aware of Ebba's existence, they must be wondering, Ester said. How did he see things unfolding? Olof stiffened.

'What do you mean, "unfolding"?'

'Aren't you afraid they'll talk?'

'But they won't tell her.'

No, of course not, Ester thought. They wouldn't talk to *her*. But they'd talk to others and then the talk would be on its way and in the end, if Ebba was lucky, it would reach her.

But this isn't what she had wanted to talk about. She wanted to know when he was going to tell Ebba that he'd met someone else.

Olof sat in the armchair and looked at the ceiling.

'Maybe she's got something going on, too,' he said with a fullness in his voice that could have been mistaken for reflection.

'But what do I care,' he added.

For a person who was in the middle of a break-up and at the start of a new relationship, this was precisely the wrong thing to say.

It was for dinner, this Saturday dinner in Arvidsjaur, that Ester had bought the new jacket and blouse. White with floral embroidery, far too summery for February but so beautiful she couldn't resist. Olof noticed that the blouse was new and touched a flower on her sleeve. He said that it was odd to see her in florals but that the blouse was lovely and he liked the way Ester dressed. The dinner took place in the hotel's dining room where they'd eaten lunch the day before. The room was decorated in light pine with rippling fabrics and lacked character.

The dinner became a test.

During the early part, Olof sat there answering his wife's texts while waiting for their food and then between bites. He smiled as he read them and the smile lingered as he typed his replies. Sometimes he laughed.

Ester was so dismayed she couldn't put words to it, for if she did it wouldn't have been feasible to share a room with Olof that night. Not even a death in the family could have made her touch her phone during dinner with him. But her situation was different to Olof's. She wasn't married. She convinced herself that he was texting to keep his wife happy and unwitting, so that she wouldn't grow suspicious about a change in his behaviour and ruin their weekend now that it had finally come to pass. Olof was answering Ebba's texts now so that later he would be left in peace with the woman he loved and wanted to be with.

There was another interpretation of which she was vaguely aware and rejected in full: that it was especially important now – after such large concessions had been made – to show his mistress that it wasn't to her he belonged, but to his wife, so Ester wouldn't get it into her head that she had any power here even if he'd displayed weakness by needing her physically.

She ate her food in silence. She ate and ate. When Olof finally noted how deep her dejection had become, he set aside his phone and didn't touch it again. He followed her gaze out of the window. The shift was instantaneous. Now it was just the two of them. Together, they took in the winter night from the dining room of the Hotel Laponia. They shared a view, shared a dinner, the wife was gone and he was compensating her generously.

'It doesn't get better than this,' he said. 'The most beautiful winter outside, toasty inside, a tasty dinner and in bed, a woman you love . . . making love to.'

Ester was sure that there was a pause between 'love' and 'making love to'. He said he loved her. There was a pause there, she hadn't misheard, 'in bed, a woman you love'. Olof definitely paused after 'love' before he realized that it was a dangerous sentence to utter, one which he might need to account for. Making love was objective fact. As for love, only he could know. His words alone were the proof. And so he added a pause and 'making love to'.

She offered a faint smile.

Olof was wrong about one thing, she thought. The dinner was not tasty. It was anything but: industrial, ready-made and then shipped through the interior of Norrland. In order to fill the growing void, she consumed more than the flavour warranted and her hunger demanded. There was cheesecake for dessert, this too from a package and a conveyor belt. She ate the entire piece, sensing the touch of mass-production over everything here, even over her and Olof, the two of them, far from home during their tryst, slick with the sleaze of sneaking around.

Olof paid the bill, which ended up being quite expensive.

He said that because Ester had travelled all the way to Arvidsjaur to be with him it was only fair he paid for the food.

They went back to the room. Ester felt over-stuffed and alienated but that disappeared the second they were in each other's arms, which they were and continued to be late into the night. The next morning, too, was devoted to erotic enjoyments. As Olof lay atop Ester looking into her eyes, where he couldn't elude the lack of reservation, he whispered to her:

'This will never work. I'm too boring. You'll tire of me.'

An hour later, he drove her to the airport.

Soon he would move on to another town in Norrland. Ester asked which one and promptly forgot. She usually remembered such things – places, dates, times – but this she forgot because it wasn't what she was wondering. There were other answers she was after.

Olof's hand was on her thigh for the entire journey, except when he changed gear. The forest around them was as still and white as when she'd arrived two days ago and the ploughed snowbanks even higher. The trees were wearing hats and overcoats.

Olof parked the car and accompanied her to the departure hall.

'Thank you for coming,' he said and held her, rocking from side to side.

'Do you think we'll see each other again?'

'There's a risk we might.'

His body. It was her downfall. She didn't want to be without it even though his frustrating ambivalence was constantly in play, even as they said goodbye.

'We'll see each other in Stockholm,' he clarified.

And she flew home. Then she walked from Central Station to Kungsholmen, the boot digging into her Achilles tendon. In Stockholm, all the snow had melted. It was dark outside and dark inside. She felt the desolation and latent despair, started making calls; no one but Fatima answered, though she'd left calling her till last. She was the most principled and least accommodating. A few years before Fatima had had a drawn-out relationship with a married man in which she'd been tossed between euphoria and misery. Now she was married and had two small children who were allowed to endlessly insist on her attention when she was on the phone, something Ester endured with equanimity, aware as she was that she took up too much of people's valuable time and energy. Fatima told Ester that once people got physical, expectations could develop. From this point forward, Ester had rights. Ester knew her other girlfriends would have given more tactical advice, but just then she thought there was really something to this notion of rights.

Spurred by the charge to make demands, if only as an

excuse to speak to Olof and tell him that she already missed him, she called him that very night. He was watching TV with the volume on high, was dull-voiced, and didn't lower the sound.

'Am I interrupting?' she asked.

'I'm watching the news.'

'I understand.'

She fell silent, waiting for insight to strike him.

'Do you want to keep watching the news?'

'I can watch while we talk. Was it nice to get home?'

'No, of course not. It was awful.'

'Really? Aha. Yeah.'

He sounded self-conscious yet distant, or as one does when one wishes to keep a certain someone and her menacing intimacies at bay.

'Are you in another hotel room now?'

'Yes. It's nice. Good TV.'

'I can hear that.'

A few times in conjunction with the production in Västerås the previous autumn, Ester had seen Olof and his wife interact. Each time she'd noticed his wife's sarcasm. Everyone who knew the couple could testify to the noxious verbal discharges Ebba Silfversköld directed at her husband, and at others. Ester had taken this as a sign of her spiritual hollowness and how bad they had it. Malice and sarcasm couldn't co-exist with a loving disposition; they were the antechambers of dead relationships, they were contempt shirking from the light, cowardice piggybacking on aggression.

Or they were the final defence of the disappointed and hurt against unjust indifference. Now, during this stifling conversation, Ester understood Olof's wife's sarcasm. She sensed in herself a corrosive contagion, heard it hissing in her words.

'I'm going to bed soon,' Olof said.

'Will you sleep well?'

'Like a rock.'

'I won't.'

Olof didn't enquire, said nothing, kept watching the news.

'Have you eaten dinner?' Ester asked.

'The whole gang went to a pizzeria.'

When she didn't ask a question, the conversation came to a halt.

'What kind of pizza did you have?'

'Calzone.'

'Folded over?'

'Yeah. One of those rolls with oozing cheese.'

'With flakes of oregano on top?'

'I didn't notice. Maybe.

Silence.

'Was it good?'

'Yes.'

'Did you have a nice time?'

'Yes. They're a nice bunch to travel with.'

'Did any of them ask about us? About you and me.'

'No.'

'So no one commented on my visit?'

'I can't say that they did.'

'Strange.'

'Why would we talk about it?'

'Indeed. Why.'

'It's nobody else's business.'

'Well it certainly is somebody else's business, but perhaps not your touring theatre company's, no.'

Olof's irritation rose, stood at attention.

'I've been thinking,' said Ester.

'Ugh.'

'Of course you can take it like that.'

'Something unpleasant is coming.'

Ester refrained from saying anything until she regained her self-control.

'Maybe you want to turn the volume down?'

She readied herself. She knew she shouldn't say what she was going to say but thought it had to be said, and remembered her rights.

'I've been the mistress before. I have no intention of being one again.'

And after a pause, to avoid any misunderstanding:

'I want to be with you in a real way.'

The TV could no longer be heard, but Olof's breathing was louder.

'You have to choose,' said Ester.

The words echoed and clattered. She knew she wasn't ready to back them up by desisting, which rendered them worthless.

Olof's rage arrived quickly as rage does.

'So I'm supposed to end things with Ebba right away or what?! Tonight? Or when the fuck do you mean? You want me to call her right now? Huh?'

He made the thought sound absurd. For Ester, it was absurd that the thought was absurd. She said that Olof had had six months to think about it.

'What do you mean, six months? Think about what?'

She felt ice cold, and when she was cold, he was hot.

Regretting the outburst, Olof wished her a good night. She would not have one, but the sentiment itself was enough to keep her hooked.

Three days went by, three days of slush outside and dejection within. Ester sat with the Gottlob Frege but couldn't work. On the Wednesday evening she went to the cinema with an acquaintance. They rarely met up but Ester still talked about Olof and her consuming worry over him not seeming to think their weekend away was a turning point. Ester's acquaintance listened and offered a quick diagnosis. Olof had been after casual sex and Ester should leave him. Ester found this analysis shallow, conventional and moreover wrong because the sex had been the hardest thing to get him on board with. She changed the subject and resisted the impulse to offer a justification.

The film they saw was being shown at the Grand on Sveavägen and was about a woman who fell in love with a Stasi agent who didn't like what he was doing but was stuck in the system and fraught with self-loathing. During the screening, Ester sneaked her phone out of her bag several times and lit up the cinema. The third time she did this, Olof had called. She wanted to leave right away, in the middle of the film, run to him and throw herself into his arms. But she was stuck in the middle of a row and besides she had her acquaintance to consider.

After the film, she listened to the message surreptitiously, making sure to do so while her acquaintance was in the ladies' because Ester understood her unspoken criticism as clearly as if she had come right out with it.

She heard how Olof was trying to sound light and breezy in spite of his irritation at having been the one to call her and not the other way around; he even asked if she was out of the country. Ester smiled to herself. Was she to have fled out of disappointment? Or did Olof think that she would only be out of touch if she was out of the country?

There was another, far worse explanation: this was one of those acts of performative speech Olof so expertly commanded. If this was the case, then he was conveying that regardless of what had transpired between them last weekend, Ester was free to travel abroad without telling him because they weren't close. The purpose of this statement was to communicate this distance in spite of the closeness implied in calling her.

To Ester it was incomprehensible that they might not be close, so she didn't even acknowledge this explanation.

When the acquaintance, now back from the toilet, noticed that Ester was more interested in calling Olof than the rest of their evening together, she said she wanted to go home. She was hurt; Ester tried to make up for it, but it was too late.

They took Sveavägen south to the subway and talked

about the film. The acquaintance noted how typical it was for the woman to die in the end so that the man can be redeemed. Ester suggested it could just as well be interpreted that many men felt women were important as romantic partners and they quite simply despaired upon watching their beloveds die.

'You're too individualist and too romantic.'

'Love can be important in a person's life whatever the normative ideas on the subject.'

'You're not talking about love. You're talking about heterosexual coupledom.'

'I'm talking about love, erotic and intellectual. Coupledom is just a symptom of the closeness implied in loving.'

'As I said, *un individu romantique*.'

Ester's acquaintance was more than nettled. Ester may have been too, because she impertinently pointed out that in the film, half of all of those who died in the end were men. It was hard to say that the women's death toll was related to their being women; you couldn't have different and pre-determined models of explanation that varied according to gender, right? That would imply you're using what you hope to discover as a starting point and seeking evidence that supports a theory, rather than trying to uncover a truth about reality.

'The very point of observation is to support a theory,' said the acquaintance, 'because the theory is true.'

'So what do you do when something contradicts it?'

The acquaintance replied that the theory was there to identify and describe a real structure.

But then, haven't you assumed what you were meant to prove? Ester wondered while she thought about Olof's call; maybe their future was bright after all.

'You should read up on this,' said the acquaintance. 'If you did, you'd also have the tools to understand what that man is doing to you and with you.'

The distance between the two night-strollers increased by a few centimetres as they continued down the pavement.

'In films women die in order to redeem men. And in reality women think they can help men be redeemed,' said the acquaintance.

'But if you already know why certain things happen to various types of people, then you don't need data,' said Ester, 'neither in the form of films nor reality, because data will never influence your interpretation of reality; on the contrary, it's adapted to keep the model intact and unassailable. Isn't that approach questionable? There could be many other and more complex explanations for what you're describing.'

'Your view of knowledge is antiquated.'

'Yes. It's as old as this street. But how do you interpret the death of men in the film?'

'I'm not interested in how men have it, but surely there's a theory if only you'd study the literature. Call that lover of yours who's using you. I'm getting on the subway here.'

And with that the acquaintance disappeared into the

entrance at Hötorget at the corner of Kungsgatan and Sveavägen.

Ester wasn't interested how men have it either, but she did have an especial interest in how one particular man had it, who she called while standing at the doors of the Kungshallen food hall with Hötorget and Filmstaden as a backdrop and Kungsgatan stretching like a black rope underfoot.

The phone rang at least ten times. He didn't answer. Dissatisfied, she hurried home on foot. She was thinking volatile thoughts about herself, about Olof and his reasons for not answering, about her view of knowledge and about her acquaintance's view of knowledge. Right then she couldn't bear the idea that she shared her acquaintance's epistemology of Olof Sten and his love life. All the sense data transmitted to her was being used to support the theory that he harboured the same romantic interest for Ester Nilsson as she did for him, and that only external and internal hurdles were stopping him, hurdles that time and her good influence would clear. It seemed no data could alter this thesis, and she presupposed a fixed structure of love and a universal human being as postulate and axiom, impervious to each refractory piece of empirical evidence; instead it was reshaped to better fit her theory.

The whole walk home she hoped he'd call her back. She kept the phone in her hand so she wouldn't miss him. Now wasn't the time to get desperate and call him once a minute, she thought. After twenty minutes, she was home and calling him from her landline. No answer. She called again five minutes later.

The sound of his voice sped her pulse. He said he was at the pub with his nephew. Ester wished he'd been at the pub with her instead now that they knew each other carnally, but thought it was nice that he cared about his nephew.

Olof suggested a date the next day, sounding decisive, as if there were something he wanted to talk to her about. She tried to set a time and place but he didn't want to. Firm commitments are to protect the weaker party, for the stronger one wants to keep everything open in case he's struck by a whim. Weak is the party who wants too much, strong is the one for whom it doesn't really matter.

'I'll call you tomorrow afternoon to confirm a time and place,' said Olof, and she would have to be satisfied with that.

Those unlucky in love and of a certain temperament are compelled to talk about it, all the time and with anyone. Speaking eases the pain. When Ester Nilsson was content, she didn't air her private matters. She didn't need to. In suffering, she became loose-lipped and careless with herself and very one-sided. She searched everywhere and anywhere for something, a word, a phrase, an observation that could help her see the connections and move forward. Hope was all she wanted, not wise words on the art of resignation.

Thus she displayed her misery for all to see. When she was out of earshot, she knew people talked and offered diagnoses, that the adjectives flowed. And yet she continued to open herself up like a wound in an inopportune place – each time hoping to be offered something propitious that was also likely, but instead, as with all wounds that keep opening up, only fresh bacteria from the exhausted audience were introduced.

The next day, before she was to meet Olof, Ester had lunch with her old supervisor at the Royal Institute of Technology. They met up on occasion to talk about things that only they enjoyed, namely their subject, which was also all they had in common. The supervisor was a pleasant woman who had been pleasantly married for twenty-five years and had two pleasant children who studied at the RIT and they too were following paths to lives filled with pleasantries. When she had listened to Ester's story, the woman offered a number of comments, all of which were in fact for her own benefit:

'How nice not to have to deal with all of that.'

And:

'That sounds awful. Can't you just forget about him?'

And:

'God, we used to run around like that as teenagers!'

Ester felt flattened but quite sure this woman hadn't 'run around like that' even as a teenager, but already then had prized her ability to differentiate between what was important and what was not.

'Oh, how nice not to have to deal with that,' she repeated.

Ester chastised herself for prattling, but she understood that what she'd just heard was a defence against a far too intimate confession coming from someone to whom you didn't feel close and didn't want to get that close to. The hostile comments themselves were a way of staving off intimacy and the draughty meagreness of one's own life. Ester wished she could rescind her confessions. This other woman was smart. The situation hadn't been equal to Ester's intelligence, and she did not want her former supervisor's life. She cautioned herself to choose who she spoke to more wisely. Slamming on the brakes twice in less than one day was taking a toll on her.

The former supervisor was warning Ester about the age difference, which Ester had barely given a thought to, much less considered relevant. She explained that Olof might be frail and infirm one day and then it might not be as fun. The supervisor and her husband were born in the same year and month, only ten days apart.

Ester nodded; there was no point with some people. True passion, fire in the blood, couldn't be communicated to those who were cast in stone. They didn't understand it. If you could resist something because at some point, one day it might cause pain, it was something you could live without altogether. But Ester could not live without this certain something.

At two o'clock they finished their lunch at Grill near Strindberg's Blue Tower on Drottninggatan.

'Is he a good thinker?' the supervisor asked as they walked downhill towards the Central Bath House and Hurtig's Bakery, as though sensing she hadn't said the right things.

'He's a good sport. That's the important part. And a good listener.'

'That's not enough for you, Ester. This is beyond me.'

Ester refrained from saying any of the awful things she could have said in reply. They parted at T-Centralen and she continued along Drottninggatan towards Old Town. On Stora Nygatan she took a seat in a coffee shop and waited. When Olof called she wanted to be close to Södermalm and City, the better to rush to wherever he was.

It was slushy and damp and there was a rawness to the air. She wondered why he didn't call. They were supposed to be in touch 'in the afternoon' and that meant any moment now. Ester sat in a corner and took her laptop out of her bag to finish writing an essay that needed to be submitted to her newspaper editor the following morning. She had to make it work even if she was feeling scattered.

It was quarter past three; she reworked a few sentences. Twenty past three; deleted an adjective, missed it and put it back. Read through the text; it was a bit too long. Three twenty-five; deleted an entire paragraph at the beginning and got the text to the right word count, but now it lacked structure and direction. Well, in that sense, it mirrored life itself. Three thirty; she considered changing careers, and spent a moment reading. Thirty-five past the hour; the telephone lay mute on the table.

Twenty to four, she decided to call him, and when she heard the warmth on the other end of the line, life was worth living again.

'I was just about to call you. I've been walking all around Söder.'

'Oh, good.'

'Now I'm at the Katarina Cemetery.'

'That one's stunning. Are you at your father's grave?'

'Yes. For the first time since he died. How did you know?'

Ester thought he might be preparing for a separation without knowing it and that's why he was at his father's grave – a separation from his wife who, presumably, held power over him by moving between hot and cold as he'd often described his father had. Now he was in the cemetery, bidding farewell to his father, that is to say his wife. She was filled with hope.

'We were supposed to meet up,' she said, 'isn't that what we said?'

'I suppose we did.'

'Can't we go for a beer? Just drop out together. I want to get drunk today. With you.'

'No. I'll stick to coffee.'

When Olof Sten refused alcohol, there was a good reason.

'I'm going for dinner with a friend at some point tonight,' he said.

Ester looked out over Stora Nygatan. The city's pavements were for the most part closed because of the risk of falling icicles, so people were walking in the middle of the street. The drainpipes were flooding and sheets of slush were sliding down the roofs.

'I thought we'd decided to see each other today.'

'Well in that case, I have to go home and change. I'm sweaty.'

'Weren't we going to see each other properly? Not just for a spell before dinner with your friend.'

'Don't try to make me feel guilty.'

I'm not allowed to guilt-trip you, thought Ester, but you're allowed to disappoint me in whichever way you like. With Olof, everything was loose, up in the air. It was a sort of virtue for him, his version of freedom, and the second Ester tried to fix it in place she was guilt-tripping him.

'But we said.'

'You're pressuring me. I haven't seen my friend in ages. He wanted to have dinner with me today.'

Ester's words ebbed away. There were none at her disposal. It went quiet.

'I guess I'll come and see you all sweaty, then. But don't complain if I stink.'

'I like the way you stink.'

He laughed his mildest laugh. Within ten minutes they were at Sundberg's bakery on Järntorget. The cafe was mostly filled with pushchairs and new mothers. They sat in a corner as far from them as possible. As luck would have it, that corner was next to the toilet, which received a steady stream of visitors.

Ester told him about the newspaper article that was due tomorrow, and Olof listened attentively and asked questions about the theme: how group behaviour could be mapped onto individual personality types, and how relationships between different groups were structured in the same way as they were between people. In short, nature was mathematical and always followed set patterns, one simply had to identify them correctly.

'How many hours do you write a day?'

'As few as possible. I'm having a hard time working right now.'

'I see. Yeah. Such is life.'

He looked away and didn't want to hear the reasons why. And then he rubbed his chilled hands together and said that he and Ebba had gone to see a Harold Pinter play at the City Theatre two days ago. He relayed his impressions and mentioned that Ebba was quite taken with one of the male actors. With what sounded like resentment, he pointed out that Ebba would never allow him to say the same thing about another woman without triggering intense jealousy.

He appeared to be asking Ester to explain what he understood to be a characteristic, one of many, common to the female sex. Ester could offer no explanation. She was thinking that the way Olof was talking about his life didn't suggest a break-up.

He seemed completely unaware that Ester was wondering why he and the wife had gone to the theatre together when they were supposed to be in the middle of a divorce, and he seemed to believe that he could offer poor Ester knowledge of a minor rift between the spouses as consolation for the time he'd spent with his wife. But that rift was for nothing. To Ester, the rift was already clear as day considering what they'd been doing together. She wanted to know why that rift didn't have any consequences. Why did people tolerate their abysmal rifts when there was something that could be done about them?

'How's it going with you?' Olof asked.

'Not great, actually.'

They drank their coffees. Around them, the mothers were nursing in groups.

'And you?' Ester asked.

'Me? I'm good.'

He said this casually, almost with frivolity. This is precisely what happens when your life is a lie, Ester thought. You lose your bearings for meaning, as well as what's appropriate to say, how and when.

'You got sad last time,' he said.

Last time? Ester wondered, what happened last time? Aren't I always sad?

'Yes, I suppose I did.'

'I can't leave Ebba.'

A short pause.

'I don't want to.'

A short pause.

'I can't hurt her like that.'

A final pause.

Ester noted the shift from 'can't' to 'want' and the retreat to 'can't'. But who could say whether it was 'can't' or 'want' that mattered. She felt poisoned, as though her body had flooded with some sort of toxic waste. She'd been wrong about Olof; he didn't despise the definite and worship vagueness and apathy. When this unfixed state needed protection, he became active and clear. Once putrefaction and murkiness had been secured, he went back to being indolent.

Yet again she noted Olof's relief when he'd finished making a difficult statement, the point of which was to get rid of Ester's taxing expectations but not Ester herself. It was the same each time. He cancelled his dinner plans because he decided he'd rather eat with Ester.

Like so often before, she should have left, but she wasn't one for power play. Especially if it was meant to conceal a great inner need, which it usually was. The day she managed to decline an evening invitation from Olof was the day she would become indifferent to him.

So they ate dinner on this night too and came closer to each other than ever before. Ester told him about her life, mostly about her unhappy romances, and Olof about his, mostly about how people had consistently failed him. His father hit him and his mother favoured his sister and early on he'd been tricked by a woman into fathering a child. He was a hard-done-by person, not an active subject in his life, but Ester didn't think so, because her heart had been made porous by the bitter melancholy of losing Olof and even more porous by nonetheless being here with him, receiving his raw confidences. She understood that his suppressed rage came from a lifetime of humiliation. She saw the world through the lens of his wrongs and wanted to throw herself in harm's way and take the bullet that was meant for him, protect him from all evil, fight everyone who threatened him. Something in the way he talked to her and looked at her made her want to do anything for him in the belief that she was dear to him.

The whole night was like one long exhalation. Now that they'd hit bottom and expectations had been checked, they returned to a state of emergency, the no man's land where other rules applied and everything started from zero, where vitality increased of itself and the riches of the soul were concentrated. Olof was a state-of-emergency man but wanted to make it par for the course. Impossible by definition, and so it was his life's paradox and grandest dilemma.

After having sat for so long in one of their regular haunts, Olof wanted to move on, so they went down to the wine bar by the Katarina Lift. There they sat on a sofa, shoulder to shoulder, thigh to thigh. The room was a warm orange-red, and a plethora of bottles stood behind the bar. The sounds around them were muffled, the other patrons were solitary newspaper-readers and chatting couples. By the window was a man who, judging by how he kept glancing at his wristwatch and the displeasure set in the small muscles around his eyes, was waiting for someone who hadn't turned up. The hour was neither late, nor early. They drank the dry, full-bodied wine. Ester was tired of drinking so much wine but drank nonetheless. More out of resignation than out of curiosity, she said:

'So we're never sleeping together again. Even now that we've finally got things going. It's intolerable.'

Olof watched the man waiting by the window and said: 'I guess it's inevitable.'

The wine bottles held their breath and Ester didn't dare turn her head, only her eyes. When everything was at risk, reserve and subtlety were essential.

'What's inevitable?'

'That we'll sleep together again.'

Her attention was so heightened that the words and the moment in which they were spoken were to her memory what a hot poker is to wood.

'We'll just have to wait and see,' said Olof. 'Wait and see.'

He looked out of the dark windows with something troubled about his expression, that concave nose, the round high forehead and those funny coin-slot eyes of his. He was at once light and heavy, imposing and frail.

'What do you mean?' Ester asked. 'What are you saying?'

He withheld his reply, gazed across the water at Skepps-holmen Island, velvet-black with gold and silver points of shining light. Then he said:

'I don't know what I want. That's my problem. I don't know what I want.'

He turned to Ester.

'Maybe you could be my therapist?'

'That's probably not such a good idea.'

'No, probably not. But I don't know what I want.'

The lights in the bar flicked on and off, last orders.

'How can you not know?' Ester said. 'You just have to let your feelings guide you.'

Olof raised his glass of red and pointed to it; the waiter nodded.

'If I gave in to my feelings, my life would be chaos. And it has been for the most part,' he said.

The wine arrived and he swigged half of it down.

'What you're really saying,' said Ester, 'is that you know what you want but you don't trust that it's the right thing to do?'

'Yes. Precisely.'

'What you're saying is that you want to be with me, but you don't think it's morally correct according to a measuring stick that isn't yours but that you're still guided by?'

'I suppose that's what I'm saying, yes. The consequences of breaking up are too big. I can't do that to Ebba.'

He smoothed his eyebrows.

'If she didn't exist, there'd be no problem,' he said.

'But she exists.'

They paid and got up.

'We'll just have to wait and see,' he repeated.

Olof was headed for Katarinavägen and Ester the subway. She didn't think that what she'd heard was anything but true: he was willing but not able. Ester had a hard time imagining a psyche that held nothing to be true or false, but only concerned itself with primal strategies against its own abandonment. That psyche, which went by the name Olof Sten, had perceived how Ester would now glide away from him because he'd declared that he was choosing his wife, which he'd done so that he wouldn't be annihilated by not choosing the wife. In doing so, he was risking being annihilated by not choosing his mistress, and thus his reptile brain had to come up with something to keep the rejected party from disappearing. The reptile brain lived in the present and on impulse. It understood that abandonment was unpleasant, but not the steps that had got him there and its logical consistency and reason. To avoid abandonment there was a set of phrases that Olof's reptile brain sent to his mouth. Ester didn't know that a person could function in this manner without at least trying to resist it by reasoning, or indeed by making up for it the next day.

She didn't yet sense that this was how language could be emptied of content and substance.

It was almost midnight when Ester was waiting for the subway on the platform at Slussen. More than anything else she wanted to stop having these nights out that always ended in farewell.

If they could only go home together tonight, if only everything was different.

Wasn't it to escape the dejection that followed these constant nights out with built-in farewells that so many people throughout history had felt one person short when they were single, but that three was a crowd? Ester wondered.

As she thought this through, it became increasingly clear that she and Olof had not got closer that night, but rather, he'd clarified his intention of never getting divorced. This was what she needed to keep in mind, and not the chink he'd also left open. He'd announced who he belonged to and that person was not Ester. He'd thought about it and had made a decision. That decision was the takeaway from this ambiguous evening and the only factor that should sway her. She forced herself to believe that he'd said no, even though the rest of the evening had looked and sounded like half a yes and definitely a maybe.

The train to Hässelby rolled into the station. As she was climbing aboard, a text arrived from Olof. He couldn't have got far up Katarinavägen before he'd written it. It read: 'Really lovely seeing you tonight.'

Ester didn't reply because the message was absurd and absurdity called for sarcasm in response.

Yet again Olof had put the brakes on just as their relationship was getting going. She contemplated this soberly on her way home. Back at her apartment, she burst into tears over her awful life and her poor choices. The tears wouldn't stop – so insistent and strident that her eyes swelled and her nose stuffed up. The following day she succumbed to a high temperature and was bedridden for seven days. Her temperature was nearly thirty-nine degrees. She cancelled her scheduled assignments and gave up all attempts at industry. When she wasn't sleeping she was half in torpor, and speculated on a loop:

One: If Olof's wife was so important to him that he couldn't leave her, why was he betraying her?

Two: Since he was already betraying her physically and mentally, how could she persist in being so important that he had to stay with her?

Three: If neither the wife nor Ester were important to him, was he just sticking with the option that caused no trouble, risk or embarrassment in his social circle? But why was he with either of them if they weren't important?

Thoughts one and two implied that she didn't understand him. Three suggested that Olof was spiritually indolent, deeply careless and cruel, and that once again Ester was in love with a negligent and shallow person she didn't understand. That couldn't be right. Therefore the premise must be false and was leading her to false conclusions. There was likely a fourth possibility, unknown to her, that would straighten it all out. She just had to work out what it was.

Days passed. The fever held and a stomach upset set in. She threw up the little she had managed to consume during this hungerless spell.

In her more lucid moments she read a book by Simenon, bought on impulse at an antiquarian bookseller: *Maigret Takes the Water*. It offered relief amidst the misery, the style was precise and light, direct and unadorned but sensual enough to avoid being spartan, that enticing hazard of literary asceticism. It gladdened her that black letters on white paper could be so reassuring.

Spring came and went. The buds broke open and the sap rose, but in Ester it sank. Twice, once in March and once in April when she was on her way out, she caught a glimpse of Olof across the street from her front door, half-hidden by a tree. On a third occasion she saw him in the distance at the Fridhemsgatan crossing. He seemed to be searching for something while wanting to hide. On another occasion she saw him wandering through the Västermalm mall. He seemed to be passing through her neighbourhood on a near daily basis. What did he want? Well, he'd said it at the wine bar: he didn't know.

Vera said it was a mirage and Ester was seeing what she wanted to see. But if there was one thing Ester knew about herself it was that she could differentiate between reality and fantasy. Vera didn't know her very well, she realized. Ester wasn't in the least interested in believing the unlikely or erecting a facade of herself for herself. If she believed something it was because she'd determined that there were good reasons for it to be true. And however she looked at the matter and Olof's behaviour over the past half year or so that they'd known each other, there had been good reason to suppose that he was harbouring romantic plans for the two of them.

And now this sneaking around in her neighbourhood.

Six weeks after Olof broke it off, he sent a blank text message.

'A blank text message is the definition of not enough,' Elin, Fatima, Vera and Lotta chimed in chorus. 'He sent a blank text so that you could fill it with content for him. No, that's insufficient. His actions have to be clearer for them to be worth anything.'

Ester didn't send a reply. Another two weeks passed. Then Olof called and asked if he'd forgotten a pair of gloves at hers. She looked on the hat rack and said she couldn't see them. Did he mean the brown ones that were scuffed on the right index finger?

'Those are the ones!' he said.

The next day they met over sausages and sauerkraut at Löwenbräu on Fridhemsplan. Ester had bought him a new pair of gloves, and after they'd eaten gave them to him, blushing. They spoke searchingly and with care about what had happened to them since their last conversation. The wife was never once mentioned. On his suggestion they went back to her place, just as it was his suggestion they meet near her place, all so she wouldn't have to travel far. Clearly he thought he owed her. As they neared her door, his voice had an odd vibrato that Ester didn't recognize:

'I'm not often in this area.'

Ester understood he was trying to tell her he hadn't

been sneaking around her building and gazing up at her window, in case she thought she'd seen him there. But nothing is as neon-bright as a denial no one was asking for.

They sat a while in her kitchen. Because she hadn't been expecting company she didn't have anything to drink at home other than a splash of cognac that had been there for years. Lust steamed the air but Ester couldn't quite sense it because she was too tense – she felt unclear about what he was doing here. Hotly, he rubbed his thumb against hers but then got up to leave with a nervous suddenness. As they hugged goodbye he bent like a pocket knife so she wouldn't be able to feel his physical response.

The incomplete, unnecessary and for its purposes unclear meeting wounded Ester. She was torn up and called him the next day to say it was better not to see each other at all than have this hankering and temptation without release. An unpleasant fight resulted, in which Olof asked why it was so hard for her to understand that he didn't want a romantic relationship, but a friendly one.

She hung up without further comment. This protracted despair was exhausting.

Three days later when she came home one afternoon, a snus tin was on her entryphone. She saw immediately that it had been placed there with intent.

Olof used two types of snus and this was the more un-usual of the two, herbal and nicotine-free. It was the kind he used when making a bid for health. His attempts at being healthier had always coincided with benevolence and making overtures with Ester and their relationship. He'd usually buy the better-for-your-health snus for the sake of her and their future so she'd see the door to him was open.

She took the tin upstairs with her into her apartment and opened the lid. A portion was all that remained, almost dry but still pungent. She held it with her fingertips and thought tenderly about how it had recently been tucked under his lip. Her longing for their moments together made her body ache.

Vera shouted straight down the telephone line:

'You're interpreting signs! He has not placed a snus tin on your intercom. Ester, I'm seriously starting to worry about you. You're imagining things. He wants to be with Ebba, you have to respect that! Who do you think you are?!'

But Ester wanted to be sure. One week later she saw Olof at a theatre festival in Falun where he was in a revival of a production of *Death of a Salesman* that he'd been in the year before. Ester had been invited to give a speech about the differences and similarities between poetic, dramatic and philosophical language. Afterwards there were drinks and soggy croustades and she talked with her good friend Zoran who'd played Olof's son in the production. Over the past half year she'd been in touch with Zoran every now and then to see how things were going and to fish for clues from someone working so close to Olof.

She saw Olof and his wife standing by the wall in the festival tent, and Olof saw Ester conversing with the younger man. Their eyes met. Olof gave her a scornful smile. Because it was appalling to stand beside one's wife while smiling scornfully at Ester it could only mean that his marriage was crumbling after all, that it was only a matter of time.

She smiled too, feebly and lacklustre. The wife looked her up and down and took a lap around the room, perhaps courting competition for her husband, far better equipped as she likely was in understanding how to turn a grindstone like Olof.

Ester touched Zoran's shoulder, excused herself and went over to Olof. His eyes glittered; he seemed happy to see her. After exchanging a few words about the festival, Ester got straight to the point and asked if he'd placed a snus tin on her entryphone the week before. He flat-out denied it, but did so with such speed, verbosity and understanding that she suspected he wasn't telling the truth. He tried to frame this assertion as crazy and bizarre but knew far too well to which event and snus tin she was referring for him to seem credible. It all became clear when, with the extra embroidery that burdens every strained lie, he said, 'Putting snus tins on people's doorbells isn't my thing.' She hadn't mentioned a doorbell, but on the intercom was a graphic of an old-fashioned doorbell symbol that he'd apparently registered subconsciously. It's difficult to outwit your own mind, and even harder to control its associations. Moreover she knew that when people said something wasn't 'their style' they were usually lying, just as when they'd studiously repeat an accusation in order to insist on its absurdity. Things that need to be lied about were usually exactly what diverged from the style one wished to cultivate. We all want to believe that what we do out of shame is in fact is not part of our personality, our 'style'.

So Olof had indeed been lurking by her front door, sending blank text messages, speaking to her through objects and signs. Clearly he didn't want to lose her, but instead to stay in intimate but unspoken contact. He wanted no personal responsibility.

Nothing was decided, nothing lost, he hadn't made a decision, that much was clear. Ester understood that she had moved him deeply, if such depth existed. She assumed it did, after all everyone had receptors for the sublime.

Influenced by this knowledge, Ester decided it would be good to have a car, and thereby hurry along this sluggish course of events. Within a couple days she had found a second-hand pea-green Renault Twingo. Cute. Compact. Fast.

She had driven her new car home and was in the middle of parallel-parking it on Sankt Göransgatan when Vera called to say she'd just left an editorial meeting on Drott-ninggatan on her way to Sergels Torg and in this short distance alone she had seen five discarded snus tins. One of them was on an electricity box. Did Ester think this tin, too, had been placed there in order to be interpreted?

'But Olof's snus tin wasn't lying flat, it was standing up,' said Ester.

'I'm worried about you. Why aren't you using your sense and those faculties of reason you're otherwise so fond of?'

'But I am. And the most reasonable thing is that Olof placed the tin with one last pinch of snus on my intercom. By now I've become quite fluent in his sign language. He prefers to express himself so that the situation can be understood without him having to come right out and explain it. Otherwise it might be held against him.'

'If he wants to be with you, he should be with you.'

'Sure. But he wants to and doesn't want to. So far.'

For the rest of the spring, Ester kept the snus tin next to her on her desk as she worked. The pinch dried out and went from dark brown to dirty brown to yellowed beige. She considered getting proof by sending it to the Swedish National Forensic Centre's laboratory in Linköping together with a trace of Olof that she could probably scrape up at home. But individual citizens probably couldn't send things to the SNFC for testing.

On one of the last days in May, Olof was to travel to Norrköping and start rehearsing yet another play, a new Swedish drama that was a deconstruction of Ibsen's *A*

Doll's House. They were in sporadic phone contact so Ester knew on which day he was travelling. She also knew the difficult season was approaching, the season during which married men disappeared.

Major delays on the rail network were reported on the news. Without giving it a second thought, she called Olof and said that if he wanted to ensure a timely arrival, it would be best if she drove him to Norrköping. He'd get to see her new car, and she'd read that book about the origins of the universe he'd recommended a while ago and wanted to discuss with her.

It should be noted, the delays were on the northern main line and the problem had been cleared up in the morning, but she didn't need to mention that. Surely electrical wiring or some such had been affected in the south too; train trouble usually had chain reactions.

Olof accepted immediately, he very much wanted to be given a lift to Norrköping. So Ester picked him up on Bondegatan and they drove through the hazy early summer afternoon. Everything was calm and agreeable. Olof was so relaxed even the lines on his face had smoothed out. They spoke about the universe. When he first read the book, he said, he realized just how unlikely it was that the universe and Earth existed and could exist. Presupposing that all the constants had been in the right configuration at a certain point in time was so incomprehensible it shouldn't have been possible.

Ester kept her eyes on the road. It was an easy drive. Not

a lot of cars were out at this time on a Monday. She replied that of course it was hard for a human brain to comprehend, but clearly it was possible because it had happened.

'If billions and billions of uninterrupted chemical reactions are occurring,' she said, 'or "attempting to create the universe", then at some point one result will be the universe as we know it, and that's the condition for our existence, which in turn is the condition for our ability to think about its incomprehensibility. The chain of events seems unlikely because we're reading them backwards. We simply have to subordinate ourselves, and not try to subordinate nature to our consciousness's understanding of likelihood. The truth is there whether or not we understand it.'

'Right,' he said and laughed wickedly as though he was reacting to something else.

'Even stranger than the origin of the universe,' Ester countered, 'is that people can go an entire life without wondering if it should be lived differently.'

She trained her gaze on the road.

'Was that a dig?'

She could tell he felt very close to her today. Only then did he catch that type of suggestion and do so with a smile. The rekindled joy of intimacy lifted her up above the Östergötland plains and made everything beautiful. Nature was at its most delightful on these late May days, she thought, as she drove along the ugly motorway. The light was ethereal, none of the beauty faded, only July would usher in staleness; then dissatisfaction would be a grimy garb cloaking existence, a swathe of mould over all that was alive.

They arrived in Norrköping around six and, because they were hungry, headed straight to a restaurant by the canal that Olof knew. There weren't many people about that night, the city and pub were theirs. They ordered shell-fish tagliatelle with white wine sauce. The portions were large and steaming hot. They talked about everything that came to mind. It was a notable afternoon and evening. And so of course Olof said:

'I don't feel good in my situation.'

He seemed to want to say more, geared up for it a couple of times, but instead looked wistfully over the canal.

'There goes a car just like yours,' he said.

Ester watched the car. The same Twingo but in another colour.

'Did you really buy it one day, just like that?'

'I had some savings.'

She didn't mention that she'd bought it to drive him around. Ester made sure that everything important she did she did on impulse, so as to avoid being hindered by reason's wise objections. To her it seemed they always followed in the footsteps of fear and encouraged passivity. If you listened to wisdom and fear, nothing would get done.

'It was cheap,' she said, 'and had plenty of miles on it. I don't know how long it'll run.'

'Don't fall asleep at the wheel on your drive home.'

'I won't.'

He clearly wanted to say more. Ester wondered about the meaning of his confession about not feeling good in his situation and how he wanted her to take it. Maybe he was also thinking about the stifling summer ahead and wanted to prevent her from meeting someone else, wanted to say that she should wait for him until the summer had passed.

'You could spend the night if you're tired. It's a long drive round trip.'

He continued his earnest pondering.

'But of course I don't know what the apartment I'm staying in looks like.'

Ester waited.

'Maybe it's better if we see each other again in a while?'

His tone told her that he was finished deliberating and had decided to resist his lust. Sense had indeed followed in the footsteps of fear and had encouraged passivity. But waiting was not difficult when he was wavering. If she only knew that everything would one day change, she could be endlessly patient.

Their interactions seemed unparalleled and rare to Ester. No one else could have ever experienced such intimacy and taken such delight in another's company as when things were good between them. And now he was on his way to her. The summer lay ahead of them, the deadliest season for marriages.

'It's light until late now; driving back to Stockholm won't be a problem,' she said.

Olof seemed relieved and disappointed, and looked out over the canal as if he was trying to catch sight of his intentions and see what they looked like.

'Please be careful,' he said. 'Drive safely so nothing happens to you.'

Ester wanted to see what he was contemplating and looked out over the canal, too.

'I'll get a lift from the station when the others turn up with the train,' he said. 'Otherwise you could've driven me to the apartment.'

He hadn't quite decided how the evening was going to end; ambivalence left it open a crack.

'I can still drive you to the apartment,' said Ester.

When that crack was resolutely shut, there would be a moment of calm amidst the ambivalence, until unease returned and the process began again. It was like the tides.

'No. I'll go with the others.'

They split the bill and drove to the station where the rest of the ensemble would soon arrive. When Ester dropped him off, she didn't kill the engine. It would have seemed too keen and could backfire. Olof made no attempt to get out. He took her hand, which was resting on the gear stick, stroked her thumb with his and said:

'Maybe you could drive me here again.'

Then he got out of the car, took his bag from the boot and walked towards the train station without looking back.

She journeyed home through grey-blue air. An early summer's eve. Ester weighed nothing because bliss makes people light. 'Maybe you could drive me here again.' Impossible to misunderstand.

She could have had him for the night. But she didn't want isolated hours. To take a leap, people always needed a summer. In August, riots kicked off, wars were declared, and people committed unpremeditated murder. And married people divorced. This evening he'd announced what was to come.

One and a half hours later, Ester was airing her apartment and so satisfied she could have endured days without contact. But only a little time passed before a text message from Olof arrived. Lying in his nomadic burrow with its scuffed corners and sterile walls, he wrote, thinking about the universe and its constants. How had she explained that the unbelievable had happened, that the universe could come into being? He'd already forgotten.

Within a few minutes, she replied:

'If everything keeps going and efforts never cease, then at some point everything will end up in exactly the right position in relation to everything else. Once is enough. A continuum of attempts is what causes that single instance. Therefore, the constant striving of chemical reactions should never be stopped, whether you're an atom or another kind of particle. Thank you for tonight. /E'

Two weeks passed – tranquil, pleasant weeks during which Ester finished the Frege translation she'd been working on since the winter and had the ease to think about something other than her desperation. Influenced by the mental equilibrium from the Norrköping trip and what had preceded it, she achieved greater clarity about problems of a political-philosophical nature that she'd previously only had a notion of. She refined her points of view, clarified their contours and drafted an essay.

What more, she'd found a way to bring about another car trip with Olof, this time to northwest Skåne.

He had a summer house in Nyhamnsläge and Ester had come to an agreement with Vera, who was renting a house in Mölle over the summer, about helping her with the rent for four weeks, so Ester could be geographically close to Olof while she and Vera kept each other company.

That's how it came to pass that Ester was lying on her bed, composing a message to Olof supposedly from her Renault Twingo. The car was writing to him to tell him about how it had enjoyed his warm body in the passenger seat and wondered if he didn't want to do her the honour again. Forget about the car's extremely trying owner, she didn't need to be involved, but imagine enjoying the weight of his body and firm musculature once more during a longer trip.

Clucking with laughter, Olof called her after a break in rehearsals to enquire about the date and time of Mrs Twingo's intended departure; he was planning on travelling down on Friday. Ester said that Twingo was probably definitely unmarried, but even that would have done nothing to stop the wanton piece of tail from standing on a cross-street near his home with a full tank of petrol at five o'clock on Friday.

And so it was decided. Ester and Miss Twingo dressed in a pea-green travelling suit waited for him there, dazzled by the fiery branches of afternoon sun illuminating his figure as he rounded the corner. He looked tanned and healthy in his slightly distressed jeans and white shirt with rolled-up sleeves. He stroked the car's body and enacted a small scene using his entire self and just the right measure of scabrousness, demonstrating how glorious it was to be allowed to enter Miss Twingo's warm, soft interior.

Ester laughed gleefully, and then they were off.

Through Sörmland and Östergötland, the colours of the summer's evening intensified as they drove. Each year she was as surprised as ever by the evening light in June, violet and marvellous. She would have wanted to keep on driving with him for the rest of her life, no part of her wanted to arrive. But when they were outside Linköping they stopped at a roadside restaurant where they ate breaded fish with remoulade and boiled potatoes which had been left out too long and had acquired a miserable oxidized membrane; she noticed that Olof didn't share her wish to never arrive. He wanted nothing more than to arrive, arrive in the solitude of his house.

After the dinner break, when they were again zipping

through the greenery and the evening light, Ester asked a question she'd been mulling over ever since she knew she'd be in the same part of Skåne as Olof for weeks.

'What should we do if I run into you and Ebba? In the shop or on the beach or street or wherever people run into each other. How should I behave?'

His face looked tense. This was not a good question, indeed it was a very bad one. It implied that he had done something that needed to be hidden. According to him, nothing had happened if it was unnamed, uncategorized and unformulated; when everything was fluid, nothing could be distinguished.

'It wouldn't be strange if we did run into each other.' He sounded besieged, under threat.

'It's a bit strange. Uncomfortable, if nothing else.'

'For whom?' hissed Olof.

A heavy sigh escaped Ester. This perpetual uphill battle.

'For you and for me. And probably for your wife.'

'She doesn't know anything.'

'About what?'

'We don't have a relationship, you and me.'

'No. So what is it that she doesn't know anything about?'

'Don't try to catch me out by splitting hairs!'

'We don't have a relationship and have never had one. So what is it that she doesn't know about us?'

'We're in a car together, that is all. And I see now that this was a bad call, too.'

'And in the winter? All our visits to the pub. Night-time kisses in passages and alleys. Arvidsjaur?'

'Once! One single time! And it was a mistake.'

Her knuckles turned white as she gripped the wheel, she had been accelerating with each sentence and now was doing 130. Calling their encounter in Arvidsjaur a 'mistake' shocked her speechless. The road ahead was straight and wide, and she kept going faster; it was the only available release. Spreading out above them was an idyllic night sky, golden with pink daubs and wisps. When they had driven ten kilometres in icy silence, she slowly and carefully said:

'Your impudence is grotesque. Once? It was a weekend. An entire weekend. A lovers' getaway planned in detail by you and staged by us; not to mention, preceded by a large number of long dinners held in great secrecy in the pub, eyes and hands meeting in the candlelight and all that. And during our three-day weekend in Arvidsjaur, that *you* invited me to, and that *you* insisted on, it didn't happen once, but seven, eight, ten times, if you're sitting there tallying instances of genital penetration in order to determine your level of guilt.'

To this irrefutable enumeration, Ester added a plea of wounded sentimentality, even though she knew it would weaken her argument:

'And since then – during this spring – you've shown me furtive devotion and restrained physical desire on several occasions.'

Olof saw an opening and slipped in so as to avoid the irrefutable.

'I have not.'

'Yes, in fact you have.'

'Where's your proof?'

She was helpless in the face of his view of existence. Why was Olof here with her if all he wanted was to deny that they'd been seeing each other? Why didn't he decline her offers and invitations if he was so intent on defending himself against them? What was his aim with all of this?

'You can't prove restrained physical desire and furtive devotion. It's in the very nature of the furtive and the restrained.'

She should have sent that pinch of snus for testing at SNFC after all.

'You interpret everything to fit your hopes and intentions,' said Olof.

'Yes. Restrained physical desire and furtive devotion are interpretations, only you can know for sure. But I don't have "proof" for what we did in Arvidsjaur either, even though I know what we did and I know it's true. A plane ticket and a receipt for thirty kronor for two packets of cotton reels don't prove what we did in bed any more than they prove what it meant to you. But we're not taking this to court, Olof. We have no use for proof and evidence.'

He sat with his palms pressed to his thighs and fingers spread as if he was in deep concentration. He said:

'It was nice, but it was one time. What happened was wrong.'

'The only thing that's wrong here is that you're afraid to take the leap even though you want to free yourself from that strait-jacket you're spending your life in.'

'I don't want to take any leap.'

'Why do you keep meeting up with me when you know I'm only meeting you in hopes that you're going to take that leap?'

'Don't ask me to travel with you if you're going to use it for extortion.'

He started packing up his things.

'I suppose I'll have to get out in the next town and take the train.'

Then he realized that the next town was Jönköping, which wasn't on the main line, and screamed that now he'd have to check into a hotel too and Ester had cost him a whole day. To her surprise, she realized that Olof thought she wanted to get rid of him, throw him out of her car. He really didn't get the unconditional part of her love. However much they fought, the last thing she wanted was for him to leave the space they were sharing.

The mood in the car was so thick you could dice it: cubes of horror, alienation and rage. After driving another few dozen kilometres, Ester commented on something trivial that popped into her field of vision. Olof was so relieved, he took a breath and grabbed hold of her arm, grateful that she wasn't angry any more.

Ester saw his agony – like that of an abused child faced with its parents' rage, the relief when it dissipated – and thought that one must show great understanding towards the broken. He pre-empted disappointment by disappointing. One must endure and be patient with those who have been damaged by their environment. Each time she had this thought, she could endure a little longer. She believed she could help him dare to love.

In Jönköping where the road ran along Lake Vättern she swerved sharply out of the way for a family of ducks walking all in a row. Olof yelled that you should never swerve to save animals, it could cause an accident.

'But nothing happened,' she said and touched his bare forearm. 'We didn't get into an accident.'

The very act of touching him increased her lust. He squeezed her hand and held it for a moment before carefully guiding it back to the wheel.

There are temptresses and there are wives. The temptress, better known as the mistress, is iconic. Wrapped in a kimono, she smokes cigarillos and drinks liqueur among bric-a-brac and souvenirs from foreign lands. She is well-travelled, blasé, self-centred, quick-witted and light on her feet. Despair is not hers to know, sorrow is alien, an impenetrable fortress is she. She will toy with a man, using him to pass the time, but love him she will not. For the mistress/temptress does not love, just like the girls at the bordello don't love, and if she does love, with all the pain that it ushers in, it's called 'hysteria', not love. She liberates the husband from tristesse and the mutual vulnerability of coupledom, while destroying the marriage – enemy of the wife and divider of womankind.

This version of the mistress/temptress exists perhaps in a few rare examples, but first and foremost she is an idea. Part of this idea is the notion that a man's biology can be cleverly exploited by woman's psychology, for he is at the mercy of his male urges, a weakness that she with her feminine wiles knows how to exploit.

To Olof Sten, the mistress was an idea he so eagerly

embraced that he never stopped to question that the traditional 'mistress' might not in fact exist. Instead, he zealously embraced the idea as reality. No matter what Ester Nilsson did or said, with however much desperation she loved and pleaded, always far less artful than him, she was relegated to the category of the wily, artful temptress as and when it suited him. This was possible because the category existed and flourished in the eternal interplay between the reality and the idea. When the idea didn't quite fit – the mistress should not yearn for the entwining of two egalitarian souls – Olof Sten remade her in his thoughts so that the idea would not be sullied.

The dichotomies that help perpetuate the arrangement are many and well demarcated. Wife – lover. Love – passion. Life partner – temptress. Mother – courtesan. Chaste – lusty. Virtuous – mercenary. Madonna – whore. Faithful – fleeting. Caring – egoistic. Lucid – mad.

The self-loathing that arises from being unable to abstain from that which makes man weak, his urges, is redirected to the mistress because she reveals the lover's weakness to himself and the world. The mistress as an idea constitutes a third counterpoint between the complementary woman/man. Her anatomy is woman's but her autonomy is man's. She is a third, the most frightening and most alluring, that which in the end must be pushed out of life's bid for dualistic order. At the same time, she is the archetype of woman, the bearer of all traits; the wild girl who needs to be tamed by her own biology in order to be rendered harmless and complete her process of maturation through the child she will give birth to, nourish, care for and subordinate herself to.

The mistress/temptress as a reality and person is of a more varied kind, for she doesn't view herself from the outside or as part of a stubborn structure in which she has replaced the harlot, but without the financial compensation. For her, the fellowship she shares with a soon-to-be-divorced man is something out of the ordinary, and she is the one who understands him best. She is the one who came along too late, who sits at home and waits without the subject of her thoughts wondering how she is. It's part of the arrangement that he shouldn't have to worry about her well-being – autonomous, capricious and well-travelled as she is. She's the one he has fun with, not someone who adds to the weight and worries that are part of his faithful, ordered life.

The mistress reads the landscape when they're out and about, always ready to step aside so she won't be seen to belong to the one the world perceives as belonging to another. Loyally, she helps the deceiver deceive, out of empathy for the lover but also to benefit the long-term outcome. She's the one who won't appear in the obituary, but in the worst case, defiantly sends in her own so she can finally be allowed to exist and to be acknowledged.

In the event of the lover's divorce, something else shifts, too. The dethroned wife becomes hysterical and capricious.

She may even submit her own version of her ex-husband's obituary in order to reveal the true nature of the situation.

Everything the mistress/temptress or the dethroned wife does, she does with full knowledge of the secret place to which only she and he are granted entry. This is where he has made all the confessions that assure her she is actually number one even though in every way she is number two.

Through all of this, the hapless spectator gets constant confirmation that this is about a particular kind of woman (a woman unlike the down-to-earth, dull maternal type), who is dreamt of by men and women alike and who nonetheless makes them suffer.

Nyhamnsläge is a small exclusive residential area near the sea, located between Höganäs and Mölle along Skåne's north-western coast.

Around midnight, they arrived at Olof's house, which stood alone by a rape-seed field. A modest but lush garden in thirsty bloom spread out from the house. The house was empty and the night was dark. After their reconciliation around Jönköping, and up until Linköping at least, Ester harboured great hopes about the arrival. She was a stranger to the region, and in this dense nocturnal dark it would've only been natural for Olof to suggest she wait until morning before beginning her search for where she was staying: an unknown house in an unknown location in a strange landscape. But he got out of the car and thanked her for the lift before pointing and explaining how to get to Mölle. Go back out on the main road, take a right and then it's straight ahead until the T-junction. Take a left and after a few kilometres left again. And then down to the harbour.

With these precise directions, he made it clear that even his ambivalent side wasn't considering an overnight stay. It was the first time he displayed certainty. This made it easier for Ester, for it was his wavering that kept her hanging on: the glimmer of possibility that always appeared when he claimed something to be unthinkable. But not now.

Ester decided to forget Olof over the summer. The liberation this implied was bitterly pleasant. It was a relief to not count hours and days, to not hope, to not devise strategies for contact, to not wonder what Olof was thinking and feeling. Longing gave way to loss. The days in Mölle passed in mild melancholy. Ester and Vera took day trips and visited art galleries, sunbathed, cooked dinner and talked long into the night. Ester's thoughts about how things with Olof could be different – the most consuming of notions – faded like an old poster. She endeavoured to be in the now, albeit under the veil of sorrow.

This resignation turned out to be seasonal. She had really only given her hopes a rest, because when she interrogated herself she realized that she still believed he'd be divorced by autumn, anything else would be unthinkable considering the year he'd had, and this is what was keeping her upright.

She lay on the rocks for hours, letting her thoughts float together and apart like the clouds overhead. The droves of tourists hadn't yet begun to arrive for the season. In a few weeks, this place would be full of well-fed families with thick, shiny hair and a clear sense of their distinguished lineage.

She spent a week like this with the summer and with Vera. Then a text arrived. Ester was sitting on the quay reading a biography about Mary Shelley parallel to re-reading *Frankenstein*. The text contained five words.

'Ice cream at the harbour?'

It was two p.m. A lone scrim of clouds was moving across the blithe azure sky towards Kullaberg. It was said that here three seas meet, as if water could be divided and delineated, but perhaps there were oceanographic criteria for when one became the other. On the horizon were barges and passenger ferries that at first glance appeared to be still, but were indeed sailing along the glittering waves.

'Ice cream at the harbour?'

She read the message several times. Her skin prickled, her ears rang, she who had almost left her phone in the house because she was no longer hoping for anything.

To seem less eager, she waited two minutes before she wrote:

'Gladly. Are you here in Mölle?'

Three minutes passed, as long as three days.

'In half an hour.'

She slipped a simple cotton dress over her swimsuit and after twenty-five minutes she walked to the harbour. There on a sun-drenched bench sat Olof, one leg slung over the other. Gingerly, she sat next to him and their fingers touched. When his hand had rested on hers longer than was appropriate he got up to buy them each an ice cream at the harbour kiosk. Did she want sprinkles? She did, ice cream with sprinkles had more character. Actually, she didn't want ice cream at all but ate it for the sake of communion and the moment.

Black-headed gulls circled the harbour square and the moored boats. Ester was disconcerted. Olof had initiated this meeting when she'd retreated. Now she knew that he too had the itch, the dreadful love itch. Through the sensors that linked them, he could always feel when she was pulling away and reacted accordingly.

One line of reasoning she'd often pursued in order to preserve the realism of her judgements was now grinding away in the far recesses of her consciousness. It went like this: does one have the right to create expectations for which there are no grounds? No. Does Olof know that this is what he's doing? Yes. So why is he doing it?

One: He's taken a fancy to me but is undecided.

Two: He's taken a fancy to me and can't help it even though he has decided.

Three: He's distracting himself and taking what's on offer, and it's up to the one who can't handle the arrangement to tell him to back off.

Through all her years with Olof, Ester was as good as convinced that it was number one. His next statement strengthened this belief.

'I went for a bike ride around the village a few days ago. Looking for your little car.'

'You did?'

'But I didn't find it.'

'You should have called.'

She knew full well, far too well, the stinging longing and emptiness that made someone cycle around in the hope of catching a glimpse of the person consuming your thoughts. It burned in him like it burned in her! All she had to do was help rid him of his pretences, he was in love!

The retreat was immediate:

'I was only out for a spin.'

The admission that he'd sought her out not once but twice cost him dear. And so he looked up at the hillside where the houses were climbing on top of each other in the glaring light. Bright bolts shot from the windows.

'I thought I might visit my friend who lives up there. That's why I'm here.'

Even if his retreat was expected it exhausted Ester. Could it never just be beautiful? She got up from the bench and prepared herself for the looming goodbye. This encounter was not worth the cost. She would pay with days and weeks of agony and sadness for half an hour's trivial contact. Not to mention the ice cream she'd gobbled up for his sake alone. Nothing was leading anywhere. He didn't even want to admit that he'd cycled all the way to Mölle for her. She was overcome with anger.

Then Olof put his arm around Ester's shoulders and kept it there as they followed the road along the water, the bike between them, and she rested her hand on the saddle as if it belonged to his body.

'I'm glad you came,' he said.

'Me, too.'

The wind was hot though it was rolling in from the sea.

'I'm going home to pack,' said Olof.

He was going to Stockholm over Midsummer where his wife and grown children were waiting, adorned with the holiday's prerequisite flower crowns.

'I'm turning off here,' said Ester.

'You are?'

'Yes. I'm going to the quay. Vera's there reading.'

He looked at her.

'We can take a day trip around Kullabygden when I get back. Before Ebba comes down. I can show you around.'

'When is she coming, then?'

'In two weeks.'

'That would be nice.'

She said this without conviction. The wife's name was enough to make the weight drop back down on her.

'I'll be in touch when I'm back,' said Olof and dusted his fingertips over her bare upper arm. Then he pedalled away.

The delicate equilibrium Ester had managed to maintain over the last weeks disappeared the moment he left, and a considerable pain began to tinge all she thought and felt. It became impossible to concentrate and nothing was truly fun any more. Everything became viscous. She asked Vera why Olof didn't just leave her alone since he didn't want anything. Or *did* he want something and that's why he had reached out? What was she supposed to be thinking?

Vera asked, eyes searching, if Ester wanted him to leave her alone. In that case, she just had to say so, for few people persisted in contacting someone who'd asked not to be contacted.

The conversation stopped there.

He kept his word and got in touch when he was back. And so they took their trip around Kullabygden in Ester's car. First they visited Flickorna Lundgren on Skäret, a cafe Olof said was famous. For what? Ester wondered. Her sandwich was dry and didn't fill her up and the coffee was bitter. Olof ate chocolate cake with cream. Ester only had the sandwich. It was a meagre lunch after a morning run and with five hours having passed since breakfast, but on days like this she needed less energy; her body seemed to produce all the substances it needed it on its own.

They sat in the floral splendour and bumble-bee buzz of the cafe's garden, chatting.

'Beautiful, isn't it?' asked Olof.

'Marvellous.'

'What are you thinking about right now?'

'I'm thinking about how life isn't made up of individual events,' said Ester.

'How do you mean?'

'Events are like a photo album. Or like an anthropologist's description of a foreign people.'

'Isn't everything that happens in life an "event"?'

'Do we see it like that? According to both the anthropologist and the photo album all people seem to do is dance rain-dances, have birthdays and crayfish parties, celebrate Midsummer, adorn ourselves before these celebrations, bring down a beast, eat cake, get married, celebrate Christmas, go on holiday, perform rituals. But events like this don't make up a life, they're the exceptions, and that's why we attach importance to them through photography and notation. It's the stream of consciousness in between that constitutes life, and that's where cultures are practised. Life happens in the intervals, when the ethnographer isn't describing and the family's camera isn't out.'

Olof waited for her to summarize and explain, but she looked out over the neatly trimmed lawn with its fruit trees and roses. He shifted uncomfortably on the chair.

'Is what we're doing an interval or an event?'

Ester smiled at Olof but didn't feel that she had permission to touch him even if their forearms had happened to collide during the car journey and neither made the slightest effort to move their arm out of the way.

'What would you say it is?' she asked.

'I don't know.'

'If it was just you or me, this would be both an event and an interval. The pinnacle of love is when two states can be united, event and interval.'

Flowers perfumed the air, the bees were on a stubborn hunt. Ester could hardly name one flower, but they smelled delightful nonetheless. Scent preceded language. But perhaps perception was refined through classification and one could more keenly sense a scent one could distinguish? The day that Ester found peace, had a longed-for body always near and a constantly available brain to share thoughts with, that was the day she'd start learning these things – flowers, trees, birds and nature's every name. It would have to wait until then, at present she didn't have it in her to expand her impressions and areas of interest. The onrush of life was something she had to keep at bay, not contend with and give her full attention to.

They drove on through the landscape. The little Twingo turned out to be a good romantic-investment. Two months old and it had already aided many encounters that wouldn't have come to pass without it. Olof showed her out-of-the-way sights and small seaside roads. They drove through Rekekroken and Arild and stopped by an art gallery near the water. Finally they reached Himmelsberg where they parked in order to make their way to the Nimis and Arx sculptures. They had to descend a steep, uneven hill to get to the beach.

The artist himself was on site, building his eternal driftwood piece. They chatted with him and he said he was about to take part in an exhibition themed around the dog in art. They wished him good luck and then bounded down the boulders towards Skälderviken's bay. The sun was just hot enough so as to go unnoticed, nature was lush and luxuriant, the animal life boisterous. Ester observed a remarkable little bird, who under a black beret and atop a pair of stumpy orange legs the colour of its beak was grimly observing a leggy bird's bobbing tail as it nervily searched for food. She pointed and said:

'Do you think that one lost its legs in a brawl at sea?'

Olof shaded his eyes with his hand, looked in the direction she was pointing and said:

'No, it was probably roughed up while on shore leave.'

Ester loved the lightness and inclination with which he joined in on her games and whims, loved it so much, it pounded and whined.

'Someone thought that if you've got those flame-coloured legs, you can't have them all to yourself, and launched an attack,' Olof continued and mimed the attack with his hands.

'But the beret,' she said, 'where did that come from?'

'The better question is how it lost its brush and easel *and* its legs. Someone was jealous of its talents and its beauty.'

Skälderviken's bay sparkled in Olof's eyes. He was entirely focused on her and she thought he might tell her something big and important about their time together before the day was done.

A while later, they were driving towards Nyhamnsläge in tepid silence. Their fellowship had shattered with one blow when Olof announced that he should go home and finish painting the frames before Ebba came down on Tuesday.

'You seem upset,' he said as they passed Krapperup.

'Not upset. Just gloomy about what almost happens, but doesn't. It has felt like you've really wanted something with me lately. I thought we were going to eat dinner together tonight. Cook at yours and, well, more. It was set up for that.'

'You'll never be satisfied.'

'No, I won't. Not as long as this is our arrangement. I would have thought that was quite obvious. Why should I be satisfied?'

Next, Olof said that he really shouldn't be seeing her at all if everything had to be so complicated, but he framed it as a question, a question she was meant to answer.

'Isn't this all just getting really hard for you?' he clarified.

Ester held her tongue.

'I should stop seeing you?'

'If you think it best.'

'I guess so.'

'Maybe you should also think about why you can't keep away?'

They'd arrived at his house. He invited her in with an indistinct wave, and because the turn was always right around the bend, she went in. There were tins of paint on the plastic-covered floor; the house appeared to be undergoing minor renovations. She sat down in an armchair and waited for some sort of decision about where to go from here with all the ambiguity and the summer ahead of them.

Through the open door facing the backyard, a voice on a loudspeaker could be heard. It seemed to come from a travelling circus but they hadn't noticed one on their way back. Olof slumped in the other armchair.

'You look pensive,' Ester ventured.

'I'm wondering what's out there making that noise.'

'It's someone on a loudspeaker.'

'What could it be?'

She looked at his listless, draping body. Everything was at stake between them and Olof was thinking about the noise outside.

'Oh, I'm knackered,' he said and demonstrated exactly how knackered by making his body even more limp and letting it slide out of the armchair.

'And yet we've been sitting all day,' he went on. 'Must be the sun.'

Ester got up and left. At the door, she turned around.

'I love you, Olof Sten. It's hard to understand for all involved, but that's how it is, and I'll continue to for a while. But not indefinitely.'

She walked down the steps and got in the car. She was putting it into gear when she saw him in the doorway, pleading and forlorn. He seemed to want to say something to her. But he said nothing, did nothing. He just stood there.

The summer trundled on. Ester took each sunny day one at a time, and finally autumn was in the offing. Back in Stockholm at a bookshop on Odengatan specializing in psychology, she procured a volume on pathological ambivalence. She read it in one sitting. Olof displayed all the symptoms. After that she read Freud's case study on the Rat Man, and the one on how ambivalence distorts the soul. For a long while, she felt discontented and despondent, then she thought that the more neurotic he was, the more he needed love to heal. In Åhlén's department store she bought a book that was stacked in piles and bore the title *Women Who Love Too Much*. Ester displayed all the symptoms.

By the start of September, she and Olof hadn't been in contact since their outing in Kullabygden two months earlier. The book she'd translated about arithmetic by Gottlob Frege arrived from the printers, and after some deliberation she sent a copy to Olof. It wasn't anything he would read, but that wasn't the point of sending it. The point was being in contact again, breaking the silence. She slipped in a card at the flyleaf that read:

I translated this. I think I mentioned it in the spring. Might be of interest to you. Ester

Vera warned her against this sort of stunt. Olof had to be the one to get in touch after the summer, otherwise it wasn't worth anything and she wouldn't be any the wiser. Vera was right, thought Ester and got in touch anyway, because she couldn't stand the emptiness he left behind, particularly because she didn't believe that it corresponded with his innermost desire.

Olof thanked her immediately with a letter in return and apparent joy that she'd been in touch. Ester had no doubt that he'd been worrying about her having disappeared from his life. As a result of this exchange, a new phase began. It was as if everything had been reset and they could start again. Short texts and telephone calls with observations about life and the times began to be exchanged. Ester's joy spiked, if temporarily, each time they contacted each other. The autumn became tolerable. It felt as though they were repairing something broken, building for the future.

Some time into October, Olof suggested she come and see his show in Norrköping, which had been on for a month. They agreed on a date a week later. And the world became beautiful, Ester's life regained its lustre. She sorted things in the attic and threw away old clutter. She gave money to those in need, helped the frail cross the street and didn't get irritated at their slowness in the check-out queue.

The day before they were to meet, Olof called and said that Ebba had been given compensatory leave and was coming to Norrköping on the night of their date.

He recounted this with an unnatural and forced matter-of-factness.

'Isn't it unbelievable that your wife managed to pin-point the only date in the entire autumn that you and I had decided to see each other?'

'Female intuition.'

He sounded as though he was relaying one of his wife's qualities that even Ester should appreciate.

'The betrayed need to develop their intuition, female or not.'

'Ebba isn't being betrayed. You and I, we're not in a relationship.'

'But then what is she developing an intuition about, if it's no big deal that I'm coming to see you? What, with this special female ability of hers, is she catching a whiff of? What do you suppose she's sensing?'

'You're pushing me again with your sophisms or what-ever they're called.'

Ester couldn't bear to speak, leaden as she now was. But her question was clearly relevant because Olof tried to explain himself.

'By intuition, I mean that Ebba might be sensing an

indistinct threat. She *thinks* we have a relationship even though we don't. Doesn't mean she has any reason to feel this way.'

'Then why are you sneaking around?'

'I'm not sneaking. But Ebba has an especially jealous disposition.'

'Or she has a husband who makes it seem that way. Maybe it's completely normal for her to want to know what the person closest to her is up to.'

Olof pondered what Ester said while Ester pondered her disappointment.

'Can you come next week instead?'

'Busy all week, I'm afraid.'

It was true. The entire following week was booked with trips and lectures.

'As you know, I don't want to have a relationship with you,' said Olof.

'I've gathered that.'

'Not a romantic relationship, that is.'

'Have a good time with Ebba.'

She was about to hang up but heard that familiar hesitation on the line, his softness when faced with her hardness. The two of them were like iron filings and magnets, helplessly oriented to each other.

'Talk to you later, Ester. Talk to you later.'

She called Fatima and told her what had happened. Fatima thought Ebba might not actually be going to the theatre that night, was it even feasible? Wasn't this him just getting cold feet when faced with seeing her and realizing what it would mean to pick things up again with Ester, Ester with her bid for an all-encompassing relationship and a love of epic proportions.

'I'm not blaming you,' said Fatima. 'I'm exactly the same.'

'I don't understand what he'd get out of wavering and then having to lie to be left in peace. But if you're right, I have to shut it down.'

'Shut it down if you can.'

At Stockholm's Royal Institute of Technology Ester Nilsson had studied technical physics and later philosophy. Among the students, there was a disproportionate number of orienteerers compared with the general population, but by that time, she'd given up the sport. It happened abruptly. She was a goal-oriented orienteerer until the Christmas of her eighteenth year when she unlaced her shoes and never returned to the forest. This decisive break came on Christmas Eve when she was at home watching a television documentary about Georg Henrik von Wright and heard him describe something called 'the problem of induction'; that we can't say anything about the world with certainty using observational data alone. She hadn't known it was so complicated to determine what knowledge was, but the insight made her body tingle as the world suddenly spread out before her, waiting to be discovered. She'd hardly anticipated that the problem of induction would come to fill her days from then on. She had been lazing on the sofa wearing her exercise clothes with the TV on when the programme started and had no desire to go out into the dark, her drive to train had been waning; she told herself she would only watch the programme for a little while, but stayed put until the end an hour and a half later and skipped her training session that day and the next because she was on the hunt for a library that was open over the holidays. The problem of induction was fascinating, but something else that Wright had said caused her to make this decision. He'd talked about sitting on his own in concentrated thought for at least three hours a day. Roughly the time an elite athlete spent training. It dawned on Ester Nilsson that the brain's abilities did not stem from brilliance, an innate unattainable distinction, but from the same source as the body's abilities: practice and more practice, toil, effort, always pushing a little harder. Everything could be improved upon and drilled.

She realized that she had to make a choice while there was still time.

Since that day she'd spent her time and energy on intellectual work in order to understand the world. Included in this were romantic projects that had occupied her for years. Only on the surface did these appear wasteful, directionless and like a deviation from her cerebral activities.

She earned a decent living with her intellectual offerings. The money went on books and telephone bills. It had been a while since the Twingo had inspired a romantic excursion, so she was mainly using it to shuttle friends to Ikea. Other than that, she only drove it when it needed to be re-parked ahead of street cleaning days.

Nothing really interested her apart from what was

consuming her with destructive force. A month had passed since their last conversation when she, on a day when the desolation was worse than usual, had called Olof to ask how he was doing. He was fine, and her? She was fine, too, she lied so as not to pressure him or seem demanding. And it helped, because they set another date for her to come and see his play.

On that date, she drove to Norrköping from Arvika in Värmland where she'd held a lecture for high-school students about writing anti-lyrical poetry. Her heart was not jubilant, but it was relatively light. More than four and a half months had passed without them having seen each other. She feared nothing for she expected nothing. See him on stage, have a chat after, re-establish contact: that was all she saw before her. It would have to do for now.

When she arrived at the theatre after hours in the car, she went to the ladies' in the foyer, splashed some water on her face and armpits, changed out of her wool sweater and into a blouse and jacket. Then she took a lap round the theatre to have a look. The walls were golden and the chairs a dark red plush. The play was about a century-old bourgeoisie and its preoccupation with honour and glory; she wasn't familiar with the playwright's work. Olof's role was one of the larger ones. Ester didn't take her eyes off him during the performance, which lasted an hour and a half without an interval.

They'd agreed to meet afterwards at the stage door. Ester waited for him in the quivering light of a crescent moon. She was nervous. And then he came walking towards her in that laid-back way of his, as though retreating from every attack the world might launch at him, while emanating an air of indifference.

That old devotion dug its claws into her heart, but Olof was less reverential.

'Hey,' he said, his mocking smile materializing through the dark, the smile that said Ester Nilsson was a funny sort for having driven all the way to Norrköping just to see him for a little while.

'Hey' was an easy-going word for innocent meetings, but it was also the word to use when one wished to set that tone precisely because nothing about the meeting was innocent.

He put his hand on Ester's shoulder. She nodded. She couldn't have pretended to be easy-going even if she wanted to, and now she was tense, which would be silly to try and hide. She said he'd given a good performance, very good, really very good, and the show was excellent, the production creative and the play interesting.

She already felt worn out, and not just because she'd had to come up with so many adjectives.

'Are you hungry?' he asked.

She was and they walked to a nearby pub. They sat all the way at the back in a dark corner illuminated by a lone candle that had stood in a draught for so long that the melted wax had formed a minor work of Renaissance architecture. Ester ordered pasta with a fillet of beef in cream sauce, which turned out to be a sticky beige mess. Olof had eaten before the performance and only ordered a glass of red wine. Ester drank sparkling water because she was planning to drive on to Stockholm. They spoke about the performance. Olof wondered if Ester thought he'd been good on stage. Using various formulations he wondered this several times and Ester kept replying that he had been more than perfect. Exceptional, wonderful. Then he asked for her thoughts on the play, the text itself, and Ester said that it had its merits but lacked depth and revealed the author's coquettish sides. Olof said that he'd been trying to see the show through Ester's eyes that night and couldn't stop wondering what she was thinking. Olof also asked if she thought his friend Max Fahlén had been better than him, and Ester replied that Max Fahlén had been good but not as good as Olof, because Olof had been more than perfect. Exceptional, wonderful.

She ordered another bottle of sparkling water, whereupon he muttered inaudibly. There was something specific he wanted to convey with the muttering that related to her water consumption; her first bottle had already given him pause. It didn't occur to her that he was planning on her staying overnight. She didn't think they'd built up to that and assumed she'd be driving home that night. Because she couldn't tell what he was thinking, he was forced to say it out loud, to take the abhorrent initiative. It would cost him dearly but the bill would be passed on to Ester later to pay in another form.

He regarded her incredulously, sitting there with her gravity and loftiness, qualities that Fatima had said were the pair's biggest hurdles but also Ester's salvation: never hiding the gravity of her longing was part of her attraction, but it frightened Olof (and everyone else) away, and dispersed any false interpretations of her intentions – interpretations that would only have added to Ester's woes.

So as not to be heard wanting – for wanting makes a person weak – he framed the question as an accusation:

'Have you stopped fixating on me yet?'

That blindsided her. Several seconds passed before she understood what Olof had said and could give a response more dignified than the question.

'It's not a fixation. You're in my heart. I miss you.'

Haplessly, he bit his lower lip.

'On a night like this, I wish I could offer you my guest room. But that's impossible if you're going to think it's an invitation.'

'I don't think anything any more. But I'm quite tired so it would be nice to not have to get back behind the wheel tonight.'

The subtle way in which Olof unloaded the suggestion that he himself had made was masterful. Through minor dislocations of language he made it sound as if he wasn't participating, had no preferences and bore no responsibility for what was taking place; that Ester's inability to understand the rules of the game was what was complicating everything and tying his hands behind his back.

'In that case, I'd love a glass of wine,' Ester said.
'I think I have wine at home.'
And so they walked the short distance to Olof's flat.

The apartment at his disposal had three rooms, belonged to the theatre and lay in Norrköping's Million Programme estate area. He showed her around and finally they arrived at the bedroom, the room furthest from the front door. It contained two beds which had barely a metre between them. Why were the beds separated? Ester wondered. Is this how he and the wife slept when she came to visit or had he pulled the beds apart before this visit so that Ester wouldn't think that theirs was a marriage flaming with passion and she still had a chance? Or had he simply felt like getting her home with him tonight and in an ambivalent counter-manoeuvre separated the beds so as to confound any forbidden thoughts and to demonstrate that he absolutely was not thinking anything erotic in spite of the invitation?

It was impossible to determine and from what she knew about Olof, both options were equally likely. All she did know was that no part of this was a coincidence or accidental, neither the beds' positions nor tonight's invitation. Olof operated in relation to Ester's thoughts and he in relation to hers.

On one bedside table lay a stiff silver necklace, on the floor a black bra. Both indicated a right to remain. And if the separated beds had been arranged, so too had the silver necklace and bra; alternatively, they had intentionally not been cleared away. The mighty ambivalence that this revealed was not second to the Rat Man's. When his beloved's equipage was to come riding by, he'd place a stone on the road so he could rush out and clear it from the path in the nick of time.

The worst part for Ester and her pernicious hope was that after twelve years the Rat Man had married the woman he'd treated this way. Ester might not be able to wait a full twelve years.

She regarded the bra and the necklace, wondering what Ebba would feel if she knew that she was standing here looking at them. She found it terrifying that it was possible to live alongside the person you thought was closest to you, but who inhabited a landscape of unknown events, enthusiasms and problems.

They sat in Olof's kitchen, drank red wine and talked, mostly Olof for a change; Ester listened and interjected. She tempered herself because she could keenly sense his hesitation and didn't want to risk being hurt by the cruelty it engendered.

When they had sat a while and a certain charge and fellowship had emerged, Olof said that he and Ebba had been thinking about going to Rome for a long weekend this month. But because they couldn't get tickets for November, the trip had been moved to Easter.

Ester regretted not driving home right after the

performance instead of once again being dragged into his hellish void of indecision where she and the wife were being used to regulate his anxiety.

'Easter is a long way off,' she said.

'Not that far, just a few months.'

'I've never planned or booked a trip so far in advance. You two must be getting on better since the winter.'

'What do you mean, better?'

'In the winter when you and I met in Arvidsjaur you had nothing to talk about and Ebba was keeping tabs on you and standing guard so you couldn't go out and see me. And everything between you was mute. "Completely mute", even.'

'I never said that.'

'Word for word.'

'Ebba and I have never had a bad stretch.'

Ester had to catch her breath.

'Believe what you want. The reason I can't tell Ebba about you is that she'd never believe that we're just friends.'

'In that way, we're the same, Ebba and I. I don't believe that either. My friendships don't look like this, I can assure you.

Olof thought for a moment and said:

'All relationships have their ups and downs, don't they?'

'That's what they say. And their entrances and exits, too. Except yours.' Ester drank more wine even though her tongue was rough and thick and it didn't taste good.

'So things are going well, then?'

'Yes. Very.'

'Congratulations.'

Olof fingered the rim of the wine glass. A fan was on in the apartment. Ester said:

'When you're not resisting it, the heat between us could replace nuclear power in this country. What do you think Ebba would have to say about that? This devastating physical attraction that's always between us combined with our appetite for conversation.'

A familiar look of amused mischief came over him and his eyes glinted with desire.

'Maybe I'm not attracted to you, Ester. Maybe it's just in your imagination. Maybe that heat is only coming from you.'

Three sentences, three 'maybes'. She could see and hear how he relished this precarious situation, and being the only one who knew the answer.

Ester went to the sink and poured out what was left of her wine, and from the guest room, she retrieved her toilet bag.

As she brushed her teeth, she heard Olof behind her. He lingered in the bathroom doorway looking meek; he'd pushed too hard and now had to reel her back in. He commented on how she had her foot on the toilet seat:

'You did that in Arvidsjaur, too.'

His precision in recalling a location, an event and their togetherness exactly when it was needed – but only ever then – must have been intuitive, some sort of biological instinct, Ester thought when she examined the situation later so as to see it in the context of a whole. He couldn't have calculated how to behave through analysis alone, of that he was incapable. Olof followed her into the guest room, put his arms around her, found her lips. When he'd planted a kiss, he said:

'Sleep well, Ester. If you get lonely, you can join me.'

He went to the bedroom. She stayed in the guest room and watched him leave.

'What did you say?'

She followed him. He'd already managed to slip under the covers.

'What do you mean?'

'What do you mean, mean?'

'By me joining you if I feel lonely.'

'Nothing in particular.'

'I don't understand what you're saying.'

'Come on then, lie down,' he said with an impatient wave, rankled by being made to articulate the sin.

He lifted the covers and invited her into the bed.

Nude and shaking she lay next to the only one of the world's many billion bodies that she wanted to touch with hers. He embraced her. All parts of their bodies met and hands caressed backs. The ecstasy couldn't be understood as anything but mutual. A few exceptional minutes of Ester's life went by before Olof, like an axe dropping, grew distant, abandoning their union mentally though his body remained. Ester compensated with extra intensity, whispering sweet nothings, showing him everything she felt, but he had become mechanical. Then he pulled out, lay on his back and said:

'Eh. I don't have the energy.'

And rolled over to sleep.

Ester touched his neck, tenderness still surging, a lag that came from not understanding. Olof's bed was narrow and his wife's bed was a metre away, it was crowded. After a moment, Olof said:

'I'm going to lie down in the other room.'

'No, I'll go,' Ester said. 'I'll go.'

Why didn't Ester Nilsson leave and check into a hotel for the night? She didn't even consider it. In her realm of experience, you simply didn't afford yourself nights at hotels, and because of her lack of pride there was no reason to. More importantly she wasn't sure how to take the incident. The largely positive can leave negative stains and vice versa. What was a background colour and what were the stains in her history with Olof and this latest episode? Should she focus on the fact that he'd invited her to his place and couldn't resist her, or on the interrupted sex act? After a lull that had lasted months, he'd taken two sensational initiatives in the space of a few hours. So a minor recoil wasn't unexpected.

The next morning Ester had determined that what had

transpired was a largely positive development with a small backlash, not the other way around. She woke to the smell of coffee and the hissing percolator. The sound was irreconcilable with a negative atmosphere and animosity, as was Olof lolling on the sofa reading the newspaper. Sure of the strength of their bond, she cautiously lay down on what space was left on the sofa. He didn't stop her. Then she touched his thighs in a way that made his bathrobe slide open. He didn't pull it closed. Ester's hand took its liberties. She saw that he was reading the obituaries. He pushed his reading glasses to his forehead, put the newspaper on his chest and said he felt uncomfortable. Ester halted her activities.

'What happened yesterday was no good. I don't want to have that kind of relationship with you.'

She went back to the guest room, packed and pulled on her coat. She gave herself permission to stop for breakfast at the petrol station at the edge of town and satisfy her ravenous hunger there, for she had to get away.

She was in the hall when she heard his voice behind her, unbothered, relaxed.

'Wait. I'll come to town with you. I've got to get something from the theatre.'

She watched him dress in haste and wondered how it was possible for a person to lack all sense of what could be said and done not three minutes after they'd said and done something else. With his profession, he should be an expert, hypersensitive to the inner dynamics of any scene or situation. Instead he kept putting the wrong foot forward.

How she could find herself driving him to town was already clear to her: she felt guilty whenever she saw how the slightest rejection rumpled him. If she'd treated him like he treated her, it wouldn't be long until she'd regret her brusqueness and reach out in order to explain herself.

A cold, hard November rain was drumming on her car. Next to her, Olof commented on the rain. Ester said he was treating her like rubbish. He said it really was a shame she felt that way but he'd been crystal clear from the start about what he did and did not want and if she took a right here and then a left they'd be at the stage door.

She stopped outside the theatre. Her reflection in the rear-view mirror was like the grey clouds hanging over the town.

On the pavement, Olof leaned into the car, hand on the open door, hesitation in his eyes, a pleading tone.

'Talk to you . . . and see you later, Ester.'

'Will we? Why?'

'Don't you want to?'

'Do you see any point in it? It seems so terribly hard all the time.'

Rain lashed the ground; the drops broke and splashed back up in new formations, inevitable and predictable. Everything followed its path. Maybe Olof couldn't help himself any more than the rain could help ricocheting off the tarmac, Ester thought. And perhaps she couldn't control her emotional life and the resulting action any more than the tarmac could stay dry in the rain.

Had she become a fatalist like him? Wasn't determinism by necessity a fatalism?

She watched him cross the street, hunching in the rain, happily greet a colleague with a wave and then vanish behind a heavy door.

Through fog and damp, she drove home from Norr-köping, unspeakably sombre.

The air was grey water. The country's entire worm population was on the march inside Ester. They perforated her heart, lungs and stomach with anxiety and pain. The girlfriend chorus said surely she'd give up now. You simply don't treat people the way he'd just treated her. Cryptically, Vera added that she felt sorry for her.

So Ester gave up, again. But what was the point of living if there wasn't any hope for intoxication or vivacity? There was no point. You could only grind away because life had been bestowed upon you without you having any say in the matter.

Christmas and New Year came and went. On the second day of the year, in the evening, Olof called. She picked up her phone, saw the number and felt her blood vessels dilate. She worshipped these very numbers and the sight of them made her body hot, as did the simple fact of seeing his name in writing. Ester answered with a hushed tone. Olof didn't open with a 'Hi' or 'It's Olof,' but by asking if Lukas Bauer was doping. Lukas Bauer was the Czech who was leading the Tour de Ski, which was on over the holidays. Going by the quotidian nature of such an introduction no one could suggest that Olof had a hard time keeping away from Ester nor that their last meeting was something that needed to be resolved. They were but two old pals catching up.

At first they talked in general but then Olof said something interesting. He'd made a new year's resolution about forming healthier habits.

'I have to take charge of my life. The way I'm going, it isn't good.'

How far did his bid for health extend? Ester wondered after they'd hung up, because he'd also said that they could (or did he say 'should'?) meet next week when he was home in Stockholm. Did the new year mean the hour of the break-up had arrived?

In anticipation of the planned encounter, she became happy and productive, but on the day they were supposed to see each other, he'd already given up on his new year's resolution. Hungover and muddled, he rejected Ester's suggestion for lunch because they didn't serve strong beer there. They met at noon and spent the next five hours together. Their previous failures weren't mentioned and his resolutions were not addressed. He took her arm as they wandered the streets; in this way their bodies stayed close. Towards the afternoon, they went into a cafe on Västerlånggatan and each had a pastry. He sampled hers and she his. He said that Ester should come to see the other play he was in, the one in Linköping which was running parallel to the one she'd already seen. No mention was made of how poorly that had gone.

'It would be fun to hear what you think,' Olof said.

They parted with a peck. Ester went home and her walls closed around her like a cell. Her skin hurt. She whimpered on the floor. The absence of physical contact was worst when they had come so close to it.

The low raw chill that had Stockholm in its vice yielded to brisk, glittering air and hard snow. For a few short hours each day, the sun revealed its cold eye, set in the centre of a deep-blue face, smooth and plain, no furrowed hesitation, no veils of clouds, no shifting colours.

Ester had finished a verse cycle about famous characters from novels who'd fled their authors to become sovereign and speak for themselves. It had been submitted and accepted. Days passed and no mention was made about when she should travel down to see Olof in Linköping. She worried he was having regrets. She worried that she hadn't received his suggestion with enough enthusiasm and had made him change his mind.

A couple of weeks after their last encounter, she woke at seven and decided to tackle the matter herself. Her life had been on hold for too long. She cancelled two meetings that same afternoon and called Olof. By then she'd made it to the more sociable hour of nine.

'I can come see you today. Like we talked about. I'll get to Linköping by lunch; we can eat and then spend the day together.'

There was a pause. Not a good pause. A pause filled with aversion.

'No. That won't work.'

His voice was like a pistol shot and as devastating.

'But I'm supposed to come to see your show.'

'Not today you're not. I'm going to the library and then I'm going swimming.'

Her unplanned visit seemed to strike fear into him.

Ester empathized with this fear of forced companion-ship and being robbed of independence. She would have had the same reaction, but only with a person she wasn't keen on meeting. That was the crux. If only she understood why he was asking her to come if he felt this aversion.

Why suggest seeing his plays two hundred kilometres away? Why take her arm as they strolled through town? Why call her when they'd been out of touch for a while, why sleep with her, if but briefly and interrupted? She was just as reluctant when faced with spending time with most other people, but she didn't enter into intimacies with them. What was this an expression of, this wavering, which psychic disposition was causing Olof's inscrutability?

'Weak ego,' said Vera.

'Weak ego,' said Elin.

'Weak ego,' said Fatima.

'No idea,' said Lotta. 'What's a weak ego?'

'I don't really know,' said Ester, 'but maybe it's this: you don't know who you are or what you want. You lack a core.'

'But how can you possibly love a man like that?'

'Because we don't love people for their perfections. We love them for what they radiate and what we want to partake in. I've seen that he's capable of being otherwise, I've seen him focus his love on me, and I don't think he doesn't know who he is or what he wants. He knows full well. He's just being lazy and making excuses so he doesn't have to make a decision.'

Against better judgement, against the knowledge that Olof always, without exception, dialectically determined, became soft when Ester was hard and vice versa, she didn't hang up, but said:

'We can go to the library together. And to the pool.'

'That won't work. I need advance warning for this sort of thing.'

There was violence in his expression. Some might call it integrity. Perhaps she provoked this violence in him by invading him, she pondered during the following week. In that case, he was acting in self-defence.

'Maybe we can find another day?' he said. 'I'm not up for it today.'

'I hear you. Because you're going to the library and the pool.'

'It's really fun seeing you, but I need more time to prepare.'

She tried to end the conversation but he kept her on. Olof Sten was not blind to the obvious, that a person in love can weather many blows but not an endless amount. A bridge and the camel's back can only take so much pressure. There's a breaking point that can be measured down to the last gram. It's precise and predictable but only visible after the fact with things that resist quantification. Carelessness comes last. Then the one who rejects can become the rejected.

People aren't loved for their stalwart character and rarely are they hated for their cruelty. Ester wasn't drawn to Olof's cruelty, but to the glimpse of what glimmered in the mud, waiting for her to set it free. She didn't love Olof because he treated her like rubbish but because of how exquisite it was when he didn't. This was the explosive contrast. But unfortunately Olof might have been treating her like rubbish because she loved him.

When they'd hung up and Ester had had a moment to think, she made a decision. These hot and cold spells were taking their toll. She had to leave him.

Could she never contact him again? asked Elin, who Ester was calling for good advice. It would be necessary if she took this step. Could she do it?

'Don't know, but I can't stand this any more, that's for sure.'

'It's time. I can hear it in your voice. Call me later and tell me how it went.'

She wrote Olof a text saying she never wanted to see him again and wished him a good life on his leash.

Then she went on a long walk, leaving her phone behind, and felt Riddarfjärden's winds of liberation nip as she walked over the Västerbron Bridge. She continued down to Tantolunden Park, along Årstaviken Bay over to the Eriksdal swimming centre, up the hill to Skanstull, took Götgatan all the way to Slussen, through Old Town along Stora Nygatan, the Strömbron Bridge to Tegelbacken and Hantverkargatan all the way to Fridhemsplan. The walk took almost two hours.

This must be how it felt to kick an addiction, she thought, to throw away the needles and leave the bad crowd behind. Clarity and gratitude in the first hours. Then the shakes. This wasn't poetic language or an analogy, these two things were the same. The mental processes were identical because the physical processes in the brain were the same. Love and drugs: the brain couldn't tell the difference. It just kept working and processing. The sophisticated, dialectical mind knew the difference but not the ungainly, blunt brain. For the brain, the same neurotransmitters were being processed, the same receptors receiving, the same reward, the same joy and anxiety that made you want to go back again and again, seeking the source of ecstasy even though you knew its costs. When love was imbalanced, the doses spun out of control, but now Ester had begun her purge. This time, she would weather abstinence.

At home, the first thing she did was check her mobile phone. It read: 'I don't understand anything.'

She wasn't about to explain herself.

For two weeks, she felt free. Then longing began to invade her conviction. Her determination wore thin.

The raw chill sat between the walls and however she dressed, it was too cold.

If Olof had wanted to get rid of her, he would have sent a different reply, she started to think. 'Yes, it's probably for the best not to be in contact any more,' he could have written. Or: 'You're right. This isn't working.'

But that's not how he'd replied, because he didn't want to sever ties. And in that moment her entire abstinence hinged on an impossible self-discipline because she believed something else to be true and correct, namely that one day he would realize to whom he belonged. On that day she had to be available and the threshold to reach her had to be low.

Around this time Ester Nilsson travelled to Oslo to launch the Norwegian edition of a book on the philosophy of language she'd written a couple of years earlier. She travelled joylessly and with indifference, said what needed to be said, did what she was supposed to do, but cared neither about what she was doing nor about the philosophy of language. It only interested her insofar as it was a tool she could use to interpret Olof Sten's language.

She thought that anxiety was a movement of troops in the brain's civil war, a strategic manoeuvre to get the conscious mind to make a decision that would end the pain, anything to stop the suffering.

She stayed at the Hotel Continental in the centre of Oslo in a large room with thick curtains and a fluffy bed that was far too large for how lonely she was. It rained nonstop. The trip was two days long. Olof was gone, and she'd done away with him. It would have been easier if he'd done away with her, then there wouldn't have been much to discuss, but he'd written 'I don't understand anything' as if he did not in fact want to lose her. Maybe he hadn't made up his mind after all. Olof was a part of her life in the same way that an inoperable cancerous tumour became a part of the brain. Remove what was running amok and you'd take something vital along with it.

During the train journey to the airport on the way home from Oslo she felt a little better, the spaces opened a crack. Her thoughts had started to circle around the issue: how to go about re-establishing contact with someone you said you never want to see again. The brain and body had made a pact and forced the conscious mind to decide, for neither of them could stand the self-imposed situation any more. Freedom had become unfree, purity turned to asceticism. To make a decision about abstinence was a relief, living with it was to live in shackles. And in these shackles, a new decision about freedom was made: take the drug again. The packet of cigarettes tossed in the bin at midnight was plucked out the next day and this act was just as wonderful as the act of throwing them away.

Ester Nilsson flew back to Stockholm much lighter than when she had left. A few days later she'd devised a plan. If it didn't go well, she would give up for good, this she promised herself. The plan went like this: in the name of research she would see *A Doll's House* which was playing at the Stockholm City Theatre and then, also in the name of research, she would compare it to the play that Olof was currently in, the contemporary deconstruction of *A Doll's House*. In order to complete this research, she would have to travel to Linköping.

She booked tickets and informed Olof via a brief and formal text that she intended to see his play a week from Thursday with the idea of writing something about how it related to *A Doll's House*.

His reply was immediate, and this in itself was answer enough.

'Didn't Miss Nilsson request that I go to hell?'

After having conducted a textual analysis of him for a year and a half, she knew how propitious this reply was. Olof Sten was in possession of a set number of mental states. They found their expression in a set number of verbal representations that moved between rejection, neutrality and inducement. Ester was well acquainted with the combinations, which feelings they reflected and which actions usually followed which turn of phrase. One of the variables was the number of minutes that passed between her text and his reply. Another was stressing her gender and civil status, in implicit contrast to his.

Heart swelling, she read and reread what he'd written. He was playing hurt but not so much so that she'd be scared off. And she played along. This was their game:

'And Miss Nilsson had good reason for doing so. But it was ever so tedious without you. I beg of you, return from the flames.'

He wrote:

'If you happen to be going to Stockholm after, I'd gladly tag along to Norrköping.'

She wrote:

'I intend to proceed to Stockholm thereafter.'

He wrote:

'If you're nice you can borrow the guest room.'

She wrote:

'I'm always nice. Except when you're not.'

He wrote:

'Niceness is overrated, unproductive.'

They were making mental love again. She felt reanimated. No twinge of pain remained. She was as new.

Alone on a Friday night, Ester went to see *A Doll's House* at the City Theatre. She didn't want company so she could feel closer to Olof and not be bothered by the demand to converse and formulate 'her thoughts' immediately after the performance. Here she was again, at a zero-balance where having a little was better than having nothing at all, and there was no such thing as insufficient. That can only arise from lack and end with lack, as soon as the assets are released, expectations rise and a little is worse than nothing and everything is insufficient.

The following Thursday, she was zipping through those 200 kilometres to Linköping southbound on the E4. February was more than halfway through. The air was bracing and the afternoons were getting noticeably longer with each passing day. She arrived shortly before six in her shiny Twingo. She had washed it near the entrance of town because she wanted to drive him around in a clean car.

Olof's performance started at seven. She parked by the theatre and ate in a pub by the main square. As she sat with her plank steak in front her, Olof texted and asked if she'd arrived and suggested she park by the stage door. She couldn't recall him showing such eagerness and helpfulness before. But now was not the time for conjecture, this time she would show restraint, she wouldn't get ahead of her herself and make assumptions, wouldn't risk rejection. The one who held their tongue was passive and could never be pushed away, neither could they be accused of being difficult. The passive risked nothing. Doing nothing took an enormous effort on Ester Nilsson's part, it was one of the most difficult things she knew, but now she'd make an effort.

She bought a bouquet of flowers in which she tucked her card, a note from Henrik Ibsen that said the contemporary author whose play Olof was in and who profaned *A Doll's House* was rubbish, rot and poppycock, and an actor as skilled as Olof should not waste his considerable talents on graphomaniac ladies who believe the world's time is better spent on their maternal lives and uterine catarrhs than on appreciating a man who supported their liberation.

The performance, though interesting in parts, was formulaic and quite dull. Olof played a minor role. Ester couldn't wait for the clock to strike ten.

At that hour, she was standing outside a theatre's stage door yet again, waiting. If you persist, something is bound to change. Olof came out with Ester's bouquet in hand and a smile on his face, neither contemptuous nor nonchalant, but egalitarian and warm. Their eyes met, and Ester's entire body registered the moment; it was electric.

'Ibsen sent me flowers,' said Olof.

'You don't say. What did he need to get off his chest?'

'He seems irascible. Doesn't like having his circles disturbed. No men do.'

Olof's clucking laughter. Ester knew this reference meant that the evening would go well. When he wanted to get closer, he pointed out these minor gender differences, when he wanted to alienate himself he insisted she was 'one of the boys'.

'May I accompany you to Norrköping?' he asked.

Ester opened the passenger door, bowed and made the sweeping gesture of a dignified servant.

'Thank you, driver,' said Olof and climbed in.

Their affinity was like the crook in the corner of a person's mouth who is used to smirking. It was just there, always accessible, always ready.

The evening chill had left snow crystals on the car windows. Ester scraped them off and then they were on their way. After barely ten pitch-dark kilometres, Olof asked why she'd been so angry and cut off contact with that terrible text message three weeks earlier. Ester had no need to articulate what she was thinking, saying and feeling at the time, not now that the distance was gone, but said something evasive about how his skittishness was hard to handle.

Then he said something sensational:

'You're going to have to learn to handle it.'

She gasped soundlessly. He was planning a future with her! A future where she needed to be able to handle his traits. The comment left no room for question.

'You know I'm not at my best in the mornings,' he continued. 'You've seen me in the morning.'

Another powerful mark of affinity. This was going remarkably well.

'And what did you mean by me being on a leash?'

'Nothing in particular. I was just upset.'

'But what did you mean? You're never angry enough to not mean what you write or why you wrote it.'

Ester concentrated on driving. The sky and forest were indistinguishable, so dense was the darkness and so clear and crisp the air.

'Did you mean that I live with a master who keeps me on a leash?'

'Something like that, maybe.'

She refused to meet his eye.

'That I'm Ebba's dog? I don't have my own will? She makes my decisions for me?'

'I can't recall.'

He didn't seem offended, more interested and probing, as if he actually wanted to understand.

'That's what I thought you meant.'

They drove to where he was staying and parked. In silence, they went up in the lift. She remembered how she felt the last time she'd been here, one unhappy morning in November that weighed on her like a black ton. That was three months ago. Now there would be another nocturnal sitting at the same kitchen table with a different Olof, careful, appreciative and grateful to have her there. He stressed how fun it was that she'd come to see his performance, how highly he esteemed her opinion and how exciting it was to discuss it with her. This praise seemed to lack the calculation of flattery. He wanted her to detail her thoughts on the play, so she offered an analysis of what she'd seen. He listened closely and asked how it compared to Ibsen's; personally he had his doubts about its merits. Ester said the two writers had such different agendas that a meaningful comparison couldn't be made. The one was about reality and the other discourse. The one about what the author saw and heard in real life, the other about what the author saw and heard when discussing real life.

'Isn't the discussion of real life part of real life?' Olof asked.

'Well, yes, but on another level. Meta.'

'Isn't everything actually on that level? If we're honest about it. Isn't everything theatre?'

'If you're a discourse analyst, yes. Then all of existence is text and theatre.'

'I don't know what discourse is. But I think everything people do is theatre. Outside of the theatre, they're playing at not playing. Because it's honest about its games and masks, theatre is the only thing that is genuine and true. It doesn't pretend to be authentic.'

Ester didn't reply. She was keeping her distance, her cool, her inner resolve, all so as not to lose herself – or what she perceived to be herself, the true Ester with a recognizable essence of thoughts and behaviours that she felt comfortable with – and crash right into old follies. She was acting, if you will.

'What are you going to write?' Olof asked.

'What?'

'The purpose of your research is to write something, isn't it?'

'What research?'

'Your research into the two plays.'

'My research, yes. I never know how that will turn out. As well you know, I can use all of my experiences.'

'So the research was mostly for the fun of it? A pretext for coming here?'

His eyes were glittering, but because Ester had decided to act differently this time she didn't admit to anything. She didn't clarify the subtext. This equilibrium was achieved at the expense of sober inner distance. Protecting herself meant that there was instantly less closeness.

'I don't differentiate between utility and pleasure. I take pleasure in utility and find utility in pleasure. And displeasure.'

'That, too.'

'Especially that.'

'Sounds worrying.'

She didn't reply, nor did she offer a disarming smile.

'I'd like to be able to do what you do, writing. Actors are so dependent on other people. It leads to fellowship, sure, but also dependency.'

These comments about affinity, these transfers from his account to hers were coming hard and fast that night.

'In which sense can't you write?' Ester asked.

'I just can't.'

'You mean you can't write anything fit to print?'

'I mean at all.'

The pale incandescent light that had seemed sharp and insidious in November was now warm and enveloping. They sat there talking for over two hours.

Then Olof spoke with new simplicity:

'Shall we go to bed?'

The beds in the bedroom were pushed together this time. No black bra was on the floor and there was no stiff silver necklace on the bedside table. They lay close together. It was self-evident and needed no discussion. But Ester was afraid of the backlash and barely dared allow her hands to graze his hot skin.

'You're not going to regret this in the morning, are you? Or in ten minutes?'

'You can tell I won't,' he whispered as if the two of them shared no history, as if the last time they'd shared this bed hadn't been awful.

Caressing her body, Olof whispered: 'Can you stay another night? You can go to Stockholm tomorrow while I'm on stage, pick up some clothes and come back.'

His impulses were like fireworks – sparkling, extravagant, dying.

'I'll stay as long as you like,' Ester whispered.

A few hours later before she fell asleep, she noted that the day that was coming to a close was exactly one year since her arrival in Arvidsjaur.

The morning after was the moment for dialectical backlash. If such a backlash were to come, it would come now. There would be no avoiding it. She had to find out the truth, so she pressed herself against Olof's back, her arm around his stomach. And she got an answer. What Olof did indicated that this was the dawn of a new era and the past had been put behind them. He patted her hand. This small gesture was a sign of affection, an assurance that she could relax, and an acknowledgement of previous poor form.

They slipped inside each other's bodies anew. The February morning sneaked a peek through the half-open blinds to find out what happiness and pleasure looked like in undiluted form. Then they showered, ate and chatted. The day awaited and Olof wanted them to go into town. Ester didn't question the reasons for or the meaning of the change. If he was asked to formulate it, it would lose its indeterminable vagueness, forcing definition's contours upon it. He would catch sight of it and feel regret. Now it was a matter of being flexible and crossing her fingers.

They went out. The winter sun stung their eyes, but was not warm. They held hands and walked to the town centre. The shapes and colours seemed brand new, box-fresh. The world was a different place than it had been the day before, and Olof Sten was behaving as if he'd crossed a border and reached a point of no return.

They talked non-stop not about themselves, but about the world. Olof recited a stanza of a poem by Tegnér, which he'd written his thesis in literature on before drama school. The stanza went like this:

'But thou, Mankind! art worthy to be lauded,/ God's likeness thou, how true, how genuine!/ Two lies of thine have also to be added:/ One is called woman, and the other man./ Their tune is honour bright and faith requited,/ Sung best while taking one another in./ Thou Heaven's child! thy single truth is plain,/ 'Tis branded on thy brow: the mark of Cain.'

'Beautiful but terrible,' Ester said. 'Deeply disheartening.'

'The truth is often terrible,' Olof said.

The number of buildings grew denser as they neared the centre of Norrköping. Cautiously, Ester mentioned what he'd whispered the night before, that she could stay another day, but Olof replied that it would be too complicated and risky. You never knew what Ebba might do even if they weren't planning on seeing each other this weekend because she was working. Theoretically, she could barge in at any time.

'At least we get to spend time together now,' Olof said.

'And it's wonderful. But it's the nights one wants.'

The change was indeed substantial, for he said:

'There are nights in Stockholm, too.'

And Ester floated forth on wadding and cotton.

They strolled the streets, visited an art exhibition but looked at each other more than at the art, walked until they arrived in an old industrial area that had been turned into a museum where they decided to have lunch. Sitting there with a selection from the buffet on their plates, Ester asked Olof about past relationships, his experience of love and how the relationships had begun and ended. Now seemed like the right time for a deepening of this kind. In his ambivalent days Olof would've been irritated, but now he told her about a woman he'd been very close to many years ago, during his previous marriage.

'Did you have a romantic relationship?'

'You could say that.'

Slippery, Ester thought and felt some of the weight return, but positive; he'd never spoken so openly before.

'So you had a relationship while you were married to the mother of your children?'

'Towards the end. While it was in decline.'

Again, slippery. His eyelids fluttered.

'Did you end up being a couple?'

'For a time. She died of cancer.'

'While you were living together?'

'No, later. A year or two ago.'

'What was her name?'

'Eszter.'

'Like me?!'

'But with a "z". Her mother was from Hungary.'

He seemed to want to lighten the mood because with a laugh that lingered in his hapless smile, he added:

'You know I'm not good with change; I like routine and repetition.'

But Ester hung on tight, unwilling to depart from earnestness now that they finally dared inhabit it together.

'Why did it end?'

Olof looked around, troubled, the questions were getting to be too many, but he answered them.

'It fizzled out.'

Fizzled out. The phrase worried Ester deeply. Things rarely fizzled out mutually. The person saying they did was usually the one who had lost interest and stopped getting in touch, fallen for someone else, wanted to make a clean break. One person's fizzling out was often another person's misery.

Ester wondered to herself how Eszter would have described it. But she was dead. She sensed something terrifying, but on a level she wasn't about to heed. What had happened over the course of the past day was far too incredible to disrupt with a moment of worry. Her passions had finally quieted, desire was stilled, body and psyche were in harmony, and without resorting to power play she was with the man who lived inside her day and night. A new era awaited them, Olof had made that clear. She'd contend with her doubts later.

They made their way home through sun-drenched streets. Ester was tired from the lack of sleep and from not being used to the light. It was after two o'clock. She said she should start making her way to Stockholm. This time, she had to be disciplined and not hang around, better leave too early than too late. Independence, if but performative, was her new lodestar. She had to attempt an approach that had not previously failed. This progress couldn't be laid to waste by showing a lack of restraint.

There was something clarified about Olof's person. His facial muscles were relaxed, cruelty and distancing jeers were no longer a way out. He said that if she didn't have to go home just yet then he'd very much like her to stay until he had to leave for the theatre around five.

'Then I'll stay,' she said.

'That makes me happy.'

When they got home, they napped on the bed pressed tight each other. They woke up at the same time and Olof said:

'Well, hello. Fancy seeing you here,' whereupon they embraced each other and the lust came rushing in. He stuck his hands inside her pants and whispered:

'Making love with you is incredible. But we don't have time.'

'Yes, we do.'

It wasn't yet twilight. Light spilled into the apartment as only late-afternoon light in February can, scattering bright squares, rhombuses and dots around the room.

Olof showered and Ester sat on the toilet seat enjoying the sight of his naked body, being with him, touching him whenever she fancied. From past the edge of the forest, the sun stared at them. She mentioned that there were five weeks until the spring equinox, meaning it was as light in the evenings now as it was when October turns into November. Olof said that was strange because the end of February feels much brighter. The difference must come down to expectation, they agreed. In February when you've got used to the dark, every ray of light was a gift, while in

October it was the deprivation of light that once was. The result was the same, but the experiences much different.

They held each other tight in the hall.

'I'd like to skip work tonight,' he said, 'go to a restaurant with you, eat steak frites, drink a large beer and relax.'

'That would be fantastic. But your public would weep.'

Laughing, he stroked her cheek.

'Hardly. You think too highly of me.'

On the early stretch out of Norrköping, she drove in the livid twilight that sheathes the landscape right before darkness falls, completely content.

The silence of the weekend that followed was unlike other silences. Ester made sure to work hard while her body was still content and the desire for replenishment hadn't yet made her restless. She wrote for half of Saturday and half of Sunday, and otherwise she read. They didn't call each other. It was his last weekend in Norrköping, he'd said he was going to clear out the apartment and then go to Stockholm for a few days before heading out on a long national tour. On Sunday afternoon, the first worry came creeping. Shouldn't he want to call her? Not be able to help it? She kept at it, but her work was heavier now. Words, words, that's all we have to confer. Words were worn down by thousands of years of use but also acquired their exceptional impact from those very years of usage. Should she desist? The world had enough books already and even if excess was a prerequisite for exceptional specimens she didn't *have* to contribute to the rubbish so that the flowers of others could grow on the dump.

She pushed through and stayed her course a little longer. Nothing ever got done if you thought it was meaningless. In order to have the energy to care about life itself, you had to exaggerate its importance.

By evening, the distress caused by Olof's silence became acute and the night grew long. She understood that she'd never have another good night's sleep without that hot body next to hers; once you've felt it, the loss will be eternal, eroto-romantic awakenings are irreversible.

By mid-Monday, worry had become agony. The fear of repetition forced Ester to take the measure that was most sure to lead to repetition; she texted him a little hello. When no reply came, she fell into a torture chamber. From down there, she called Olof and asked how he was doing.

'Fine, thanks. Just great. The birds are chirping, it's spring.'

His carefreeness did not include her, just the spring. A person in possession of great longing and a hole that isn't being filled with what she has chosen can even be jealous of birdsong. No mention of the incredible turn they had taken was made. The wordlessness was difficult. For Ester, a phenomenon didn't really exist until it was articulated. For Olof, it disappeared with articulation.

'Have you been thinking of me at all?' she asked.

'Yes.'

'What have you been thinking?'

'That we had a nice time.'

Nice? Wasn't it more than nice?

'What do you think will happen now?'

'With what?'

'Us.'

'If we've got to talk about us all the time, I'm going to lose interest in this.'

Not a great comment but she clung to the word 'this'. They now had something he called 'this'. Olof said that he'd read about an exhibition on the origin of man in *Dagens Nyheter* that morning and wanted to see it with Ester. She'd also read the article, but she wasn't after companionship at a museum. Last week's reset had been for naught; what had prepared her for happiness then was misery now. The old fear consumed her: that all would be snatched from her as soon as she was holding it in her hands.

'So we're not going to sleep together?' she asked.

Olof sighed. 'Aren't both possible?'

'Indeed they are. In that case, I'd gladly go to the museum with you.'

Thus they set a date for Thursday at noon at the Fältöversten mall on Östermalm. Olof must have chosen the place because of some errand he had in the area, Ester thought, because it wasn't on the way to the Swedish Museum of Natural History where the exhibition was; he was probably thinking they'd take the subway together to Frescati.

At five to twelve, she was at the Valhallavägen entrance. She began to freeze in the harsh cold, so she went into the mall to warm up, came back out, waited. At ten past twelve Olof hadn't shown up yet. When she, with certain hesitation, called and asked where he was, he was at the other end of the shopping centre at the Karlaplan entrance.

His negligence had returned, the touch of disarray before their dates. There was a marked difference between her arrival on Thursday night in Linköping when he'd sorted out her parking as well as their exact meeting place and time. Now everything was loose and approximate again. If there was even the tiniest sum in his account, everything went wrong, was done by half and left hanging. Annoyed, she walked through the Fältöversten mall. She was sure they'd decided on the Valhallavägen entrance. Her heightened suspicion towards this kind of negligence and its root stemmed from eroded trust. It had been worn down long before she met Olof and was further eroded with each new love.

She walked on to Karlaplan. There Olof was, waiting and his face gave nothing away. The first words from his mouth were that it was lucky she hadn't shown up right at noon because a friend of Ebba's had come along and stopped to chat. Olof's concern bewildered Ester. He must have decided to leave Ebba, anything else would be incomprehensible considering what had transpired between them over the past fifteen months, culminating this past week. Most likely he was mentally preparing for the day when all his friends and enemies would find out that his relationship with Ebba was over and he'd started a new one. So why worry about a friend of the wife seeing them together? Rather, he should welcome such an encounter because it could help him spread the message that he was having such a hard time voicing.

Ester didn't ask about it. It wasn't the time. It was never the time. She walked towards the subway and Olof asked where she was going.

'To the Natural History Museum.'

When he understood that the exhibition about the origin of man wasn't at the Swedish History Museum down by Djurgårdsbron Bridge as he'd thought, which to her relief explained why he was at the Karlaplan entrance, he suggested that they go to Liljevalch's spring exhibition on Djurgården Island instead.

They did and afterwards, they lingered long in each other's arms, huddled in a corner of Liljevalch's cloakroom.

On the bus from Djurgården, Olof's sister called. Ester heard him say that he'd 'never been better' which filled her with a well-being greater than any she'd ever known. She touched him as he did her, they were sitting as close to each other as they could get.

They were en route to the Passport Office on Kungs-holmen. Olof's passport had expired. He was going to Rome over Easter, to Rome with his wife, on the trip they'd arranged in the autumn. Maybe they couldn't cancel it? Ester thought Rome would deal them a death blow. Travelling together with a wife one was about to leave couldn't be anything but unbearable.

At the Passport Office they saw an actress Olof had worked with on a production a few years before and who he'd been wary of since, which really meant that he thought she was wary of him and his talents. Olof didn't go over and say hello, instead he waited for her to notice him. She didn't. This made him feel neglected, insulted and under-appreciated. Ester pointed out that the woman had in fact not seen him. He asked if Ester didn't think that actors were an unusually silly sort and acting itself was ridiculous. All that posturing and dressing up?

'Of course not.'

'Actors are so affected.'

Through this exchange, Ester understood that Olof was in close mental proximity to her; only then did he speak ill of his work and those who engage in it. When he wanted to push her away, he'd reference his guild to underscore her status as an outsider.

Ester observed these shifts with tormented empathy and thought that when he was with her, this self-loathing would disappear.

The Passport Office exit on Bergsgatan was near Ester's apartment. When the errand was complete and they were walking towards the Hantverkargatan bus stop, she asked if they were going back to her place. She thought it seemed natural. It was four o'clock.

'What would we do at yours?'

'Something suited to a domestic environment.'

'No. I'm not inclined.'

'But I am.'

'You're always inclined.'

'Because it so rarely happens with you, I am, yes.'

'Rarely with me? Is it happening with someone else in between?'

The somewhat troubled sharpness in his tone didn't pass her by. Being reminded that he was replaceable always put him on the alert. Ester had no intention of exploiting this, she wanted no game-playing, and the truth was that he, for the time being, was irreplaceable.

'No. It is not.'

'I'm meeting my son tonight. We're going out to eat.'

The restaurant they were going to was on Rörstrandsgatan across the Karlberg canal, a kilometre or so away from Ester's neighbourhood, and she said that if he wanted to, he could cross the bridge when he was finished and ring her bell.

'But it might be late,' he said.

'Doesn't matter. If you end up ringing my bell at 3 a.m., then so be it.'

His bus came rolling down the hill from Polhemsgatan and they parted with kisses. She walked home on Hantverkargatan filled with perplexing thoughts. He hadn't said the weekend was a mistake or a one-off event, he hadn't even suggested it or distanced himself from it. This was new, and this was good. He wasn't taking anything back. Everything looked promising, but it didn't feel promising. It was going too slowly. He was too inert. She wanted to get going with their life.

People are always looking for an escape route, she'd read, even out of sweetness, especially out of sweetness. But why, then, didn't she want to find a way out with Olof or anyone else she'd loved? Throughout her life, she'd fled confinement and coercion, but never romantic feelings. Those she rushed into each time. Why didn't any of the people she fell in love with do the same?

That night Ester attended a dinner meeting with fellow members of the editorial board of a magazine about politics, society and ideas. The meeting was held at Elverket on Östermalm where meticulous rustic food was served alongside dishes-in-miniature and foamed sauces.

Ester liked these editorial meetings. Interesting conversations were always had, giving her new material to contemplate, and something always came up that she'd never before considered. They met four times a year, which was seldom enough for intrigues not to develop, in spite of the ideological tensions in the group.

They decided that the next themed issue would be

dedicated to philosophy of the mind and the problem of free will from a political and judicial perspective. Considering the latest research about the brain, how should a modern judicial system be shaped?

They divided topics between them, to be further investigated, and discussed which articles they'd assign to other writers.

By eleven o'clock, they'd wrapped up. Ester walked for a while with one of the other board members, an economist who was pragmatic in her moral perspective and for whom pragmatism was the only principle, and so they didn't share many views, but Ester thought she was pleasant, not to mention well-read and conversant. They often kept each other company after the meetings and talked about modern tendencies. This time was different; Ester immediately started talking about the Olof situation. Because she wasn't safely in the harbour, she had an urgent need to talk. She was still hoping that someone would be able to explain what she couldn't understand: why the men she went out with couldn't stay away from her and yet wanted so little and set so many boundaries. This behaviour was foreign to her, she who in romance either wanted or did not, never giving a second thought to the difference.

The other woman responded with unexpected severity. She encouraged Ester to break up post-haste or to stop hoping that Olof would get divorced and resign herself to the crumbs being thrown her way. These were the only two options and she had to make a decision if she didn't want to face even greater unhappiness.

They walked up Kungsgatan, alone but for the odd night walker and dog owner. Ester said that for the life of her, she couldn't imagine why you'd want to stay with a wife you weren't happy with if you'd met someone you'd preferred.

'It's not a question of rather or more,' said the economist. 'He wants a little of both and to assure himself that the resources will never run out.'

'But the sum gets diminished this way. Everything is halved and less complete than it would otherwise be.'

'He doesn't think so. From his perspective, it's like a friendship. You prefer to have more than one friend, don't you? Otherwise, it simply isn't smart. You risk suddenly finding yourself very lonely. You have different friends for different functions and needs, right? He does, too, but the difference is that they're secret and he's sleeping with them.'

'But I'm not as close with my friends as I am with a romantic partner; that relationship is more diluted, distanced and friendly, cordial even. I could never stand seeing them all the time precisely because it's diluted and friendly, and it has to be that way so that I won't feel invaded. Intimacy with a romantic partner must either be total so that you can live together, or as diluted as it is when it's shared between several people, and then it's impossible to live together. It's the razed mental barrier to the beloved that makes the spatial proximity desirable and possible, where being with the other is like being with yourself, but better. When you unite, which literally happens during intercourse, the boundary between the lovers is erased, making it possible to be together all the time. When two individuals have no mental or physical barriers, you're alone when you're with the other. If the two of you keep the barrier intact, you have to police your borders and think about how you're behaving, be obliging and careful. The alienation is greater and the friction less, but you can never really be at ease with the other person. It gets tiring and so you have to recuperate by being alone. Romantic relationships only work if the barrier is gone, when you slip in and out of each other's mental and physical spaces without limitation, where you share everything without noticing, precisely because the barrier has been dissolved. Otherwise it's as mentally taxing as constantly being around a person you revere but aren't mentally intimate with and who makes you perpetually aware of your contours. That's why children and parents can only stand living together until the child becomes its own person; then it's impossible. And it soon follows that the child will seek a new barrier to destroy with another person. For only in a barrier-free existence does one feel whole.'

Ester's monologue had lasted all the way up Kungs-gatan, with the economist only interjecting small noises and comments.

'I like your theory, Ester: a barrier to the beloved that

disappears. That's just how it feels, that's what you're looking for and what makes you want to be in the same room
day in and day out, night after night, year after year. But
people have conflicting emotions. Not everyone wants as
much intimacy as you do. They want to live diluted lives.
Intimacy frightens them. Intimacy is dangerous. You take
a big risk getting close to someone. You risk being discarded or losing what you've had or hoped for. You risk
really getting to know yourself and presenting your entire
unguarded self to someone else. That's why lots of people
have two relationships or even more. Not because they're
particularly bored with their marriages and not because
the more fun the better, but to cover themselves a little,
insuring themselves against losses and vulnerability.'

'Risking unhappiness is the cost of happiness,' said
Ester. 'It's the price of the sublime.'

'You can't always use yourself and your own understanding as a starting point. Your goals in life differ from
those of the people we're talking about. I lived like you
once, in involuntary surreptitiousness. For fifteen years, I
hoped he'd get divorced, and each time I despaired, something would convince me that a divorce was imminent;
there'd be a minor shift that made me sure he would end
his marriage one day after all, out of exhaustion if nothing
else. He just seemed to be waiting for the right moment. I
thought we were on a spiral staircase turning towards the
light, but it was one of those spiral staircases that stops at
a locked gate. The right moment never came. One day, he

had a stroke and died. I read about it in the paper. There was a notice of his death, including those who survived him.'

They stopped by Hötorget, where their ways would part.

'Were you ever able to get over that?' asked Ester.

'It took me a long time, and as far as that kind of relationship goes, I'm done for ever.'

Ester nodded in sympathy but knew that the same was not necessarily true for her situation. No two relationships, or people, are the same.

'Take care of yourself,' said the economist. 'Be careful. It's easy to wreck your life for those moments of euphoria, they're lethal. As well you know, the years go by.'

From there, the walk home took twenty-five minutes. The air was cold and dry. Ice floes drifted in the canal, whitish grey on the dark water. Tomorrow, Friday, Olof would go on tour. However she behaved, he drifted away. If she wanted to live close to him she'd probably have to do so in obscurity; an existence of constant preliminaries and with no other choice than to let it go or let him decide. She couldn't have that. She couldn't have it any other way either. She'd rather have some of Olof than none. In the brief moments they were together, she felt the fullness of life. Then the hole in her closed up, the cry was silenced. She couldn't let herself be guided by the disappointments of others.

Around midnight, she arrived home and saw that Olof had called her landline a few hours earlier. The blood began to rush, her heart leapt from her chest. She understood that she'd finally got behind his bulwarks; he wanted something with her, he was approaching. Olof wouldn't be able to resist her love in the long run. With a satisfaction that started deep in her marrow, she went to bed. She'd only just nodded off and begun to dream when the ringing phone drew her back.

'Did I wake you?' Olof asked.

'Not at all.'

'I just wanted to hear how you're doing. I'm about to go to bed.'

He was hot and loose with alcohol and longing. This was when she liked him best.

'Can't you come here?'

He fumbled with his surprise as you do when you hear what you were hoping for but didn't dare suggest.

'How do I get to yours, then?'

No one but Olof could sound so helpless. She loved this clumsy timidity when it surfaced, and entertained no thoughts about Olof's awareness of its viability.

'Taxi,' Ester said. 'Take a taxi. My treat!'

Fifteen minutes passed. Then Olof was standing outside Ester's door wearing a pair of gleaming Italian loafers she hadn't seen before. She'd never seen him in loafers or in anything polished. They were too thin for the season, but she was touched by the effort and the sacrifice implied in not playing it cool; he'd often dressed down, was uncombed and unkempt so that Ester wouldn't get any ideas about him attaching any importance to their dates or that he was making an effort for her. Because there was something unusual about dressing down, the inversion of dressing up, she'd always taken this to mean that these dates did in fact mean so very much to Olof.

Standing in the doorway, he was smiling bashfully and pleadingly. His desire and inability to resist it seemed to embarrass him. So Ester had to be extra-careful now. With people who are motivated by shame and self-loathing, great care had to be taken when they indulged their longing. When the pendulum swung, then it swung with considerable force into the one who provoked the shame. But in this case, the manifestation was mild. Olof did no more than comment on how remarkably ugly Ester's pyjamas were.

For a while, they sat at the kitchen table talking, but soon they went to bed. The fires of tenderness and lust burned in the hours that followed, crackled and burned.

The next morning, Ester drove Olof home through a hot, humid haze that made Rosenbad, the Parliament House, and the town hall look like a romantic stage set. She rolled across the Central Bridge at a good speed, through Old Town and up over Slussen, rosy-cheeked and with that dreamy look in the eyes that follows a successful dalliance. She soon stopped outside his door, turned off the engine and put her hand on his thigh. Once again the time had come for them to part. These partings seemed to come far too often. Did he feel the same way, too? She didn't know, and he didn't address it. Maybe he was happy to see her sometimes rather than unhappy about always having to say goodbye.

Their kiss over the gear stick was witnessed by one or two passers-by. Then he crossed the street and waved from the entryway. In a few hours he'd travel to Göteborg where the tour was to begin. She didn't know when they'd see each other next, but for the first time it felt like they would definitely see each other again.

She went back home and tended to her day. It wasn't long before Olof called. He said he'd had a nap and a cold shower but was still completely drained after last night's exertions. They shared a knowing laugh. He geared up to deliver his statement.

'So,' he said. 'Maybe we should lie low with the phones over the weekend.'

Ester waited to hear the rest.

'Because Ebba's coming to Göteborg.'

He was using the same turn of phrase as he had before Christmas a year and two months ago, when they were to 'lie low with the texting over the holidays'. And like the first Christians thought that the kingdom of heaven was close, truly believed it, and lived and acted accordingly, and like so many socialists believed that only revolution could be waiting behind the next stock-market crash, Ester truly believed, now and on all future occasions, this one included, that a break-up really was imminent, and she behaved in accordance with this dream. Should she now do what St Paul's and Lenin's followers had been forced to do: realize that there was no kingdom come?

How was it possible for him to receive his wife in Göteborg the following weekend after what had recently changed and happened? How could he even consider it? And how was he going to leave her if he didn't even dare say that this weekend wasn't the right time for her to visit? He had to begin his break-up! Averting Ebba's visit would be a reasonable start, a way to signal that nothing would be as before. Surely he didn't need any more time to think or prepare?

'Hello?' she heard Olof say. 'Are you still there?'

Or maybe he had a plan? Maybe he had to keep his wife in good spirits until they'd been to Rome! When that trip was out of the way, he'd surely tell Ebba and leave her. That must be it.

'You won't hear from me until the coast is clear.'

'Thank you, Ester. We'll be in touch soon. Talk to you later.'

He sounded intimate; rarely had she felt him so close to her. Soon he'd announce his divorce and that he was free to meet without restriction. He simply didn't want to involve her in the dirty details of the split. An honourable move, she thought.

Olof toured southern Sweden. With each passing day, Ester wanted to consolidate their alliance, be reassured that the two of them were a couple who in a couple's way wanted to see each other as soon as possible. For a couple they were, if as yet an odd pair.

So Ester wrote to Olof about an idea she'd had. If she drove down to Halmstad where he was performing next week, the two of them could go to Copenhagen over the weekend and then she could drive him to Hässleholm before Tuesday's performance. She did have a lot of work on, she wrote, but it could be done anywhere.

As far as she could tell, the plan was flawless. She could picture them rambling through Copenhagen, the bedroom, suppers and breakfasts. The idea should fly and she eagerly awaited his response.

It didn't come. Twenty hours passed. Twenty hours without an answer were equal to a 'no'. It was also equal to abuse. That's not how a loving, longing person behaved towards the person he'd just entered into a romantic relationship with, this Ester Nilsson understood. What she didn't understand was what he wanted with her and what he was feeling. Entering into a romantic relationship with someone while keeping a distance seemed irrational to her, but it must serve some purpose that made the behaviour seem rational to him.

After twenty hours, Olof wrote that he and his friend from the ensemble Max Fahlén had decided to spend their free days in the house in Skåne.

Twenty wasted hours. One and a half wasted years. Ester felt tired of life and of allowing Olof to steal it. She didn't reply. There was too much to say to say anything at all.

After a few days of silence, Olof called her at home at one in the morning. The ringing woke her, and Olof sounded embarrassed and said he'd sent a text fifteen minutes ago and hadn't received a reply.

Ester had taken to turning her phone off at night to keep herself from constantly checking it. It took a while for it to get going.

'I thought you might be at a party,' he said.

'No. I'm sleeping.'

'Oh good.'

Anxiously, he reminded her of his text message, he seemed to be wondering why she hadn't answered yet. Ester didn't mention the twenty hours she'd endured without reply. When she pulled up the message she read it just loud enough for him to hear:

'Ester. Of course I want to see you, spend time with you, meet you. But it's complicated. We can see each other next Sunday evening after Ebba goes back to Borlänge.'

He opened his balcony door by the sea in Falkenberg and asked her to listen to the waves breaking.

'Of course I want to be with you,' he said.

Had he been thinking otherwise lately? Why else was he insisting on something Ester thought they'd already agreed on?

'Aha. Yes. Good.'

'Does next Sunday work for you?'

'It's far off. Over a week.'

'The tour is going by fast and so is the spring.'

'You think? I think it's creeping along.'

'No, it's going fast. I'll be home soon.'

'And what will happen then?'

'We'll have to wait and see.'

There was that expression again. Did he remember he'd used it that first time at the wine bar under the Katarina Lift exactly a year ago today?

'Then we'll see each other Sunday in nine days, as soon as Ebba has gone.'

'Do we always have to be governed by her?'

'We have all the time in the world, you and I.'

'Do we?'

He rummaged through his things and cleared his throat as if preparing to confess. She didn't recognize this throat-clearing. When he finally spoke it was halting:

'I spent a while talking to Barbro Fors, a colleague in the ensemble. We talked about writing something together. A

LENA ANDERSSON

variety show maybe. Take it to a summer stage somewhere.
Or get a small theatre together. Barbro's nice.'

She heard something off-kilter in his tone and in the
transition, something he felt obliged to report, that was
weighing on his conscious. His voice had that odd vibrato.

'Are you and Barbro Fors close?'

'We talk a lot. I think she has a thing for me.'

'And you see each other every day and work together
every night and travel around in a travelling theatre company. That doesn't sound good. Do you have a thing for
her?'

He chuckled, with a little too much clucking pleasure
for being the only one who knew where they stood.

'Oh. She's not my type.'

These words drove a spear of ice through Ester. He had
used the same formulation when answering his wife's jealous question about her. *She's not my type.*

'Hello?'

'I'm pretty tired. I want to sleep now.'

'Talk to you later,' Olof entreated. 'Sleep well.'

But Ester didn't sleep a wink. She worried. That woman
he'd been so close to once, the one who'd died of cancer,
Eszter with a 'z', was it possible that it 'fizzled out' because
Olof's wife had left him because of his relationship with
Eszter? Was it possible that when the woman who had
been his mistress became Olof's only woman, she was no
longer exciting, no matter who she was or what she was
like? To Olof Sten, were women merely functions, chess

pieces on a board locked in predetermined relationships to each other? If what was secret became official, did he have to find another secret to regain equilibrium and to maintain the balance and distance between the both of them? If he only had one in an equal reciprocal arrangement where both were equally vulnerable and naked before the other, did he feel weak and resigned? By starting a regular relationship with her, had Ester taken the place inside him of the demanding, boring wife, whereupon he had to immediately start something with Barbro Fors to balance Ester out, like he'd acquired Ester in order to balance out Ebba?

Impossible. It had to be impossible. Early the next morning, she called Fatima, who knew about these things. While the phone rang, she thought dreadful thoughts about Olof, that he had a slavish nature but fought against it by being defiant and with infantile authoritarian uprisings, but he never truly sought freedom, hence the obsessive oscillation between devotion and contempt. For appearance's sake, he jangled his chain so the audience would feel sorry for him and not see it was a slave he wanted to be.

Ester Nilsson knew that a slave seeks his own slave to push around. Was that her? She who patiently waited for him to display greater maturity, who wanted to free him from his shackles and show him the way into reciprocal love, no, that couldn't be described as slavery, unless all self-appointed liberators sooner or later end up subjugated to the object of their reforms and rescue measures.

Or was she the fly, pinned down by the cowed child,

wings torn off and haplessly gunning its engine, not knowing why it can't take flight? All the while the child marvels
at the stupidity of the insect which allows itself to be dom-
inated by such an unimportant little person.

When Fatima answered her phone, she was on her way
to work. She listened with concern. Unfortunately, it isn't
impossible, she said. Nothing suggested that Olof wanted
to cut himself loose, or that he was planning on it, because
it didn't interest him. Fatima thought Ester's concerns
about Barbro Fors were credible.

By the time they'd hung up, Ester felt like she was suffo-
cating. Was it because he'd started sleeping with Barbro
Fors too that he, on the phone from Falkenberg, spoke
of her with the guilty-party-in-love's awkwardness and
warmth? Was it because things with Barbro Fors were developing that he had disappeared for several days only to then
reach out with fresh, delicate intimacy: 'Of course I want to
see you, spend time with you, meet you. But it's complicated.' Had he come straight from her bed and felt the need
to compensate Ester, always the servant to his swings? And
had he sounded exactly like this when he'd come home to
his wife, guilt-ridden and sticky with regret after his and
Ester's trysts, while displaying a new determined vitality?
'Darling Ebba, of course we're going to Rome. I love you
and want to be with you, travel with you, encounter you.'

It was so vile she could only bear to graze the thought.
It had to be pushed away if she were to continue oxygenat-
ing her blood, and being able to see him. All of this was but

speculation that arose when despair was whirring at its worst. If she could only see Olof again, this delusion would be proven to be as grotesque as it had to be. But even Fatima was speculating. No one knew for sure. Of course he wasn't also in a relationship with Barbro Fors! It would be madness, it was impossible.

So they were to see each other the following Sunday when his wife had left for Borlänge after their weekend together. He'd spent the previous week touring small towns and villages in Skåne and Småland. They were in touch sporadically and only to the extent that she was checking in. Olof wasn't interested in having contact between their encounters, other than when he felt insecure about her devotion.

Around lunchtime two days before their date, Olof texted her: 'See you Sunday night. Be well. O.' Ester was talking on the phone with Vera when the message arrived, and Vera said:

'He's so eager to see you, Ester. I'm glad it's turning out the way you've been hoping it to. Finally. You've fought so hard for this and for him.'

Vera was in many ways fantastic. Ester could call her round the clock without her being irritated or distant, and she was often ready with a sympathetic interpretation. But she had a malicious talent for slipping what she actually wanted to say between the lines, leaving you defenceless

and her impervious because her words were ostensibly full
of praise and encouragement.

'I don't know about "fought",' Ester said wanly. 'But I've
trusted my judgement and the testimony of my senses, that
he was saying one thing but meant another.'

'One might think you trust yourself too much sometimes. You can get a bit overbearing. I wish I had your
self-esteem. I almost want to say it makes you brazen.'

Vera was like glass wool to Ester. Ester sought her out
in order to be swaddled in the soft warmth of being listened to, but lo and behold, she got cut.

So as not to seem brazen, she said:

'Well, it might be that he got in touch today *not* because
he can't wait to see me, but because he wants to make sure
I won't bother him while he's with Ebba.'

'Oh, let's not think like that. But if we did, it's because
he's still handling his situation. He'll be yours one day,
Ester.'

'You really think so?!'

'Depends on how long you can hold on.'

'I can hold on for as long as it takes. What makes you
think that?'

'How should I know?' Vera interrupted. 'I'm no oracle.'

There would be no dinner on Sunday after all. Olof's
wife decided to stay in Stockholm until Monday morning,
which he called to say on Saturday afternoon. By then,
Ester had perused cookbooks for a couple of hours in the
morning, scrubbed the apartment with soapy water and

had already returned from the Hötorg market hall where she'd bought everything she needed for the meal. This included, but was not limited to, a shoulder of lamb to be stuffed with fresh spices and string to tie it all together.

'You haven't started making preparations, have you?' Olof asked.

'No.'

'I really did want to see you.'

Ester heard cars around him and a siren in the distance. Maybe a dying person was on their way to the Söder Hospital. In the hour of her death many years from now perhaps another similarly sad conversation would be playing itself about between two other lovers while her death siren interleaved their unfinished affairs. She wished those two better luck than she was having.

'What are you thinking about?'

'Nothing,' said Ester. 'Where are you? It's noisy.'

'On Folkungagatan.'

'Did you go out to buy snus?'

'Yes.'

They laughed, the one resigned, the other self-conscious. Ester wanted to be with him there on Folkungagatan. If only he could be less important to her, so everything else in her life could feel like more than mere filler.

'Can't you catch up with me on tour instead?' Olof said and his tone, which had been weak and flat, brightened. 'In Växjö next weekend. Then you can spend two nights with me, all the way to Monday.'

Ester thought she was living in an echo chamber. Go there instead, at another time, to another place – not now but later. But with each repetition came a tiny development that fed her belief in change, a change that was being made by taking one small step at a time. Those steps were worth noting. Olof's echoes gave rise to other echoes inside Ester: Now something is happening. Now a decisive step is being taken. Now he's coming. Now.

And then it was March. Spring awaited as did Växjö. For the trip, Ester bought spring clothes and shoes in pale colours. The Saturday she was to travel she was so filled with uneasy hopes that she didn't get anything sensible done in the morning. Instead, she distracted herself with a seven-kilometre run. Being physical was automatic, it demanded no discipline, no character, no great act of will-power, it was pure habit. And just as habitually, the endorphins started their shift right after. Just as she was stepping out of the shower, Olof called and said:

'About tonight . . . You do understand that you can't wait for me in the lobby, OK?'

He sounded like he was speaking to someone who was coming to Växjö in order to insinuate themselves against his will and without his having had a say in the matter.

Ester heard only his usual floundering, as fleeting as any other sensation passing through him. She was the bedrock and he the butterfly. Sometimes the butterfly landed on the bedrock and stopped fluttering.

'No, I shan't sit in the lobby, and I shall hide as soon as we see someone, and I shall pretend as if I don't know you.'

'We have to be careful. The whole ensemble is staying in the same hotel.'

How was this different to Arvidsjaur, where he hadn't been at all careful around the ensemble, but had introduced Ester to them and hadn't seen the issue when she'd brought it up? Was the difference Barbro Fors?

If Ester didn't go to Växjö, she didn't really have any other plans. Staying at home with only emptiness and the rest of her life ahead of her wasn't appealing. Moreover there was no evidence, he hadn't said that he didn't want her there, and her thoughts about Barbro Fors were unreasonable and bizarre. And now she could hear how Olof was pulling himself back together. He had aired his anxiety, the pendulum swung back; he was no longer torn nor wavering when he said:

'It'll be lovely having you here. I'll be waiting in the room.'

There are 460 kilometres between Stockholm and Växjö. Ester drove the final stretch through twilight and when she parked on the main square near the City Hotel, it was dark. Hesitantly, she ascended the steps that led to the entrance and cautiously navigated the lobby, a quiet space that had a distinguished character and features preserved from the 1950s. Everything in this hotel was soft:

the music, the wall-to-wall carpets, the armchairs, the receptionists, the facial expressions and hairstyles. With soft steps, she glided up the stairs and because her arm was limp with nerves, she knocked on Olof's door softly. He greeted her with a soft smile and said:

'That was a discreet knock.'

'I'm a discreet person.'

They sat down in the armchairs, he poured the red wine and they drank. Soon they were both sitting in the same armchair but agreed that they would eat before they went to bed. Ester suggested a restaurant she'd found on the web that looked like it had a good kitchen. It was a few hundred metres away on Storgatan. They decided to go there.

'You go ahead, I'll follow behind,' Olof said. 'I'll see you on the corner.'

This hurt Ester deeply. She found the insouciance with which he asked her to help him sneak around both offensive and cruel, because he knew full well that Ester didn't want it to be this way. But they couldn't afford to be fighting now that they were finally together, so she held her tongue and contained herself. But one question managed to slip out:

'Is there someone in particular who you don't want to see us together?

Olof turned his back to her, arranging something.

'I'll be down soon.'

So she went down and stood on the corner. After two minutes, he came strolling along.

'Look who's here,' he said, face lit up with a smile.

'What a coincidence,' she said dully and then he took her arm and they walked down Storgatan. It was a pedestrian street; all the shops were closed at this hour. The wind whined. It was just the two of them. Even the restaurant was empty. They were shown to a table and then discussed the various dishes before they ordered, he a saddle of venison, she the house hamburger with potato wedges.

As they waited for the food, they made small talk. How pleasant, sweet and wonderful it was. Ester's rippling contentment returned, the quiet joy of togetherness. The food arrived and it was good. After a few bites, Olof looked at Ester and said:

'Why did you come all the way here to see me? I don't understand, because I'm not worth it. I have nothing to offer you. Nothing to bring to the table.'

He paused. Ester thought of the echo chamber.

'I should be the one teaching you things. Instead you're teaching me. Why have you come all this way to see me?'

Ester put down her cutlery and wiped her mouth so she could reply with the care this serious question deserved.

'If you want to know the truth, your actions often give me pause, your awful ambivalence and the cruelty that it causes. You use these two things as rudder and keel to stay your course and keep from capsizing.'

'Am I really that bad?'

'Occasionally, yes. But when I think of your essence, your presence in a room, the way you receive me sometimes, not to mention everything that radiates from you – inside and out – and all the things that just have to be right between two people, because they can't be engineered ... when I think of all this, I never hesitate.'

He looked puzzled, but happy to hear her words.

Since Ester had met Olof, she'd vacuumed up the world's stories of couples where the one misfired at the start but after a long time decided that it was indeed love, and then devoted himself fully. She searched through weeklies, Hollywood movies and anecdotes about people who'd got each other after three years or seven, of imbroglios, misunderstandings and circumlocutions that occurred because the feeling was so immense it was frightening, that the decision was a life decision and therefore not to be made lightly.

'The most difficult thing about you,' Ester said, 'what pains me most, is your far too keen and quite astounding sense of your assets.'

'What assets?'

'Fluctuations of capital. Relationship capital.'

He encouraged her to elaborate.

'Inside you, there's an account from which you make automatic transactions. You, more than anyone else I have known, have a sense of your balance down to the last öre, and you base your behaviour towards me on that. Do you need to make a deposit, perhaps by being considerate, or can you afford to make a withdrawal by being scornful, cold and indifferent, or do you even have to touch your balance at all? Everyone has an account like this inside

193

them, all people keep track of when they should make an effort and when they can sit back, when to make a withdrawal or a deposit. But your capital calibrator is much more finely tuned than most, and far less impacted by moral judgements. You don't seem to want to adjust it based on outside or competing perspectives, for example the well-being of your fellow man or partner. And it doesn't seem to occur to you to simply disregard it – which you can, you know. You only ever do as much as you have to. I'm sorry to say it's unsettling to watch.'

Olof was silent. Ester felt she'd said too much, but knew it had to be said at some point. Maybe he felt exposed and monitored, but what did it matter? What was said was said, and they had to be able to talk about these things if they were going to live together one day.

When Olof finally opened his mouth, several minutes had passed, during which time they'd finished their main course. Wasn't she expressing an objectionable economic world view, he wondered, one that he, with his politics, didn't feel he could stand by?

She shook her head gently and said that Olof was thinking about it backwards, the order was in fact the reverse. Economics was nothing in and of itself, it merely reflected nature's most inescapable structures of debt and repayment, mine and yours. Economics was but a deeply seeded insight about what things demanded, cost and corresponded to in the form of investments. Pay and be paid was how it went, if not with money then with something else.

'Either we incur debt or someone is indebted to us or we're in equilibrium. These are the three options. When someone has something that someone else wants, there is the potential for a transfer, but also an imbalance of power, which can be regulated by various means. What I'm saying is that you have extra-sensitive instruments for assessing this transposable power and how to regulate it.'

'And what kind of instruments might they be?' Olof asked, resting his elbows on the table and pushing aside his plate, where a lick of currant jelly was left along with the last of the cream sauce.

'Because we are aren't dealing with money – how awful would it be if this were a case of prostitution – only nobler means are at our disposal for regulating power and imbalances.'

'And what means are they?'

'Doubt, reassurance. Lack of definition, definition. Clarity, ambivalence. Honour, dishonour.'

Ester noticed Olof's air of misgiving.

'That sounds metaphysical.'

'It is.'

'I have to go home and think about this.'

'It bears thinking about.'

'Do you have an account inside you, too?'

'Everyone does.'

'Then why are you talking about my account as if it was something special?'

'Because I've never met anyone with such an exceptional

awareness of their balance. And as I've said, I've never met anyone who makes no effort to resist his awareness of IOUs, promissory notes, fees and cash flow. Most people don't want it to be like this, and so their actions counter this awareness.'

'So according to you, I'm wrong? I'm all wrong?'

He wasn't succeeding in sounding injured. Ester attempted a reply but couldn't come up with a decent formulation that was both conciliatory and true.

Soon they were out on the pedestrian street heading back to the hotel. It was, if possible, even more desolate now, the wind more harsh. They seem to have built Växjö in line with ancient Mediterranean ideas about architecture, where one built for maximum shade in the burning sun, Ester said to Olof. To fend off the cold, they held each other close. Ester thought that this might end up being a wonderful weekend after all. They'd just had a frank and in-depth conversation, and tomorrow they'd be going to the Kingdom of Crystal. In a moment of amnesia, she believed they already belonged to each other and could celebrate Easter together. This must have been why she with certain expectation said:

'Easter's coming up.'

To which Olof replied:

'I'll be in Rome over Easter.'

This fact had slipped Ester's mind because it was incomprehensible. Incomprehensible facts never really make their way into the centre of cognition. You can learn to rattle them off, but they'll never become real knowledge. Ester had assumed the trip had been cancelled simply because it should have been.

'How can you go to Rome with Ebba now that you've met me?'

'Because I live with her. People who live together take trips together, don't they? Isn't that what people do who live together?'

It sounded like he was actually wondering what people do when they live together. Ester thought that when you weren't motivated by longing for your partner, then you resorted to mimicry. Conventions and templates existed so you didn't have to work out what you wanted and needed, they stood in for this kind of examination. But if you were together because you couldn't bear to be apart, then there was no need for mimicry. Modes of togetherness would arise spontaneously; you never had to think twice about them.

'We should be the ones going to Rome.'

'It is what it is.'

'You make it sound like you're a helpless victim of life and its progression. When you talk about your marriage to Ebba it's like you're talking about the changing of the seasons or the inevitability of death. Like you're being *afflicted* by life at all times, and by your wife. You're just along for the ride. You don't have an accelerator, just brakes.'

'And maybe I like being this way and just having brakes.'

'So you're content with your life?'

'I would say so. Yes. In fact I am.'

Olof nodded thoughtfully at this statement, his contentedness, and his life.

Back in the hotel room, Ester lay down on the bed, waiting to be joined by Olof, who was drinking a glass of red wine in the armchair. It was just like in the hotel room in Arvidsjaur: her eagerness and him stalling with phrases like 'we have all night', which was closely related to the phrase 'wait and see'. Ester found the whole thing mysterious. They did nothing but stall and wait and see. Was it the waiting itself that spurred him on, which also gave him the advantage of being the one to decide when she would get what she was thirsting for?

'Talking to you is so stimulating,' said Olof, tucking in a portion of snus. 'Our conversations are fantastic.'

'I didn't come all the way to Växjö to talk.'

'No?'

His expression was lewd and amused. He thoroughly enjoyed being the object of her helpless desire.

'You're impenetrable,' said Olof and leaned against the back of the chair, his legs comfortably outstretched.

'Impenetrable? I'm wide open. What do you mean?'

'I don't know. I just think of you as opaque. Hard to get close to. Averted.'

'You've got to be kidding me, Olof. How can you think I'm impenetrable?'

'Do you want to be my mistress?'

His hand was moving up and down, fingers gently drumming the tabletop.

'No, you know I don't.'

'Indeed. So you've said.'

The question was so bizarre Ester almost forgot it that instant.

The phone rang. Olof glanced at it and let it ring. As Ester digested what he'd said, the ringtone faded. It rang again within ten seconds.

'It's Ebba. I'll get it now so I don't have to later.'

It occurred to Ester that Olof might have asked Ebba to call after she finished her rounds in order to make a show of his innocence: how chaste and faithful he was, spending his Saturday night in a hotel room in a small town far away and wanting nothing more than to speak with his beloved wife. Was everything with him choreographed and calculated? Were they all actors in his play: Ester, Ebba, Barbro Fors, Max Fahlén, his children and whoever he needed to fill a supporting role? Was Olof Sten in fact a demonic director, not the anxious extra Ester thought him to be?

Olof put his index finger to his lips and the phone to his ear. Talking to Ebba while Ester was in the room: that was new. He'd always tucked himself away before. What did this imply? She couldn't decide and soon had no idea what to think about any of it. All she knew was that she hoped and believed that her every suspicion was false. They couldn't be true . . . weren't allowed to be true.

He sounded normal and pleasant on the phone to his

wife, hemming and hawing and saying mm-hm, chuckling and listening attentively. No, it did not sound like he was in the middle of a divorce at all. And Ester couldn't believe her ears when he said:

'I'm going to drive around the Kingdom of Crystal tomorrow.'

And then came more hemming and hawing, mm-hms and ha-has.

'I'll keep that in mind. I will. Yes, well, let's leave it at that then. Lovely. Yes, and you. You, too.'

Ester was staring at the ceiling, hands clasped behind her head. Desire had fled. Now she had to keep her mouth shut or else her voice would betray her.

But even silence betrayed her.

Olof set the phone on the plastic surface of the desk and waited for Ester to guide them to the moods that lay beyond the thick mist that had rolled into the room.

'Did that upset you?'

She didn't reply. They had to look after their fragile eroticism and cherish these moments that were so few. When poison seeped in during these brief encounters, it imperilled their bond. Was this why he'd asked Ebba to call? So Ester wouldn't get any ideas? Or perhaps he hadn't asked her to call; it was but a thought. And yet something made her sure this was in fact the case.

'Wives who want to ruin things for husbands and their mistresses are clever to keep ringing their men,' said Ester. 'It's effective. It creates a tiny tear, a slight wearing in the material. Break-ups and breaches are made up of many tiny tears and worn patches. So ring! wives, ring! if you want to undermine the relationship between your fickle husband and his mistress! Ring out the new and ring in the old!'

Olof took a gulp of wine and sieved it through his snus.

'You sound bitter.'

'Oh, I have such good reason to. What was it that you were supposed to keep in mind?'

'Huh?'

'You told Ebba you'd keep something in mind.'

'I told her I was going to the Kingdom of Crystal.'

'And what did she ask you to keep in mind?'

'Her collection of Iittala glass.'

'So you're going to the Kingdom of Crystal with me, and there you'll buy Iittala glass for your wife?'

'I'm not buying glass for anybody.'

With a playful, wolfish smile, he joined her on the bed as if none of what had just been said or done had happened. Ester hugged him from behind, pulled up his shirt and pressed her palms to his skin. Desire came rushing back. It was in moments like these that she knew why she was here, and it was in moments like these that the thought of giving this up drove her mad.

The next day, they went from one glassworks to another, browsing but not buying. They travelled over one hundred kilometres that day. Ester drove, Olof sat next to her, his hand on her thigh. Ebba called once but then they were left in peace. By the afternoon, they were back in Växjö. Though not yet hungry, they planned dinner, the high point for secret couples and their clandestine encounters. Before returning to the hotel they reconnoitred a Greek restaurant on the other side of the railway tracks that Olof had spotted in the distance. Thought it was situated at the foot of a hill almost at the tracks, it went by the name 'Acropolis', the high city. It looked shabby. The soiled menu hung outside the squat, grimy house, white with blue trim.

'The others would probably never come here,' Olof said.

'Can't we just forget about where the others go and what they see?'

'No, we cannot.'

'How do you find the energy to always be thinking about not being found out?

Ester angrily kicked an empty plastic bucket littering the kitchen entrance. The label revealed that it had once contained crème fraiche.

'They'd probably never come here,' Olof repeated and walked ahead of her up the hill towards the car.

Ester's hands were shaking as she slipped the key into the lock. On the way back to the hotel, she was so upset she drove over the kerb at a roundabout. Olof grabbed the handle above the door and asked her to cool it.

'What's the worst that can happen when your wife finds out about us?'

'It would be a catastrophe,' Olof said flatly. 'An absolute catastrophe.'

'What do you mean "catastrophe"?'

'My life would be destroyed.'

'But why?! You don't love her! You don't care about her!'

For a moment, it was quiet in the car. Then Olof said:

'I'm not going to sacrifice Ebba for your sake, if that's what you think.'

Ester took a long, slow breath. She must have misheard him. How could he say that? You couldn't ask someone to drive over a thousand kilometres one weekend and then say that.

She drove onto the main square, parked, switched off the engine and waited; he offered no redaction. Then she asked why he kept inviting her to visit if he knew that nothing was going to change, knowing full well that change was all she wanted, that she was visiting him only because she hoped and believed that things would change.

Olof said that he'd explained what needed to be explained a number of times already.

'How can you be so unsympathetic? You haven't given me one reasonable explanation.'

'There's no giving you a reasonable explanation unless it aligns with your point of view and how you want things to be, is there?'

'I'm sure there is. But it has to have some measure of internal consistency.'

He got out of the car and walked towards the pedestrian street, the one they'd strolled along the night before. Ester went up to the room and gathered her things, heavy-hearted. She was zipping up her bag when Olof returned. With a gentle laugh, he said that Ester was a bit nuts but funny. The sight of the packed bag made him earnest.

'You're leaving?'

He sank into a gloomy lump on the bed.

'Now I really feel stupid,' he said.

Ester felt sorry for him and wanted to ease his pain but she needed more if she was to stay another night. As slowly as she could, she put on her jacket and gloves, but slowness did not help; Olof was just lying there, saying nothing, and eventually she had to leave.

Even as she walked to the car, she was hoping he'd come after her. She waited a minute in the car with her head on the steering wheel, but no one came running after her. She drove off. She drove all the way to Stockholm in the dark without food or drink, without stopping, robotic and numb. Around Jönköping, her phone beeped. She had driven for over an hour and a half, but was prepared to turn right around at the first available exit.

The message was from a distant acquaintance who was wondering how she was doing these days.

At seven thirty the next morning, Ester Nilsson woke up in her bed on Kungsholmen and thought: I can stop caring about him; what a relief. His words from the day before were echoing in her head: 'I'm not going to sacrifice Ebba for your sake, if that's what you think.' That's precisely what she'd thought, it had been her basic assumption. She got up and ate a hearty breakfast that Hippocrates himself would have appreciated: rye porridge with chopped apple, freshly ground coffee and whole-grain bread with smoked salmon. Today marked the start of a new life. She was counting on never hearing from him again. But she couldn't get rid of Olof Sten that easily. At ten past eight, he texted to say he was really sorry about what had happened, and he hadn't meant to cause any pain.

'I thought you understood,' he said.

Understood what?

Ester tied herself to the mast and continued her solitary voyage. A new message arrived at eleven: 'You forgot the earbuds for your phone. I'll post them to you.'

When the package with the earbuds arrived two days later she spent a long time examining his handwriting, in which was written her name and address. She pressed it to her cheek and thought about him buying a padded envelope at the post office, taking pains for her, making an effort for her.

The days passed. She grew more tender. Within a week, she was receptive to any and every proposal. In other words, everything was back to normal. Easter arrived. She followed the weather in Rome on the international weather service online. Rain: *6 degrees, feels like 2.* When did meteorology start reporting how the weather feels? Well, this bad weather felt mighty good to her. It was helping her endure Olof's time in Rome with his wife. But nothing prevented the thoughts of what those two were doing in the warm indoors.

She spent all of Good Friday working, then she ran out of steam. She spent the rest of the weekend eating Swiss roll in bed, keeping an eye on their weather. It had stopped raining in Rome. It hadn't rained in Stockholm for a while. At this point in the spring, the sunlight had whitened and motes of dust were dancing in the sunbeams, all the while the air receded like ageing gums.

Nature knew what month it was, like the body knew its age. Though it hardly seemed possible, the landscape of Ester's soul became even more desolate in the bright, harsh light that arrived with spring, that *was* spring.

Olof had been back from Rome for one day when he called. He told her how tired he was of travelling and now

Skövde of all places awaited him at the weekend. When she didn't suggest anything, he said:

'If you happen to be in Västergötland, there's space in a bed for you in Skövde on Saturday. Just so you know.'

They agreed on an arrival time. Ester offered to call the hotel and upgrade his room from a single to a double.

For the rest of the week, Ester was buoyed by the great calm that came from being longed for. Everything was light and easy again, no desolation, no angst; she cleaned the apartment feeling sweetly disposed to the world around.

On Saturday morning she was in her hall, about to switch off the last lamp before catching the train when Olof's ringtone sounded; Ebba had announced that she had some sort of business at Tidaholm's general hospital and intended to carry on to Skövde since she was already in the area. Ester listened, put down her bag and offered no reply in spite of Olof's attempts to get her to help him palliate this thing that kept on happening. He sounded deeply troubled, especially by her unvoiced disappointment.

'I have to call the railway before the train goes, or I won't get a credit voucher for the ticket.'

At the time of purchase, she had hesitated but ultimately had chosen the flexible ticket option. She wondered why these clashes kept happening. Was it by chance, or did he get cold feet and ask Ebba to visit so he'd have an excuse to cancel on Ester?

Fatima thought Ester was being gullible. Maybe Ebba

wasn't visiting him when he said she was. He was probably making it up.

Ester swept this thought into the dustbin of her mind.

'Do you think women have a sixth sense?' Olof asked in the way he did when he wanted to connect.

'No. I don't. What I do know is that we've had this conversation about "women" before.'

'But isn't it strange?'

'Not in the slightest. The only thing that's strange is that you choose to be a pushover. You could've asked her not to come. I've got to go, I have to call the railway.'

'But one starts to wonder.'

'The women who are close to you have to be extremely vigilant of the atmospheric disruptions that announce your actions. But of course, you don't think anyone notices your skidding and sheering. If you want to stop being plagued by "women's" sixth sense, here's a tip: stop cheating on your wife or divorce her.'

As with all else, love follows the ineluctable principles of evolution. When put under strain, the feeling mutates in order to survive the change in conditions and like all life, it wants first and foremost to remain. People want to love. It's more important to them than being loved. Ester Nilsson went to great lengths and disregarded what she needed to disregard to keep loving Olof Sten.

During a short break in Olof's tour the following week, they met up at Ester's place and had a home-cooked dinner. She was once again restrained and impartial, free from expectation. They talked it out, and Olof said they had the rest of their lives and being with Ester was wonderful. They made love for half the night, ate breakfast and travelled to the Hellasgården nature reserve where everything held the same promise as the small, hard buds on the trees. They walked for ten kilometres, then spent the entire day and night together as well as the following night.

The heat arrived suddenly, twenty degrees in the middle of April, and spring burst into bloom. But the season was treacherous, the ground still cold though the sun overhead was warm. This long period of reconciliation gave them time to sync their rhythms and find harmony. Their connection became more earnest and fun, less breathless and fragmented. From this point forward their encounters were light and filled with wondrous desire. Olof was a changed man and didn't once push her away. No ambivalence was apparent, no complications; she could count on him. As soon as he was back from touring he was with her and if the tour brought him close to Stockholm, she was with him. For Ester, it was like swallowing a capsule of joy with an easily digested casing made of gelatine and doubt. At the weekend he had a duty to his wife but because, according to Ester Nilsson, it wasn't possible to live like this in the long run, she was sure that time was on her and Olof's side.

They often strolled through town, and on one of these occasions when Ester felt a little down and was fretting, he stopped in the manicured garden behind Parliament, leaned over and kissed her worries away. After that they walked into Old Town, where the air offered no resistance and gravity had lost its pull. They floated along Västerlånggatan, their arms around each other, passed Slussen, went up Götgatsbacken and turned on to Tjärhovsgatan, a backstreet that was less trafficked and more anonymous than the lively Folkungagatan. Halfway down Tjärhovsgatan, it was time to part. Acquaintances of his might spot them here, Olof said, and kissed her again with the same intensity. It was Friday; the weekend was fast approaching. He and Ebba were going to spend the night with friends on Runmar Island. Ester imagined it would be an insufferable weekend and each insufferable weekend brought him closer to the inevitable break-up.

With light steps, she crossed Katarina Cemetery that balmy evening, his kisses lingering on her skin and in the heat of her lips.

One night, after they'd spent a month in this trusting and reciprocal way, they were lying close together, naked in bed, talking. Olof told her that when he was very young, around seventeen, he became enamoured with an older woman who lived in the building across the street from him; she often sat on her balcony smoking cigarillos. He didn't know anything about her and didn't try to find out, but he fantasized about her. She became a fixed idea. The woman had a slender neck and slim arms, and her hair was always arranged in a loose, pretty up-do. He became obsessed with the woman on the balcony but was content having her at a distance and wanted nothing more, so his image of her would never be distorted by the mundanity of the flesh. In his daydreams, he called her Ilse. One day a removal van arrived and the apartment was emptied. Soon it was filled with other people's items. He never saw Ilse again.

Olof said that he'd never told anyone the story of Ilse before. He seemed deeply moved by it. Ester was touched by this confidence but found the story so completely conventional she wondered if he'd experienced it or had read it in some embarrassing autobiography.

This was how she came up with the prank in Karlstad, when 'Ilse' was to be waiting on the square at 10 p.m. with an oxeye daisy in her buttonhole.

They'd laughed so hard and played so earnestly for the past month that Ester couldn't imagine the flower and the card would be received as anything but a flirty lark, drawing them even closer together.

It was on the day before Walpurgis Night that Ester Nilsson asked a florist in Karlstad to go to the Scala Theatre with a gerbera from Ilse and a written request for Olof to meet her on the main square. For the rest of the day Ester was filled with her whim and looked forward to Olof calling her right after that evening's performance, laughing at the joke. She declined Lotta's invitation to join her for dinner just so she could await his call at home.

Three days on, he had yet to get in touch.

They were back to their old ways, that inevitable return. Was the flower from Ilse too intimate? Did his thermostat read: You've given Ester a taste and now she wants to devour you. Shrink your flame, push her away, hold her at a distance, put her on a diet of bread and water because this is not working.

For one week it was silent as a grave. She worried that she'd hurt him.

On a hot Sunday in May, Olof called. Ester was polishing a collection of texts that were to be published in the autumn and had planned on working the whole day through. She hadn't counted on hearing from him, and so the joy rippling through her was all the greater.

'You want to come with me to Hellasgården?' he pronounced.

'Yes, I do.'

'Or maybe you're working and I'm interrupting?'

'You're never interrupting. I'll swing by yours as soon as I've showered.'

'Do you have to shower?'

'Yes.'

'Well, shower quickly then.'

And so they travelled to Hellas again and walked through the tender green. They ate lunch on the patio of a timbered cabin. The conversation flowed, topics bounced in, were discussed and bounced out, but no mention was made of Ilse or the gerbera. Olof had to go home and take care of something in the afternoon but said that he'd very much like to meet up again in the evening. They could, for instance, go out to eat in her neighbourhood, so they didn't have to think about cooking. Clearly, he was compensating for something.

Had he snuffed out the flame he carried for Ester after the Ilse incident, but regretted doing so when he noticed how senseless, quiet and unpleasant life became? Was this like when he set out to lead a healthier life in the new year – sticking to it for a few days before it got boring?

At seven that evening in May, they met at La Famiglia on Alströmergatan. After dinner, they went back to Ester's and fell right into bed. The gerbera had still not been mentioned, and Ester needed to bring it up in order to fill the vacuum that was still between them. So she asked if Olof might have seen Ilse recently, perhaps when he was in Karlstad? She must be getting on in years.

Now, Ester thought, they could at least laugh about it. But instead something peculiar happened. Olof arranged his expression and voice to sound surprised with a hint of indifference.

'Were *you* the one who sent that flower?'

The surprise was well-played, so she couldn't be sure.

LENA ANDERSSON

'But you've known that all along, haven't you?'

'I thought it was Ebba.'

By the time Ester had collected herself, she'd understood that a new distancing measure was in play. She sat up to better see his face since he was probably lying to her.

'Never for a second did you think Ebba sent you that flower.'

Olof looked into the middle distance, where there was nothing to see.

'First I thought it was the stage technicians joking around. But they didn't know what I was talking about. Then I called Ebba and asked if she'd sent flowers from some Ilse.'

Ester's body was no longer close to Olof's. She couldn't stand the physical contact. This was like living in a play by Ionesco, she thought.

'You'll never convince me that you thought it was Ebba.'

'But I really did. She's got a good sense of humour.'

'At least you thought it was comic. That's good.'

'The first thing everyone says about Ebba is that she's funny.'

Ester was far too sure of their compatibility for her to see the roads down which his emotional life led him. She didn't know what it was like for Olof, always begging for his cup to be filled and feeling too hollow inside to ever believe he might be swindling her.

She was already on her feet and fully dressed. It felt like she never wanted to be near Olof again, but knew that

214

tomorrow she'd be filled with longing and would be explaining away his shortcomings.

Olof stayed in bed, consumed with directing his play and his role in it. He said:

'Ebba was quite surprised when I asked her about it.'

'I can imagine, because you knew it wasn't her. How could you know that and still call up to ask? I don't understand. What you're saying and playing at right now is frightening me; it actually sounds like you're trying to convince yourself that you thought it was Ebba. Lying about your life is bad enough. If you're trying to convince yourself of your own lies and want me to believe them, too, then we have a real problem.'

'It hadn't occurred to me that it could've been you.'

Could this be true? Did he think so little of her? When he received the flower from Ilse, did he really not think of her first? Ilse, whose existence no one but Ester was aware of until recently. But then what kept him coming back to Ester? Why did he want her if he never thought of her? And if he never thought of her, why did he need to cultivate this forced distance?

A vicious circle of questions. There must be a missing thought, one that was hidden from her and which falsified the premises and as such the conclusions; the simplest and most inaccessible of all being that not everyone took life as seriously as she did.

Olof's birthday fell on a Saturday that May. He celebrated on a rented boat in the archipelago with family, friends and his wife. It was the hottest day of the year, and Stockholm's sheer beauty pained the city's more sensitive souls. Ester spent most of the day with Elin, and as usual they conducted a detailed analysis of their relationship woes and tried to understand them logically. Elin was having problems with her mother and had qualms about a friend. Ester had her eternal topic.

'When Olof and I see each other, it's wonderful,' she told Elin. 'But it doesn't go anywhere. I don't see him reflecting on the fact that two relationships are one too many. He seems to think it's just enough. But when we talk, it's not clear if this is in fact what he thinks or if it just happens to be this way. His thoughts and feelings seem to lack a backbone.'

Elin replied dryly, matter-of-fact.

'No backbone, no morals. And you still want him?'

'I'm afraid so. And I believe everyone has morals. Somewhere deep down, everyone knows what's right, even if they can't work out why.'

'Sure. We all have some moral sense.'

'Fatima thinks he's also seeing Barbro Fors.'

'Excuse me?'

Elin gave her a questioning look.

'To balance out me and his wife. But surely no one can carry on like that, no one can be that misguided?'

'Sounds highly unlikely. Have you seen anything that suggests this might be the case?'

'Not really, no. But if it's true, then I've been so wrong about him that I'll have to sever every nerve in my body that is tuned to him. And I can only do that once I really believe it. Until I'm sure, I'll always find some way to believe it to be otherwise. And sometimes, quite often really, I do believe Olof loves me.'

Elin adapted easily to Ester's needs and said:

'Maybe he's caught up in something we don't know about.'

'It seems that way, doesn't it?

'Let's say it is until we find out more, and we'll think about what it might be. But I don't believe what Fatima said.'

'Thanks. What a relief. Neither do I.'

They ate an early dinner up on Mosebacke, where the breeze was mild and warm, sitting with the best view of the harbour entrance and the water, the lapping of which could not be heard at that height. Perhaps one of the white boats returning from the archipelago was carrying Olof and his party.

These bright May evenings were difficult for the

existentially wretched, more melancholy than those in dark November. May nights were for the happy and content, and birthdays were among those moments when mistresses were made aware of their number two status, however much they felt themselves to be number one in secret.

The temperature didn't drop though night had fallen. The heat lingered in the tarmac and the walls. No cool relief rolled in from the water. You could hardly tell where your body ended and the surroundings began.

'Next year you'll be there on his birthday,' Elin said.

'You think? Do you think that disintegration is inevitable?'

'There's always some disintegration in the end. Everything is constantly changing even if you don't notice it. Even inside you.'

'Not inside me. I'm in a hermetically sealed chamber. Nothing gets in that changes my feelings. I'm sort of frozen. Love gets freeze-dried in conditions like these. Just add water; everything's intact. That's why I fear this could go on for ever.'

'No one is in a hermetically sealed chamber. No such vacuum exists.'

The boats were like seashells on the water. Ester considered her friend's words and wondered which boat Olof might be on, but then she realized that the archipelago boats didn't tie up here, but at Strömmen, a bay further along. Had this occurred to her sooner, she would've suggested they find a spot on the veranda at the Grand Hotel, just to be close by.

Olof's tour had come to an end, and he was back home. The two final performances were at the Stockholm City Theatre and Ester was in the audience, watching with an aching heart but without flowers and without making herself known. She didn't want to intrude or embarrass him in front of others.

His first morning off, the free time that began now and would last all summer, Olof called and asked to meet right away. Ester hurried over to him on Bondegatan. They jumped right into his marital bed, the saturated light and colours of the budding summer that spilled through the window. It was the first time they'd met at Olof's in this bed. It was a clear shift, one of many, and it had to mean that a breakthrough was nigh. Until now, he'd put the brakes on this step. Ester felt utterly hopeful. Long did they lie in each other's arms.

At 1 p.m. they took the bus across the bridge to Djurgården and went to Blå Porten. In the courtyard, bubbling with life, the gulls and house sparrows eyed up their lunch trays. Ester remembered them eating herring here in November one and a half years before, and how heavy her body had become when a few short words left his lips. But now there was lightness in the shade of these lavish trees, and she was savouring it with an agreeable mix of listlessness and acuity. But soon summer would be in full swing – a dejecting fact. The question of the coming months was an abyss, but it had to be asked. And so she did.

'What's going to happen this summer?'

'I'll be in Skåne.'

It sounded so simple. He was going to be in Skåne. And where would Ester be while Olof was in Skåne? He gave her a kind look. She remembered sitting here before, asking a man who she was helplessly in love with what he'd be doing over the summer and getting the same unfeeling reply. She sat with Olof amidst Djurgård's greenery and lay in his marital bed but had no impact on his life. He was the engine in hers, but she wasn't even a tiny propeller in his. She would have moved to the desert with Olof Sten; he wasn't prepared to change anything.

On this point, Ester was incorrect. She exerted a veritable force on Olof's life, the force that mistresses exert – no more, no less – a force whose vectors follow a traditional script, wherein summer is the time for the wedded pair and the mistress enters patent quarantine until normalcy is restored with the arrival of autumn.

Soon Olof would travel to his beloved Kullaberg. After the long tour and nearly six months of temporary living arrangements, he looked forward to a summer of rest and relaxation. Ester felt she really should respect this sentiment.

She wanted to be generous and tolerant and meet Olof half-way when it was important to him.

'Maybe you could text me sometime during the summer,' she said.

'Of course I will.'

They sat in silence with the birdsong.

'I can visit, if you like,' said Ester.

He furrowed his brow with agreeable puzzlement.

'That might be difficult.'

She nodded several times to show that she understood just how hard it would be and how complicated his situation was.

'But I can come and see you in Stockholm,' Olof said.

Ester studied his face to see if he were kidding.

'You mean during the summer? You'll come to Stockholm just to see me?'

The heaviness waned and her heart sped.

'Or we could check into a hotel for a few nights,' he said and turned his blithe self towards the sun and shut his eyes.

'A hotel in Skåne?'

'No,' he said, changing his mind and gently shaking his head. 'You and I, we're not going to stay at any hotel. We'll stay in a castle.'

Ester's flickering breaths became shorter and hotter.

'A large castle for us. With fountains and feather beds.'

'Where is that?' she asked, breathless.

In many ways, Ester Nilsson was unsuited for this life.

She thought Olof was talking about a real castle-turned-hotel in Skåne that he was actually imagining them checking into that summer when Ester came down in person for a few actual days and nights that they had officially put in their diaries.

She knew imagery and symbolism were formidable tools, but she didn't see the point in using them to illuminate the beauty and strength of a tragic saga. If they could have a real relationship, why resort to poetics? All he had to do was unshackle himself and take that step. Dreaming and symbolism were superfluous; everything they might want together was within reach. But Olof didn't share this view, so the fantasy of the castle was his gift to her.

'Should we go to Skansen?' asked Olof and stood up before Ester was clear over his intentions of seeing her over the summer.

Embracing each other, they wandered around Skansen. They kissed in front of the seals. By the flamingos, Olof took out the camera his children had given him for his birthday, and Ester asked him to take a picture of them. Olof said no, he couldn't have Ester on his camera. They rested on a bench. Olof had an ice cream, Ester was watching her weight. Then they took the 47 to Norrmalmstorg. There they changed buses and parted at Slussen. Ester had thought they'd spend all evening and all night together now that they had the chance, but Olof had to clean the apartment. She offered to help. He said he wanted to be on his own. She was about to say that she could go with him and be there while he was being on his own, but held her tongue at the last second and returned home to disharmony's dark little dwelling.

At ten the next morning Olof called, wanting to see her again. So they went for a walk in Hellas and dipped their feet in the cold water, spent the day, evening and night together. The next day was the same, as was the next, they didn't let the other out of sight. On one of these evenings when they were sitting at Olof's eating fettuccine with a mushroom and Bolognese sauce for dinner, he dealt her a blow:

'I don't know why you carry on as you do, Ester. With married men. Why do you allow yourself to be satisfied with so little? You can't get what you want if they're married.'

Again, his statement was performative, an act in itself. His choice of words could be relatively arbitrary, as long as they worked to create distance. She shouldn't be getting any ideas, the speech act said, just because they'd spent a number of close, tender days together and he'd shown his dependence on her.

'I don't carry on with married men,' Ester said dully. 'But to find the men who interest me I cast the net as wide as possible.'

'Married men can't give you what you're longing for.'

'You give me a lot of it. When you choose to.'

'But that's not enough for you.'

'Of course not; I want to have a real relationship with the one I love.'

'But that's what married men can't give you.'

'None of the men I've chosen have been Catholic.'

The air felt icy this mild summer's eve. Olof reached for the wine bottle's neck, stroked it fondly but absently.

'I just don't understand why you agree to these terms. You're worth more.'

'Give me better terms, then.'

'I have my situation. But there are others.'

'Others? Do you really not understand me at all?'

Olof cleared their plates and put them on the counter.

'This is wrong,' he said, his back to her. 'I'm treating you unjustly.'

'What do you mean?'

'I'm taking advantage of your feelings for me.'

Ester corrected him; she thought she detected a flaw in his thinking:

'But you can't take advantage of me, can you? We love each other. So you're not taking advantage. Taking advantage means that even though you don't feel anything, you draw benefit from the other's feelings.'

It didn't occur to her that this might be what he was admitting; it didn't occur to her because it was illogical. Why would he expose himself to risk and pain if he didn't love her? It didn't add up. Thus, he could not be said to be taking advantage of her.

Olof looked out over the rooftops, gazing into the

distance. When he didn't confirm her assertion, but appeared to be holding fast to his own, Ester went to the hall and put on her shoes and her outerwear.

'Are you leaving?'

'Yes. Of course. I can't stay here and allow you to keep taking advantage of me.'

'But you could stay the night.'

Who would reproach Esther for not losing faith and hope under these conditions? There could only be one reason for him not ending it, even though he knew he should: she was the woman for him. Ester Nilsson had a little too much confidence in a person's internal stability and constancy to be able to orienteer in this world.

They spent this night and the next together. Recently they'd been spending more consecutive nights together than ever before. After all that had happened, shouldn't it mean something? And when they were lying close together, Olof whispered:

'Put your arm like this instead, so we can be even closer.'

Even closer? They were as close as could be.

'I can't get my head around it,' he said. 'We meet by chance at a read-through and now we're lying here after all these months. It's unbelievable.'

No, when a beloved whispers such words, who can blame Ester for her eternal deductions and conclusions? It was obvious that she was witnessing his resistance crack. This was exactly as contradictory it seemed. The fear of life-changing love made you keep it at arm's length until you couldn't any more. Isn't this what she'd been reading and hearing everywhere?

'Each time it's like meeting for the first time,' he went on. 'My nerves are always wracked before our dates.'

He said her name and touched her cheeks, pushing himself inside her with a deep breath, moving carefully while his clear eyes met hers, free from intrigue and foul play. And Ester believed that in this moment, they had stumbled past the point of no return. This was it. Just one more summer.

The day was upon them when Olof was to leave and not return until the autumn. They hadn't arranged to see each other, but Ester couldn't imagine not seeing Olof one last time, so in the morning she walked to the Nature Company on Kungsgatan and bought hiking gear to the tune of a thousand kronor. Olof had mentioned that he'd be going hiking at the end of August with an old friend from drama school and had asked Ester for tips on how best to prepare. So he could practise during the summer's test hikes in Kullaberg, she bought him a cup, compass, map, special socks, belt, water bottle, a book about Abisko, where he was going, and trekking food. With all of this in a large plastic bag, she went over to his place. From the street, she called to ask if she could come up and say good-bye. With pounding dread, she ascended four flights in the cool stairwell; he'd sounded gruff on the phone.

And it was indeed the day of recoil. Olof was in a foul mood, immediately apparent in how he opened the door, just a close-fisted crack that she had to widen herself, and then she was greeted with his back as he made his way to the other room where he was still packing. Her kiss landed on his cheek because he'd turned his face away.

As she handed him his presents, she could tell that buying them and coming here today had been a mistake. Troubled, Olof merely glanced at the gifts.

'How sweet of you,' he said and set aside the bag.

He went back to his luggage, added a pair of jeans, a linen blazer and the polished loafers he'd worn in the winter when he'd visited her. He responded to her silence with that irate, sardonic look, and she sensed the source of his irritation: the demands made by her sheer presence, her insistent claims and lofty principles, her singular difficultness.

'What are you up to today?' Olof asked.

'This. Saying goodbye before the summer.'

The precision of his distancing methods was astounding. Experts should be flocking to him, Ester thought – psychologists, sociologists, economists and politicians – to study the ur-form of ambivalence and the perfect technique for rejecting someone while holding on to them, never letting them go and never letting them in. Olof had perfect command of it; it had to be natural, for he was hardly capable of devising these methods himself or perceptive enough to have studied others in order to copy their methods. His techniques had to be an evolutionary by-product of something else that was steadily and systematically working towards unknown goals inside him.

What were the goals? That was the question. What did

he want to achieve with his behaviour? Ester thought he wanted to love, but didn't dare.

All of Olof's gestures and statements on this, their final day, were intended to tear them asunder. Ester was burning in the flames of her own misfortune and yet wanted to spend these final hours with him.

He rummaged through his things. And like a child who finally has a friend over, he offered Ester whatever he was finding in drawers and hiding places: small pieces of jewellery, stones, souvenirs, books.

Once he'd told her that he had a hard time with partings and goodbyes. Maybe that's why he was so uneasy today, she thought. He didn't want to be apart, didn't want to travel, but wanted to keep her here with him by giving her his things.

Ester joined Olof, who was taking a break on the bed, and held him. He refused her caresses but asked her to accompany him to the train. First he'd visit Ebba in Borlänge for a few days and then he'd weave his way through the countryside towards north-west Skåne.

They took the number 3 bus to Tegelbacken. As it turned towards Katarinavägen, right where Fjällgatan opens up and Stockholm's splendour shines for all to see, Olof looked at Ester and said:

'So what's your summer going to be like?'

Ester froze in the heat. The question was full of violence. Maybe he was being cruel because she'd been so puppyish with her hiking gifts and her yapping. She saw the mechanisms in play yet kept on yapping, because she wanted to break through to another level, one where they were true to each other and thoughtful, where neither was dog nor master. She wanted to act as if they were already there even though this had never worked.

'My summer will be filled with longing,' she said.

'But you have tons of friends. You can see them.'

I'm not going to reply, Ester thought. I'm going to get off at Slussen and find someone who can prescribe me a pill that will erase everything my heart has ever felt and everything stored in my brain. She looked out of the window. Gröna Lund was in action. Olof had visited the amusement park once with a young woman he was courting. Since he'd recounted the episode, Gröna Lund had pained Ester.

They got off at Tegelbacken and walked to Central Station. Olof's long strides carried him ahead of her, and he disappeared into Pressbyrån's kiosk in the main hall without checking to see if Ester was with him, so she went to the top of his platform. When he turned up with his evening paper, drink in hand, he said:

'People might see us.'

'Which people?'

'I feel uncomfortable being here with you.'

'Then just bloody stop feeling uncomfortable! Or don't ask me to come with you to the train in the first place.'

With instant regret, he took her hand.

'Be well, Ester. Talk to you later.'

He disappeared into the train. The platform's chill pushed through her light summer clothes. To reach Klaraberg's sunny viaduct, she walked along the platform for the trains to Arlanda Airport. When she was on the street, unsure of where to go and which of her friends to call to ease her sorrow, a text arrived. Olof wrote: 'This is tough for me, too. Hugs, O.'

Three minutes passed. He must have written it as soon as he'd sat down. He didn't usually write 'hugs'. Olof, she thought, was like faulty electrical wiring running through her life. Shocking her each time she brushed against him, but also the source of her energy. She answered warmly and wished him a lovely summer – her eternal trust in good deeds begetting good deeds, that the means and the end were one and the same, that the only way to encourage decency was by being decent.

Ester told her friends she'd be spending Midsummer with her mother. She told her mother she'd be spending it with friends, so her mother wouldn't worry about her well-being. On Midsummer's Eve she was home alone, finding fellowship only with the television. On Midsummer Day, she read a book, and continued to ignore the growing chaos of her apartment. On the Sunday she travelled to Hellasgården and traced the routes she usually took with Olof.

On the Monday, right after the lunchtime news, a text

arrived from Olof, ending their relationship. The reasons
he gave were their many fights and her constant dissatisfaction, as well as feeling like a scoundrel around his wife.

'I can't take it any more,' he wrote.

Disappointment is a wasteland, physical devastation, burned-out vigour where all that remains is a singed smell. As she walked scores and scores of kilometres through Stockholm in the months that followed, Ester Nilsson wished for mankind's demise, in particular the demise of Ebba Silfversköld.

Summer was made for families with old inherited mansions in the archipelago and half-timbered houses by the sea, where the owners sat on the veranda slowly destroying their livers. It was tedium in the guise of relaxation and the anticipation of life beginning again in autumn. Summer was what had to be endured. And there was something about heat that Ester couldn't stand.

One day in mid-July she walked from Kungsholmen all the way to the gardens of Rosendal. There she bought a jar of posh jam and pale sourdough bread as a treat before continuing to Djurgården, sweating, and finding the bag rather cumbersome to carry. She should've bought the bread and jam on the way back, she shouldn't have bought them at all. Treating yourself didn't help; there was no help for the abandoned. Love's foundations must be excised at a cellular level, she thought.

In a conversation with Elin, she dwelled on Olof's low self-esteem as a reason for what had transpired, the esteem that had been destroyed in childhood, and for which Ester had to show understanding when faced with his whims and fancies because he pushed her away when he was most desirous and rejected her when he was most afraid of approaching wonder. Elin listened and interpreted along with her. But in the end she said it might be simpler than all this: Ester might just have met a real shit.

It was like being filled with cement.

After an hour, Ester called Elin and said that maybe it was that simple, maybe Elin was right, but she asked her to please not use that word again, because all that would happen if she did was that Ester would withdraw from her.

'I understand,' said Elin. 'There are always reasons why we end up the way we do and anyway, we know that no one is only one thing.'

'Thank you, dear Elin. Yes, that's precisely what we know.'

Weeks passed. The gulls screeched outside the windows as she lay in bed wondering how Olof could choose Ebba Silfversköld over her. She offered something completely different to Ebba's hollow quips and nervy laughter. She knew Olof knew this, and such knowledge could unleash anxiety so deep it made you want to be rid of the problem and the decision. Her next thought was a given: she should reach out to Olof to see if he was satisfied with the break-up. If he was, she'd never bother him again. However, she thought it unlikely considering how close they'd been in the previous weeks, how he'd sought her out, needed her, how he'd caressed her and spoken to her about their exceptionalism, and whispered that it all was unbelievable. Breaking up after these gestures of love suggested a strain so great that the decision could only have been made in haste. But if he'd changed his mind, he'd never dare tell her. He'd rather spend the rest of his life regretting than risk giving her the upper hand. So, she'd have to dare. Pride would not be allowed to determine their future. She, with her strength, had to take it upon herself to be vulnerable and risk making a fool of herself.

As always in the space between their encounters, the heart forgot all the negatives that the mind still recalled.

So after the summer, Ester rang Olof. He sounded happy about it, grateful even. She began to rush and rumble inside, imagining that the divorce had taken place over the summer. He asked how she was doing. She said she was well, and the summer was good, she's been in the archipelago, which she had. One cold, rainy day she and Lotta had taken the ferry to Ut Island and had been gone for twelve hours.

With the muted tone he often assumed in moments of intimacy and mutual understanding and that made Ester feel chosen and close, Olof said:

'It was good of you to call.'

She asked if she could invite him for lunch at the Opera Bar. She'd received an award the week before to write a book about the intellectual history of subjectivism and its political roots, but it could stretch to buying Olof lunch, too.

'It was in the terms and conditions. Write a book and invite Olof Sten to lunch.'

His laugh was warm; he wanted to meet the very next day.

At five to one, Ester arrived at Kungsträdgården wearing a new autumn skirt and new patterned tights. The graphite blouse was also new and it matched the skirt. It was late August, too hot for tights and too cold for bare legs. But the pattern was nice. Each year, Ester tried to usher in the arrival of autumn by wearing too many layers.

It was an ordinary day. No sun, no cold, and the sky's white haze had something uningratiating about it. They were to meet at one o'clock. As the delicate clang of St James's bells began, Ester was at their meeting point, slightly obscured by a tree. She was looking at her legs, wondering if the pattern on the tights wasn't too much after all.

One minute past the hour, Olof texted to say he'd be five minutes late. Because Olof only made as much effort as his needs and interests demanded, she knew he felt like he'd run out of credit: he didn't usually let her know if he was going to be five minutes late.

The statistics were in their favour. People got divorced

after the summer. And it was just before a divorce that one desperately and abruptly cut out all temptations to show resolve and that what one had was good enough. How many summers could Olof last in this marriage? Maybe it was already broken and that was why he'd been so pleased and sounded so devoted when she'd called.

Ester saw him sauntering across Charles XII Square – tanned, relaxed, stubbled and sloppily dressed for summer. Clearly, Olof had some funds in his account after all, otherwise he'd have shaved and dressed properly. But the sloppiness could also mean that this encounter was so important to him he had to regulate the pressure he felt by stymieing her assumptions. He had done that before. Interpretations were not easy to make if you wanted them to correspond with the truth.

The Opera Bar was a dark and muted winter bistro with few patrons around this time in August. When it was still so light outside, people felt too summer-fresh for its dusky interior.

Ester heard herself babbling, part nerves, part embarrassment. Among other things, she said that it was in this pub that the engineers Andrée and Knut Fraenckel met for a bite to plan their balloon expedition to the North Pole at the start of that P. O. Sundman novel. This introduction seemed to give Olof pause, and he said that he'd read the book ages ago but didn't remember anything about it, especially that scene.

'They ate lobster and after that, cream cake,' Ester said

and thought about the linguistic oddity of his words: if you didn't remember a book, you couldn't assert that you, above all, could not remember a particular scene; you couldn't remember less than nothing.

They took a seat, took no notice of their own self-conscious glances, took in their menus.

'We can order appetizers, mains and dessert, and have wine and beer. My treat,' said Ester, who had pictured an extravagant reunion meal.

'No, I don't want to.'

Olof pushed his reading glasses to his forehead.

'What don't you want?'

'A main and a small beer are enough for me.'

She knew he wasn't talking about food.

'How was your summer?' she asked even though they'd gone over all of that on the phone the other day.

'Excellent.'

How could it have been excellent? Is your heart made of stone? Ester screamed on the inside. On the phone he'd seemed needier, as though he had less in his account; then he'd said his summer had been 'all right'.

'And you?' Olof asked, but only to be polite.

She didn't have to answer because the waiter arrived, and they each ordered salted salmon with dill potatoes and a medium-strong beer. They ate quickly and didn't say much.

An hour later, they left the restaurant and made their way towards the Opera, crossing the Parliament House

Garden where once they'd kissed, and carried on to Old Town. They always followed the same path through the city. Ester had nothing against it, as long as they were walking together.

'I've never seen you in a skirt,' Olof said.

'Yes, you have.'

'Have I?'

'Last time you saw me I was wearing a skirt. When we said goodbye at Stockholm Central before the summer. But you've never seen me in patterned tights. I thought this skirt was more autumnal. It's a new season.'

They went to the Café Sundberg on Järntorget; the same cafe they'd gone to shortly after their first carnal encounter and Olof had said: 'I can't hurt Ebba like this. I don't want to.'

As they sat there, Olof's phone rang. It turned out that he had to dog-sit for his son in the evening and they were sorting out the details.

Ester was so used to setbacks that they felt like that old sweater you do the cleaning in. This resignation gave her a cooler and slower, almost forestalled, mien and this shift made Olof more attentive. He became interested when she was resigned. She became resigned when he was uninterested. When he took a step closer and she did the same, he would push her away, and then she became cool and austere, which sharpened his attention. It was a closed circle.

Ester looked out over the square instead of at Olof. It wasn't her intention to capture his interest, it never was;

she didn't have the energy to be calculating, even though how to be was clear enough.

'Shall we go to a museum?' Olof asked.

Always with the museum visits when he wanted to be close to her and yet not.

'No. I think I'm going to go home. I'm a little tired of museums.'

'You don't want to?'

He looked at her searchingly. It wouldn't take much kindness for her to give in.

'Nothing will come of it. Nothing comes of anything we do and you'll leave as soon as it doesn't suit you.'

'What did you think was going to happen today?'

'Nothing. I was just looking forward to seeing you.'

Scrunching his forehead, he searched for the right words.

'How's the car?'

Ester smiled sadly.

'It runs well whenever I re-park it. Otherwise, it sits there.'

They walked towards the subway. Outside the entrance he held her and she felt his body respond to hers. So she didn't take the subway; they went to his place and to bed.

Afternoon slipped into night. Olof called his son and told him to find another dog-sitter. They made potatoes au gratin and steak and talked about all of their shared interests, such as the hiking trip in the mountains the following week. He said the things she'd given him had been very useful.

Around midnight when they'd been talking non-stop for eleven hours Olof asked if Ester could imagine writing a play. The amateur theatre group he'd directed off and on over the past few years wanted a play written just for them for their next season. He'd been considering Brecht but over the summer he'd thought they could perform something by Ester Nilsson instead. A one-act play for eight people was what was needed and soon; the start of rehearsals was imminent.

A cautious jubilation was unleashed in her chest. She was right. He had regretted the Midsummer break-up and wanted to reconnect, he'd even come up with a sophisticated way to do it. A play implied a more enduring tie.

Olof looked at the clock. She could tell he was preparing to say something ambiguous about how she should leave, but preferably not. These were his words:

'Are you off now?'

'No. I'm not going home now. It's the middle of the night.'

He didn't object to her staying, but neither did he invite her to. When they'd brushed their teeth and he'd crawled next to her quaking, longing body, he said:

'You can't ask a man to resist a naked woman lying next to him. A man has his urges.'

Ester thought she could get him to make better and

more loving analyses later. Everything in its time. Now it was their reunion that mattered.

The next morning she took the bus home and started on the play. Spurred on by a fantastic energy, she wrote for a week, breaking only for meals, and then was finished. It was about a married couple and the third person in their relationship, as revealed in the presence of their friends during a melancholy crayfish party. Olof read it as soon as he came home from the fells, made it known that he was aware of her digs at the wife's role and at the husband's/lover's role, but said nothing more about it, accepted the play as it was and said he was very pleased.

Autumn arrived. It grew darker, colder, barer, and Ester Nilsson's one-act play *Cog* was in rehearsals one night a week under Olof's direction and Ester's supervision. He'd asked her to sit in on the rehearsals 'as often as possible'. It was always possible. During these autumn months, Olof called her often to discuss aspects of the text and to hear if his portrayal was in line with her intentions. They kept things strictly professional; they were in a phase of recuperation and reconstruction, as happened in the autumn, so they could slowly move towards a new spring, yet another spring. The closer winter came, the more enticing his tone and language, the longer his gazes lingered; everything was vague and intimated, noncommittal but full of meaning for her to identify and interpret. When there was nothing to resist, he became more clear-cut.

In January, rehearsals entered an intense final phase, and it was only natural that the director and playwright met to agree the finishing touches and to deliberate. Each time their bodies sparked with memory and possibility. Olof seemed to like testing his capacity for restraint, to see how close he could get to the forbidden without giving in,

approaching the fire and withdrawing. As winter progressed, the heat and tenderness in his gaze increased.
They'd arrived at the date when they, as part of a reliable
seasonal rhythm, had gone to bed together for the past two
years in February. His inner atomic clock counting down
to it again. Ester marvelled at its precision: meeting at the
cusp of spring, leaving around Midsummer, repairing and
rebuilding during the autumn and reuniting in the spring.

According to cultural narratives, spring was for romance. In the summer, you were married and cleared out
the cupboards. Olof heeded the accounts and schedules.
They went to work on his psyche and he put them to work.
These patterns gave structure to all that was loose and
unclear inside him.

Soon it would be spring again.

After a theatre premiere, one eats and drinks. So too it
went after this modest premiere one Thursday in March
with an audience of fifty in a worse-for-wear basement
theatre serving up sandwiches and red wine. Olof Sten
wasn't just performing that night, he was in overdrive. No
provisos or conditions could be discerned. He was completely focused on Ester, forthcoming, attentive, lovelorn.
His charge wasn't only apparent in how he looked at her,
but in his body's position in relation to hers, in what he
said and didn't say, in the expressions he made and didn't

ACTS OF INFIDELITY

make, the direction the conversation was steered. In short
it was one of those evenings when he didn't mention his
wife once, in fact actively avoided mentioning her. There
was no duplicity or contradiction. If everything was a game
and staged, then tonight he was playing at not playing.
Pure and true, honest and vulnerable, he was meeting Ester
halfway. That's how it was each time Olof felt ready once
again. They were on their third winter, only a few weeks
delayed compared to the two years before, and his erotic
light was shining brightly. Ester was familiar with it all,
but her enjoyment was no less rapturous. With each passing year, his opportunity to say it was a mistake and all her
doing diminished.

Olof had invited an old friend to the premiere, a
scenographer, but a scenographer without a stage and
embittered by that fact. He introduced himself as Göran
Berggren and had a suspicious countenance that seemed to
be permanent rather than situational. His heavy head was
set atop a short neck, and he had a disagreeable way of
offering praise in the way people do who spend their lives
in conflict with others: praise shrouding an ever-present
scepticism. So after the performance, when the three of
them were talking around one of the tables, Göran Berggren said to Ester:

'Congratulations on the play. It was good.'

'Thanks,' she said, upon which Göran Berggren said:

'This time we could even understand your writing.'

Ester focused on Olof's willing body next to hers

instead of Göran Berggren's comments. In honour of the occasion she'd worn a nice skirt and blouse with a matching waistcoat and leather boots. Olof said it was beautiful and suited her. Göran Berggren kept insinuating himself into their conversation, even when they were speaking in low voices, and because he was Olof's friend, Ester wanted to be accommodating. That's why she spent a while asking him about the essence, challenges and history of set design, which he expounded upon in an engaging way, though muttering and with offish reluctance. They might never be rid of him. Everyone else had gone home including Fatima and Lotta who'd come to see the performance and winked knowingly at her sitting there next to Olof. Only Ester, Olof and Göran Berggren remained. With a loud voice, Göran asked how Ebba was doing. Ester crumpled up, and her rippling desire and ease faded, but not for long because Olof said she was well last he'd heard and didn't the subway go all the way to Göran's place from here?

And then it was just the two of them. It was midnight. Olof had the keys to the venue, a little basement theatre on Västmannagatan. They emerged on the gleaming-wet tarmac, Olof locked the door and they became one with the dark. They walked one block down to Odengatan. Nothing had been articulated and yet it had been agreed. Olof looked at Ester and simply said:

'Your place or mine?'

'Mine.'

He flagged down a taxi with one hand and took her

hand with the other. Ester wondered to herself how many times a person could come back before he understood that every return to the other devalued the marriage he claimed to prize so highly. Because their encounters were equal to their atmosphere, she couldn't ask.

They arrived at her flat. She put the premiere flowers in a vase. Olof's touch was hungry and urgent. They undressed, got under the covers. Clasping her hotly, he said in that absurd way that only Olof Sten in his ambivalence could:

'We'll just lie here next to each other, nothing more.'

'Will we?'

'Yes, let's just sleep next to each other.'

'I can't.'

'Neither can I.'

'I'll explode if all we do is lie here.'

'Me, too.'

He brushed the hair from her forehead and tucked it behind her ear.

'But you can't have such high expectations of me this time around. I can't live up to everything you want from me.'

'I don't have any expectations other than wanting to be with you always and never letting you go.'

He pressed his finger to the tip of her nose.

'No. That's just it.'

And so the night began.

Ester could see she was running inside a wheel, but

believed the two of them would soon veer onto the same path; they were people, not hamsters, after all.

Early the next morning, she drove Olof home like so many times before and dropped him at his door.

'My body is completely satisfied and at ease now,' she said.

He held her hand, stroking the back of it with his thumb.

'Good, that's good.'

'If you want to aid public health, you should visit me regularly.'

'Are you "the public" in this case?'

His eyes narrowed into coin slots when he smiled; Ester never had her fill of seeing those coin slots, feeding in a coin of bliss and watching him liven up.

'Everything is its parts,' she said. 'If one person's health improves, public heath improves, as long as it doesn't occur at another's expense. And it doesn't.'

'I'm not so sure about that.'

'No, I know. And that's unfortunate.'

They were silent.

'Shouldn't you have a word with her anyway? You're drawing out the suffering of three people. You'd be doing her a favour if you left her.'

'I'm afraid you're wrong,' Olof said. 'But I'd probably be doing you a favour if I left you.'

He got out of the car and went through the front door, waving.

Caresses from the one who wishes to be loved or needed should come as surprises, should not be given out too generously. They should be offered in a way that seems arbitrary, like an unpredictable yet regular exception. Then the recipient counts them ten-fold and they bind her tightly. Just look at how God holds people's interest. No one understands the psychology of dependency and double binds better than him. He knows how to chain people to him with the perfect dosage of love and aloofness so that they can never be free, so that he will never be left. And people know to arrange themselves so that they never have to stop loving and needing their saviour.

After what happened, it seemed natural for Ester to ask Olof the following week if he wanted to see a play in Uppsala, a play for which she had already procured two tickets. He didn't reply, but when she sent a slightly barbed text a day later asking for a decision so she could know if she should ask someone else, he immediately accepted. Like so many, he couldn't bear losing what he did not in fact want to have.

On the night of the play, Ester knew within seconds

that this date had been agreed to out of a reactionary impulse. She waited in the car outside his door and the moment he sat in the passenger seat he cast a scornful glance at her pleated skirt draping across the seat. It was the kind of look that a schoolchild gets when the other children notice that an effort was made to look nice, but that effort had misfired.

After Olof had complimented the previous week's skirt, the one she wore to the premiere, she'd gone and bought another, and now it was clear that it wasn't her style; it looked ridiculous. She'd hesitated but bought it anyway, emboldened by his praise.

They hadn't even turned onto Folkungagatan when his next jibe came. He stated that spring was in the air and it had a special light, distinctive and ethereal. When Ester agreed and took it upon herself to describe the magnificent violet glow of a clear early-spring evening and how it persuaded the senses, Olof said:

'And no one has captured the spring in oil-on-canvas quite like Ebba's father, Gustaf Silfversköld. His paintings are still unparalleled.'

The manoeuvre was so subtle she couldn't adduce it without seeming oversensitive, but he might as well have said:

'Don't get your hopes up about tonight. Just so you know.'

Their mutual understanding had been slain, and he'd made it clear to whom he belonged without having to get sticky with intimacy. He even got Ester to see how plebeian her last name was compared with Ebba's.

It was a terse trip. Ester was silent at the wheel. This made Olof wonder if his message had been received, so as they drove into Uppsala he told her a joke from the theatre world that Ester didn't understand or in any case, didn't laugh at, whereupon he said it was a joke that probably only actors would find funny. Tonight, he was one with his craft. He added that Ebba had always felt at home among actors, and there was something about a doctor's job that was like an actor's.

'I wonder what that might be,' Ester said.

'It's hard to put a finger on,' Olof said.

Because she was the one who'd chosen the play, he was ungenerous about that, too. He offered a didactic explanation during the interval that this was the type of theatre regular people like, people who hadn't been to the theatre much.

When the curtain came down, Olof had rushed to the bar with the thirst of one who is lost in the desert and guzzled his red wine, the foyer murmuring around them, carefree people who did not seem to be corroding inside. Exhausted and full of woe, Ester clutched her bottle of sparkling water.

As they sat there across from each other, a high-spirited gaggle approached their table, old acquaintances of Olof's and Ebba's as it turned out, but Ester didn't need to know this information to read Olof's desperation over being seen with her.

She empathized when she noticed his fear and left the table by pure reflex, disappearing into the crowd before the merry bunch had a chance to suspect that Olof and Ester were there together.

Once, she turned around and saw him sitting there, trying to hold his life together, Ebba Silfversköld's husband conversing with mutual friends.

The journey home was as terse as the journey there. Around them, the plains of Uppsala were dark but for lingering patches of snow.

Drip drop, love is drained, drop by drop. One day wear and tear will outpace the shine. One day the lack of change will be the same as stagnation. One day you'll be done. One day even the invaluable will lose its value. Drip drop, joie de vivre, joy and trust drain away.

Drip drop.

Drop, drop.

Drip.

But it wasn't quite that time yet for Ester Nilsson.

It was April again, muddy and wet but the evenings were getting lighter and the trees' branches were bare and accusatory. The morning after the Uppsala excursion, Ester received, for the umpteenth time, a slightly reproachful text from Olof declaring how it was wonderful in every way to be with her, but that he couldn't have a sexual relationship with her and he'd 'explained this a number of times already'.

It was simple-minded to send yet another message like this – every variation of 'I want to but can't', and you're forcing me to do what I shouldn't be doing'; 'I don't want it enough to do it and you're pressuring me into concessions I shouldn't be making'; 'I'm not allowed to want to and you have to stop in order for me to want to'.

Ester was tired, tired.

Within an hour, Olof called to ask why she hadn't responded to his text. She said there was nothing to respond to. He wondered if they should go out to Hellas in this beautiful weather. Ester said she wasn't inclined, because she was tired. And with this, the telephone line caught fire. Olof could sense something was about to break, that Ester Nilsson had been gnawed to the bone. Olof told her that he'd spent the past week rereading all of her books, 'had really felt their power', found patterns and themes that he hadn't noticed before and 'was impressed'.

This made her feel even more tired. He was so transparent, it was disheartening.

'A walk would be nice,' said Olof.

'I think I've walked enough,' said Ester.

'I'm not feeling good in my situation.'

'You'll pick yourself back up. You've done it before.'

'I don't know what I want.'

'And yet it's always gone your way.'

'Are you free on Saturday?'

'I don't know.'

Olof said that the amateur theatre group really wanted Ester to write next year's play for them, too. This made her very happy and she decided on the spot to tackle an old idea she'd been carrying around, a comedy about the first Council of Nicaea in AD 325 and the Christian Trinity. Olof thought it sounded promising.

On Saturday, they went to Hellas. Rarely had he been this insistent, so she wanted to see where it would lead.

Nature's perfume was pungent, its verdure writhed and strained. Snowdrifts and rays of sunlight were engaged in a battle that the sun would win. As happened this time of year. Everyone but the snow knew it. Though doomed to be eradicated, it fought to the very last snowflake, forming a protective crust so sharp it could cut human skin. But it was helpless against the sun.

Ice floes were still drifting on Källtorp Lake, and a few young men were skinny-dipping by the pier. Ester and Olof sat on the rocks, from where they could see the youths howling as they took the plunge with dangling delight. Olof playfully covered Ester's eyes, proprietary, protective, as if she were his. But Ester was not amused, she was drained. Because he always reacted with vigour when her interest seemed to wane, the relationship began to accelerate.

With his incredible sensitivity for the fluctuation of capital, Olof could tell how close to the breaking point she was. He started visiting her in the evenings after rehearsal, he called and asked for her opinion on things he'd read in the newspaper, they spoke nearly every day and there was no friction.

Moreover, Olof wouldn't be in Skåne this summer; he'd be working at the open-air theatre in Stockholm, while the wife was recuperating at her parents' country home on Yxlan. She was exhausted, unhappy and out of sorts after a tough year at work, Olof said. Ester thought that she'd be exhausted, unhappy and out of sorts, too, if she was Ebba Silfversköld. Maybe they were suffering the same ailment.

But she also thought, mostly out of an old reflex, that there was no way back for a couple who didn't spend the summer together.

Unfortunately, Barbro Fors would be in Olof's open-air theatre production this summer; she'd even been the one to ask the director if he could give Olof a part in the play, he told Ester.

Then it was June and they continued to meet often and intensely, just like at this time the year before. For the first time in years, Ester wasn't dreading the summer. She wasn't happy exactly, but sufficiently satisfied and pleased to be able to give in to whims like buying expensive salt 'from the Dead Sea' when its beauty and health benefits were demonstrated at a pop-up stall in the Västermalm mall.

With this salt, she scrubbed away dead skin over the Midsummer holiday and thought about the bright nights stretching out before them, theirs for the taking.

The Monday after Midsummer, Olof called Ester to break up with her.

'My regret and guilt are getting to be too much,' as he said.

Well, it just keeps going, Ester dryly told Vera. This year he called, last year he texted. Vera explained that Olof was just closed for the summer. Didn't Ester know by now that he shut up shop in June and opened again in the autumn? Mistresses had to tolerate locked shops.

Ester asked Fatima if she thought that Olof would be with her if Ebba died or left him in some other way. Fatima didn't think so: he'd find new excuses, new hurdles, new women. She forbade Ester to go to Olof's summer performances, that would be beneath her.

Ester spent her days reading early Church history and the doctrine of the Trinity while she was writing the play. In the middle of the summer, she was commissioned by Swedish public radio to write a short essay on the 'orienteer's soul', which would be broadcast during the world championship in Falun in August.

An hour after it was broadcast, Olof called and asked which way the needle was pointing. South, she said.

He cautiously enquired about how the playwriting was going; that's why he was calling. He needed to start preparing the direction. She hadn't sent him any drafts over the summer. It sounded like he thought that was strange.

'No. I haven't sent any drafts.'

He suggested they go for a swim in this beautiful weather, then she could tell him about the play and share her thoughts about its staging.

Because Ester didn't have anything better to do and, moreover, was not burdened by pride, but rather a teeming loneliness, she agreed to go for a swim.

After swimming for a while, they returned to shore and Olof unfolded the blanket he'd brought for them to lie on. It was quite a narrow blanket, and they had to lie close together so as to both fit on top of it. The sun was scorching. Soon they took another dip, swam out to the islet and back. And then they took another rest on the blanket, shut their eyes against the sun and didn't say a word about Ester's play. She felt his skin against hers even though she wasn't allowed to touch him. Olof said he hadn't seen her at any of his performances. He'd looked for her each night.

'No, I didn't go. You left me again at Midsummer.'

'Yes. This isn't easy for me.'

'I thought we'd be seeing each other every night this summer. I'd so been looking forward to it.'

'I wouldn't have been able to, in any case. It would have filled me with too much regret.'

'Regret? Do you suppose Ebba thinks it's better if you betray her every other rather than every night?'

He didn't reply.

'Maybe you've been seeing Barbro Fors this summer instead? Maybe that was more practical and comfortable since you two were sharing a stage every night anyway?'

Ester's tone was not snide, but neutral, as though she was saying something ordinary. She'd said this so he would object.

'Ebba wondered that, too.'

'And what did you say? She isn't your type?'

'How did you know?'

After walking for a few minutes through the greenery along the water Olof said that it would be nice to stay in the green grass until evening, with Ester and some grilled chicken. Ester could recall the date of each instance he'd expressed his longing for communion with that exact content and analogous phrasing. It struck her that Olof Sten was a sort of automaton, the same thoughts, actions and language where one thing led to the next in a loop in which he was stuck and in which she for some reason was stuck with him.

Why did she love an automaton?

Why didn't it help that she knew he was an automaton?

Why did nothing help?

A month passed. Ester finished her Nicaea play and rehearsals began. She didn't attend them, the inclination and ardour were lacking. One early autumn day when the sun was still hot but the leaves were dry, Ester and Elin were sitting at the Eldkvarn outdoor cafe next to the town hall. Elin commented on how perpetually low Ester was lately. Because Elin knew it was fruitless to state the obvious about moving on and forgetting, they discussed strategies for inciting action instead. Would it be worth it to anonymously inform the wife? Elin wondered.

'I've written at least ten of those letters and never sent them,' said Ester. 'Remind me why?'

'Bringing the situation to a head. Breaking the cycle and the deadlock.'

They took out paper and pen. For instance a letter could arrive from someone who had been sitting at a cafe, recognized Ester or Olof, and had seen and heard things that they thought the wife should know. They wrote a few preliminary lines.

'He won't choose me when Ebba's read this letter.'

'We don't know that.'

'We probably do, I'm afraid.'

'*She* might not choose *him*. And then he can choose you. Eventually. But it might take time.'

'How much time?'

'You have to figure out if you want to be chosen in this way.'

Ester put down the pen and considered this while taking in the sparkle of Riddarfjärden's rippling waves and the jagged silhouette of Söder Mälarstrand.

'Of course I don't. But that's nothing I need to take a

stand on because Ebba will never let him go. A rival only makes him more interesting.'

'Have you ever thought that this might be precisely what Olof knows, and he's using you to make himself interesting to her?'

'No. Because using each other like that is a crime against a person's humanity.'

She glared defiantly at the town hall's golden crowns, crowns that someone risked their life polishing until they gleamed.

Mostly to entertain themselves, they kept drafting the letter to Ebba Silfversköld. Ester was reluctant. She wasn't ready to find out who he'd choose if he had to.

'We can't, Elin. I can't.'

'I understand.'

The letter was half-finished. Ester folded it up and kept it.

Vera suggested that Ester wasn't actually afraid of finding out who Olof would choose if he had to, but wanted to avoid finding out what living with Olof was like. This was also what a number of acquaintances, long befuddled by Ester's behaviour, thought: she didn't actually want what she was fighting for.

Ester found this reliably recurring thought about a lover's capacity for self-deception tiresome, not to mention tainted by its own simplicity. Via sunken Freudian cultural goods, people had come to understood that beneath the longing for love was a more genuine misery, hidden from the unhappy one herself but not from the spectators, and therefore she should first contend with this more genuine lack that she was fleeing through the romance.

When Ester was presented with submissive ideas about the unconscious, she asked herself why they were making love so complicated. There was no doubt an encounter with another person could spell the difference between misery and well-being. That this existential fact was an unfortunate biological vagary, one of the horrors of existence, didn't make it any less true.

Nature was dressed in all its finery. The trees were adorned in deep red and yellow, spots and speckles. At the mouth of the Djurgård Canal, the leaves looked like marzipan treats, but the earth, grass and stones stuck to a more sober palette. Ester's walks took her out there sometimes. It was the middle of October. The theatre company was rehearsing her play one night a week under Olof's direction. The troupe had decided to go out for a drink together after rehearsal and one of the actors called to see if Ester wanted to join them for both. The invitation made her happy and she accepted. It was a weekday, and they had dispersed by ten. Olof wanted to walk a while with Ester and have another round so they went from the centre of town to Old Town, where they found somewhere that was open.

'Where are you tonight?' Ester wondered.

She'd just found out that Ebba was at home on Bondegatan, on sick leave for occupational burnout.

'I said we were all going out together.'

'And she was OK with that?'

'Of course. I'm not . . .'

He didn't finish his sentence.

'Does she at least know if I'm at rehearsals or not?'

'She doesn't worry about it.'

'She should.'

'But you and I, we're not in a relationship.'

'No. But we have been.'

Olof had to take the number 3 from Mälartorget up Katarinavägen. Ester was going in the other direction on the same bus. According to the passenger information display, her bus would arrive a few minutes after his. They went to his bus shelter. It was cold in the small hours of the night and Olof was shivering, hands stuffed in his pockets. He was only wearing a light jacket. Ester rubbed his back to keep him warm, and he wrapped his arms around her. Then his bus arrived. He kissed her goodbye with the same tender, hot desire as during their very first kiss one winter night up on Folkungagatan, the snowflakes settling in their eyelashes. She remembered it as if it was yesterday.

During the weeks that followed, they often spoke on the phone about the realization of the play and the state of the world; Olof liked discussing politics with Ester. She started turning up at rehearsals. They went for coffee and talked about a scene that was particularly challenging to perform. Soon Ester invited him to dinner.

Elin pointed out there was a chance that Olof was reading the situation the same way as Ester was, but to the opposite effect: each time she let him back in, even though he was clear about never leaving his wife, it strengthened his belief that she approved of the arrangement. By returning to him time after time even though he'd stated that he didn't want what Ester wanted, she was agreeing to be his mistress.

The thought knocked the wind out of Ester, and it would not be dismissed. With as much rightness as her, he could indeed assert: You say one thing but do another, and actions are more important than words. You say you don't want to be a mistress, and yet you keep agreeing to be one. Of course I take this as proof that your words have no value.

Olof wanted very much to meet at Ester's for dinner, he said, but only to talk because they couldn't continue as before, no matter how glorious she was in bed.

'It's true,' said Ester. 'We can't carry on as before. But I don't just want to talk. And if you only want to talk, then there's no point in you coming.'

'Are you giving me an ultimatum?'

'Yes. I can't guarantee that there will just be talk.'

'Neither do I.'

He sounded as though he was tired of himself and his meagre attempts to stem the onrush of desire. So he came over once more and their romantic relationship began anew, a little over three years after the first time they met. It was a rain-slicked black October evening. They ate chicken casserole with rice and after talking and eating, they went to bed; two familiar bodies, unabashed.

From now on, she had to be able to trust him, she said,

because she couldn't bear another backlash. This time couldn't be like the other times. Their communication had to improve, and he couldn't just up and leave when he got anxious.

'I agree with both the description and the analysis,' Olof said. 'We'll do things differently now.'

Olof hadn't admitted anything like this before, Ester thought, and big changes are a result of many small shifts in existing patterns. Wasn't that how the Soviet Union fell? Even that fall was preceded by minor reforms and greater openness.

Fatima suggested Ester shouldn't think so hard about Olof's life and should focus on her own. Ester tried, but found she wasn't particularly interested in her own life.

They carried on into winter, which arrived early, and through the new year. Never before had they been lovers in the autumn, which suggested the pattern really was broken. They met up and they made love, they talked and strolled, exchanged ideas and reflections, they ate and drank and enjoyed each other's company and bodies. She gave him lifts, they drove to exhibitions and went places. Once when she'd come to collect him and he called her car a 'pick-up mobile' while smiling mischievously, the distancing effect was so mild and playful and his eyes so alive with amicable joy that it could only be seen as part of their connection.

This new equilibrium included them emailing when he was out of town; he was rehearsing a children's play in Gävle now. 'Thanks, you' began a reply to a message she'd written about how happy she was about the development of their relationship, then he wrote that he looked forward to another 'sitting with Miss Nilsson'.

'Sitting' was of course a little boring because 'lying' was the decisive factor but at least he'd replied, met her half-way, wasn't disappearing, there was nothing fickle about his behaviour even if his emails were a bit cool for her taste. He still seemed to be fishing his feelings out of a tin, rather than being driven by them. But she was convinced that his timidity in writing was due to shame and clumsy language. Not for a second did she think he was exercising discipline in the face of the written word's endurance, the risk of leaving a trail.

Over New Year, Olof was with his wife on Yxlan. Ester continued her tradition of celebrating alone with a meal she'd cooked from scratch and three rented movies about people who, after many hurdles, got each other in the end. She felt a sort of ease. The ease carried into New Year's Day. But on the evening of 1 January, the worry came creeping in. It was her fourth New Year's with-Olof-without-Olof. On the second day of the year, the agony was already so deep that she lay on her bed taking short, quick breaths, unable to get up. Nothing had happened except him not getting in touch, but she'd gone from peace to a wreck in a few hours, precisely because nothing had happened. The seconds trudged on.

At 11 a.m. on 2 January the anxiety was so consuming that the mistress went against the prohibition of contacting her lover while he was with the wife. The prohibition was clearly articulated:

'You're not allowed to call when I'm with Ebba.'

She called.

Olof declined the call.

She could picture him sitting with his wife in a villa in the archipelago savouring a well-tempered brunch as the snow billowed outside the rustic kitchen windows, a white landscape stiff with cold.

Ester couldn't even concentrate on the skiing competition on TV, she muted the sound. Soon she couldn't stand the pictures of the skiers' mountain-high vitality either, and turned off the television.

One and a half hours passed in this way. Then Olof called; the cramp in her chest released and Ester was so grateful she hardly needed to speak with him, it was enough that he'd called. But they spoke anyway. She said that longing was leaving her breathless and she'd rather be a snowflake in his hair than this creature in the bed being devoured from within. He was on the bus from Norrtälje, laughing warmly at the idea of the snowflake and said that if she picked him up at the bus station, they could see each other as soon as he arrived in Stockholm.

Ester leaped up, made the bed, showered, got ready. The pain was gone, her air passages opened and she was steeped in confidence. She was biochemically dependent on one individual's presence in her life.

She thought: He's calling me from the bus. He's suggesting we meet. He doesn't want to hide his longing, but show it. The break-up is nigh. This time he'll come. This winter, this spring.

—

She was parked on Valhallavägen near the bus station and in the wing mirror, she saw him approaching. *Objects in the mirror are closer than they appear*, it read on the mirror. Ester Nilsson believed in the accuracy of that line. And right then he seemed very close.

A backpack was slung over Olof's shoulder, and he was taking small steps to keep from slipping. Once in the car, he gave her a suave look, but his appearance was shocking. He looked awful. Unshaven and grubby with filthy hair and a whiff of must. She'd never seen him like this.

Didn't this speak to the state of his marriage, of Olof and Ebba's lack of respect for each other? Did this suggest loathing and self-loathing laced with the indifference implied in not dressing properly even if they were in the countryside? Or did it suggest how comfortable Olof and Ebba were with each other, so incredibly close they didn't need to put on airs, so close that one of them was looking elsewhere for a spark and flare of unpredictability – as well as for a reason to wash?

Ester read and read, interpreted and interpreted, making eternal deductions, but didn't come any closer to certainty.

She drove with caution through the city because she wasn't just transporting them, but their delicate mood. The snow that had fallen over Christmas muffled every sound. Even the snow on the carriageway was white, so dry and new it was.

It took less than fifteen minutes to drive to Olof's. She

parked on a side street in the neighbourhood. While he went up to his apartment, she went to buy them lunch at Cajsa Warg. Within ten minutes she arrived with two trays of lasagne, and he was freshly showered, clean-shaven and smelled of soap. Soft, hot and rosy, he sat in his bathrobe at the table. As they ate she ran her fingertips over his bare thighs and their bodies responded. He took her hand and they went to bed, the one the three of them shared.

Darkness arrived in haste and dropped like a theatre curtain. The love-making was short and fast but intimate. Olof sounded apologetic when he said that his 'urges were pent-up'. That set of words – pent-up urges – could only mean that the level of sexual activity with the wife was zero and he wanted to communicate this and nothing else to Ester, so she would know they had a shot. The married couple's sex life was dead, that's what he'd said, and no words could have been sweeter. Ester knew that Olof knew she interpreted his subtexts and his messages were being received even when he was being cryptic. If he spoke plainly she could hold his words against him, so instead he indicated where they were heading so as not to have to spell it out.

He wanted them to have a drink in the kitchen. This eternal red wine that they kept pouring into themselves at all hours of the day. Ester had never craved alcohol like Olof did and was never interested in a glass of wine other than with food, but if this is what it took, she'd keep drinking until everything was in order. She'd have to leave the car here and pick it up in the morning.

On the way to the kitchen he took a robe from the bathroom door and handed it to Ester. It was made of silk and threadbare in places with holes by the belt loops. Ester assumed it was the wife's. She was taken aback by how casually and thoughtlessly he was handing her the wife's robe. It was unacceptable for them both. She didn't want to put it on, but neither did she want to break the mood.

Or maybe the robe was further proof of the change that had occurred? The wife was already out of the picture, formalities were all that remained. The one who wore the robe was the one who he considered his partner.

They hadn't been sitting in their robes drinking red wine long before Olof became nervous and said Ester had to go. Ebba might be on her way, she had only been taking care of something in the house before returning to Stockholm. Ester better hurry. This brand-new level of risk-taking also must mean that his brain was breaking free from the marriage even if his conscious mind was still resisting.

'It's best you go,' he repeated.

His jitters made his tone recklessly harsh.

'Ebba might get here any second now.'

Ester put her hands on his cheeks.

'What would happen if she were to arrive right now, as I'm standing here in her robe and holding your face in my hands?'

'I can't even imagine. My life would be in pieces.'

'How could that be? I don't understand. Explain.'

Olof lost his temper and shouted:

'You think she's got a hold over me or what the fuck do you mean?'

Stunned, Ester took a step back.

'At least that would help straighten a few things out. What kind of hold would that be?'

'She'll be here any minute now. Hurry.'

Soon Ester was walking along Skeppsbron Bridge. The road was picture-perfect, frosty with yellow lamplight. The black sky encircled the stars' flickering holes.

A week went by. On Sunday evenings, the rehearsal was held in a space near Huvudsta, and as usual Ester gave Olof a lift home afterwards. It was their little ritual. Before she started the car she touched his knee, and he put his hand on hers. Then she drove off and soon was on Klarastrandsleden, heading towards Södermalm. She drove slowly to extend their time together.

'It would be so nice to go home with you,' said Olof.

'Do you have to go to your place?'

'I suppose I do.'

'Is Ebba there?'

'Unfortunately.'

Klarastrandsleden is a few kilometres long. They didn't say anything else for a while. A hundred metres before the Kungsholmen exit, Olof said:

'It's a pity I have to go home.'

'Maybe you can be late?'

'But not too late.'

'Should I get off here? Decide, quick.'

Thirty metres to the exit.

'Take the exit,' said Olof.

Ester drove steadily and accelerated up Fleminggatan. It was green lights all the way and right outside the building was a free space that was always taken. They walked the few metres to her front door. Something incredible was happening.

And then Olof said:

'How naughty of us.'

The comment didn't sit right with Ester, something was out of whack. This was part of the preservation, not the break-up – in the way that a mistress is part of a marriage and not of its dissolution.

Once, when they'd felt very close to each other, Ester had asked Olof to describe his feelings for her. He'd replied that the most incredible thing about men is that no one can see what we're thinking or feeling, which constituted an individual's freedom in relation to others. Society was a dictatorship of truth, especially the women with their constant demands for soul-searching. Olof was a dissident of the dictatorship. He refused to search his soul. Thank God, he said, that we can't see inside each other, even if he often felt the world could see right through him. It was a ghastly feeling, and each time he realized that his interior was his and his alone, it made him all the happier.

Recalling that exchange, Ester wondered if secret-keeping was the attraction for him. Was she just a pawn in their power game, the person Olof could be 'naughty' with in order to prove to himself that the wife didn't know what he was doing, giving him the upper hand?

She banished the unease, pushed away the knowledge that she could never have a lasting exchange with a person who wanted to keep his interior hidden from her, and thought about the breakthrough she was witnessing. Never before had he taken such initiative.

They were standing in the hall. Ester asked if he wanted something to eat. He replied by embracing her with hungry lust, kissing her, taking off her clothes, and steering them to bed.

Ten minutes later, no more, they were on their way out of the door. Olof had to go home to the waiting wife before she had a chance to get suspicious.

In the snow that kept falling and falling this winter, Ester made a handbrake turn at the crossing and took Hantverkargatan towards Södermalm.

As always, she drove him home after love-making with a feeling of affinity and sorrow. It was a quick drive, hardly any cars were out that night. At about ten to eight, or 19:53 according to the clock in the car, Ester Nilsson dropped off Olof Sten. She'd almost be home in time for the eight o'clock TV programme she'd been looking forward to. With one last kiss – and this was indeed their final kiss – he disappeared into his building with half a wave.

Driving down Katarinavägen, Ester could picture him opening the door and forming his features for the wife, to appear as though he hadn't just spilled his seed inside another woman. Was he being evasive? Did the wife notice? Was he compensating with ardour and prattle?

She rolled past Slussen. Crowds of people were out and about, and the groaning accordion buses were all in a row. What she and Olof were doing was wrong, Ester thought. One shouldn't allow people, that is to say Ebba Silfver-sköld, to believe their lives were something they weren't. People should be able to reject the truth if they didn't want it, but it had to be proffered. However, this was Olof's job, not Ester's. He had to be the one to tell Ebba about them.

Reeling with emotion, she passed the town hall. She thought about the things he'd said over the years that made his actions seem less immoral because they were supposedly part of an imminent divorce: 'I'm slow, Ester.' 'Break-ups are hard for me, you know.' 'We'll just have to wait and see.' 'We have the rest of our lives.'

A new week began for Olof and Ester. It would be their last. The next morning, Olof went back to Gävle, and the telephone was silent for four days until Ester called on Thursday.

He was curt at first. She suspected he was afraid of being embroiled in relationship talk after Sunday's events, afraid he'd transferred too much of his capital from his account to hers, for as soon as she asked what he thought about the morning's news about the culture minister's blunder he relaxed, expressing his surprise at the minister's poor judgement, and added that he'd sat next to her once during a performance of *Richard III*, which she'd slept right through.

The conversation didn't feel great, but laughing together about the minister made it better. Olof said he was recovering from a bad cold. There was something intimate about colds, Ester thought. When director-generals had colds while being interviewed on TV or the radio, it made them seem less powerful, closer, more human. Presumably this was the reason heads of state never made appearances when they were under the weather. She was gripped by tenderness at the idea of an ailing Olof. It struck her that he was often ill. Was it because he didn't 'feel good in his situation'? The lies and secrecy around his emotional life were taking their toll on his immune system.

They talked about the up-coming day-long rehearsal with the theatre troupe. In the final phase of rehearsal, they sometimes worked full days, and this Saturday was one of those. Olof said he would arrive in Stockholm late on Friday afternoon. Ester asked if she could meet the train. He made it clear that he would go straight home from the station but, sure, she could meet him there if she wanted to.

He seemed to have lost his sense of urgency. It puzzled and troubled her, but still the next day, she was there waiting at the platform for the trains arriving from the north. In her pocket, she was clutching a packet of bright red goji berries that she'd just bought at the Hötorg market hall. They were supposed to be good for colds.

The train arrived on time, and there was Olof and that aimless gait of his. His legs didn't seem to know where they were going and yet were transporting his upper body, which was even more clueless. Ester was wearing a black winter coat that went down to her ankles and which she thought was beautiful, like something out of *Anna Karenina*.

She didn't think there was anything strange or submissive in waiting for Olof at the train station. They were lovers, and lovers were equal in their gestures of love.

Olof's smile flickered between mocking and warmly amused, as though he was undecided.

He said:

'You look like a stationmaster. In that long coat and with the brand on your hat.'

She was wearing a black cable-knit hat with a pale leather patch on the front.

He didn't touch her and didn't stop. They walked side by side towards the main hall. His coolness made her feel silly, but it didn't stop her from offering him the goji berries.

'These are good for colds. Full of antioxidants.'

Olof stuffed the packet in his pocket. They walked down Tegelbacken and caught the number 3 bus. As his eyes wandered across her body in the crowd, Ester sensed vague disdain streaming towards her. But she didn't agree that she was degrading herself, that would be a conventional opinion. Degradation was impossible between lovers. It was only natural to steal twenty minutes when the opportunity presented itself. Until Olof dared make his big decision, this was how they'd have to carry on. Only those who were careless with life would find this pathetic.

The bus lurched. She remembered other lurching buses and their bodies eagerly swinging towards each other.

'See you tomorrow?'

'At rehearsal, sure,' Olof replied with indifference.

'What are you doing tonight?'

'Eating dinner with Ebba.'

Ester deliberated before continuing. Beyond a certain

degree of torment, pain stopped mattering, and at least things became interesting.

'What are you going to have?'

'Ah, well, I've got no idea what Ebba's come up with. Something tasty, I'm sure. It usually is.'

Her heart was being burn-beaten and the smoke stung her eyes. He hadn't been this married since October, before they'd ushered in their era of openness and trust.

'Maybe you could have goji berry for dessert,' she said. 'And give one to your wife. So you have a long and healthy life together.'

'Have you poisoned them?' Olof chuckled.

They arrived at his stop. Ester wasn't expecting any pleasantries upon parting, but got off with Olof in order to walk home from there. It was a fair distance. Sometimes the toxic stuff that had accumulated in her needed cold, crisp air to evaporate.

She had taken but a few steps when Olof called after her to say they could walk to rehearsal together tomorrow. She turned around.

'I'll call when I'm on my way,' he said.

She set her course for home and mulled over the situation. She really had believed and felt that they'd progressed during their last rendezvous. But here she was again, a distant being, a stranger waiting on platforms, someone who resembled a stationmaster, tendering goji berries without invitation or request. It was as easy as ever to regress. Maybe because nothing was developing. Only Ester had it in her head that progress was inevitable.

After almost an hour in the slush, she reached Fridhemsplan. She rented a movie and bought pizza. She thought about Olof's dinner with his wife. 'Something tasty, I'm sure. It usually is.' The words made her shudder.

The rehearsal started at noon, so at eleven Ester was waiting by the Karlberg Canal. Nothing had been arranged, but there really wasn't any other way. She waited; Olof didn't come. Eventually, she risked being late for rehearsal and called him. He had badly misjudged both the time and distance. Walking from Söder to Huvudsta took at least an hour and a half under normal conditions, but now the route was thick with slush and powdered with fresh snow. With each step forward, her feet slid backwards. She'd be over half an hour late if she waited for him, but they couldn't do anything without the director anyway. And she wanted to walk with Olof, wanted to be with him as and when she could, and to set yesterday right.

Ester thought that the negligence Olof was showing towards the ensemble was precipitated by a self-loathing that came from living a lie. Negligence was his conscious's way of inciting action. The pressure had finally found an outlet. Like all things in nature, the will followed the paths available to reach what it needed to reach, do what needed to be done. Sloppiness and a lack of concentration were ways for the psyche to trigger changes that otherwise would not be made. Olof's life was quite simply falling apart at the seams, Ester thought.

To intercept him, she walked southward along the Karlberg Canal, but even his coordinates had been diffuse and imprecise when she'd called to hear how far he'd come:

'I see a red-brick house on the left and a sign.'

She'd already passed Barnhus Bridge when they crossed paths. It was noon. He didn't mention his delay or that the ensemble was being kept waiting. Wearing a dirty jacket and a nonchalant air, he stumbled forth in the slush, ill-tempered and hungover. They walked to Huvudsta in silence.

By the time they arrived, the actors were already in action. Apparently, he'd forewarned them about the forty-five-minute delay; they were restless but not surprised. He hadn't called to forewarn her.

They worked for several hours straight. The parts were beginning to stick. Now all they needed was to be fused into a whole. They carried on until five, and when they were done, dinner awaited them all in Birkastan at the home of one of the actors. The group deliberated walking or riding the subway.

'It would be nicest to go on foot,' Ester said and looked at Olof without arranging her features so they would display something other than the hopeful ardour she had no reason to be emanating. Somehow, it had fixed itself into a habitual expression.

Olof glanced at her. To her dismay, the sediment of disgust lingered in his gaze, and the following line unleashed clouds of toxic spores, as from a deathcap mushroom:

'You're not the only one who wants to walk.'

Vera said:

'What if you were faced with a starving person who was allowing themselves to be satisfied with a stale crust of bread once a fortnight? Stop holding out your hand, Ester. Get your own food, free yourself from bondage. People diminish those who ask to be diminished.

Fatima asked:

'Where's your self-respect?'

Ester explained that she was not a beggar, nor did she lack self-respect. Quite the contrary in fact, she had so much it allowed her to overlook the weaknesses of those who were afraid to love. She'd never play or be steered by their power games.

Shrill with vexation, Vera yelled that Ester was arrogant, did she think she was God?

Ester asked how this fitted with her being pitiful, pitiable. An arrogant beggar in divine guise? This made Vera yell even louder.

'The more interesting question,' Ester said, 'is why Olof

keeps stuffing that crust into my mouth. He could just stop, but he doesn't. He wants something.'

'But he doesn't want enough!' Vera shouted. 'The world isn't a mathematical equation.'

'And yet no one is surer of what x and y represent than you.'

'I can't do this any more. I give up. I need some time away from you. I'm taking a break.'

And she did. They took a break from each other.

From rehearsal, the group braved the snow-slush; their route took them past Karlberg Palace, under the railway and up the hill towards Birkastan. Olof lagged behind Ester, conversing with one of the actresses. Though Ester was also talking, she could sense Olof's mind as keenly as if it was her own; he was aware that he'd trodden too hard on her, and this was not good. But she also sensed this awareness was paired with a furious desire to trample her and cut her off once and for all, destroy what he harboured for her, crush her so he could find equanimity. His sensations were as clear as ice inside her: he couldn't live without her love nor could he live with it; he wanted to have it but didn't understand what it turned him into; he wanted to avoid it but didn't dare relinquish it; she showed him that there was a better version of life out there and for this, he despised her.

Towards the end of the walk, her sense seemed confirmed. She saw his need to reel her in, to re-establish contact in order to neutralize his guilt. Meanwhile he wanted to keep their intimacy in check and was irritated by how flaccid her sullen severity made him seem. The sum of all this was a chipper yet contemptuous exclamation in which admiration was swaddled in caustic irony:

'Or what does the poet and philosopher say to that?'

And then some of what had been discussed behind her was relayed. When she turned around, his expression was inviting. His response disarmed and appeased her.

Soon they were at the home of the couple who was hosting the dinner, and the stew was simmering on the stove. They drank wine and ate snacks; in the living room, the group split in two to chat. Ester sat in Olof's group and sensed how clingy he thought it was that she had joined his group and not the other one, which would have been the strategic choice, but she rejected strategy and the fight. She'd sat with his group because that's where she wanted to be, in hopes he'd reach an insight about his humanity. Ever in sensory contact with his consciousness, Ester was aware that he couldn't stop feeling irritated with her, for their relationship had once again ended for him and one-sided love is a leech on the beloved's neck.

She was silent and encumbered. The others spoke all the more, and Olof in particular. They talked about the EU's expansion and Russia's superpower ambitions; never at a level higher than what the headlines and decks of daily newspapers offered. Skimming the surface fatigued Ester, and she found it uninspiring.

And then the conversation got interesting. Someone in the group told a story about a man he knew whose wife had recently left him for another woman. A comment was made about how it probably wasn't as bad being rejected for a person of the opposite sex, because then you didn't have to think it was a personal failing, but a category of physical desire, which was probably easier to accept.

That's when Olof chimed in.

'No. I don't feel that way. I really don't. In fact I think it would be worse. If Ebba left me for a woman it would be awful. Unbearable. I'd be devastated and feel like I wasn't good enough at all.'

Ester stared at Olof, stared to see if there was any subtext, perhaps a confused admission of this monumental hypocrisy.

But there was none. He looked sincere, as though he honestly loved his wife and truly dreaded being left by her.

So as not to make a scene, Ester resisted the impulse to go home. Instead, her shaky legs took her to the kitchen where their hosts were putting the finishing touches on the food. She was hiding that she was drowning inside, but could hear the strain in her voice when she said it smelled fantastic.

The stew was served, and everyone gathered around the kitchen table.

287

Over dinner, Olof desperately bestowed recompense. As they helped themselves to the food, lamb with vegetables and couscous, he sang Ester's praises, quoting from an article she'd written for one of the morning papers a week ago and complimenting the idea behind it. He linked a line in the play they were rehearsing with a stanza from one of her poems, which apparently he knew by heart. Throughout the dinner, he referenced things she'd said – 'as Ester usually says', 'as you once wrote, Ester'.

And for the first time, she lost respect for him. The compensatory subservience he staged when he had to was among the more deplorable things she'd witnessed. She was as disgusted by the aggressive flattery as by his hostile rejections, but most of all by the pathological oscillation between the two.

When they'd finished the main course, Ester excused herself, saying she needed to go home, a difficult day's work awaited her tomorrow. She thanked her hosts for dinner. The couple tried to entice her with dessert, chocolate mousse cake, but she declined.

As she was putting on her shoes in the hall, Olof came after her.

'Are you leaving?'

'Yes. I am.'

'But why?'

Ester looked at him, his wine-stained shirt, his drooping body and cheeks, bottle-like shoulders and his saggy neck. She'd never considered them – these body parts – as parts before, she'd loved him as a whole, intensely and indul-gently, loved him in waking and in slumber, while eating and working, while reading the paper and taking walks, while on the toilet and while showering, in scorn and in dis-appointment, loving him in every moment without pause.

Before her stood a pathetic figure with awkward arms dangling from his slack frame and a clumsy incompetence that no longer warmed her heart.

'You know precisely why. Never in your half-lived life of slack ambiguities have you ever known anything so pre-cisely.'

'I don't know what you're talking about.'

A ray of hatred punctured Ester Nilsson's membrane. Previously, when hatred had appeared in moments of despair, it had been on the other side of red-hot yearning. Now the hatred was cold and spoke through her when she said:

'You've done what you wanted to do, Olof. You've achieved the desired effect. You've never quite managed to hold back your disdain for the only person who has over-looked that you allow yourself to be a remarkably small person. Only in fleeting moments have you managed to not look down on me because I've persisted in loving you in spite of this.'

What she said was met with far too great understand-ing, and Olof stayed silent. Then he rejoined the others.

—

She'd been home a little while when Olof called. He must have left the dinner shortly after she had and was now in a taxi home, his voice soft.

'What happened there?'

Ester's ire halted, like a gushing tap being turned off. But the washer was leaky. It continued to drip.

'What happened there?'

She was surprised by the harshness in her tone. She had always helped him in these situations, helped him in order to help their cause, but ossified disappointment caused her to refrain.

'You got really angry,' he said.

'Yeah. I got really angry.'

'I did something wrong as usual, of course.'

Ester waited a few seconds so as not to be rash.

'Do you have any idea how you've been treating me since I met you at the station yesterday?'

'Actually, no.'

'Do you want to know?'

'I guess not, because you're so mad. But go on, so we can get past it.'

'We probably won't.'

'Aha. No. I guess not.'

'Why would you be "extremely sad" if Ebba left you? It's incomprehensible considering our escapades for the past three, almost three and a half years.'

'Of course one would be sad. We're married.'

'Yeah, you are. Wouldn't it, then, be extraordinary if the

wife you've failed, deceived and betrayed fell in love and left you, if she was allowed to be happy?'

No reply.

'Wouldn't it be a perfect solution to our problems if she met someone who cared about her, so that she could leave you and your wretched marriage? You should let your wife have that.'

Olof was quiet for a long while before he said:

'You probably don't understand. I like Ebba. I really like living with her.'

The words struck Ester like rivets. Actually, it was the rivets holding her together that were being pulled out, but it was hard to tell the difference.

'You've got a strange way of showing it.'

'I can see how it might seem so. But I've never wanted to leave Ebba, and I've been clear about that from the start.'

And that was it. Only curiosity spurred Ester on to the next line; she was sitting beside herself, studying the course of events.

'I have to ask, Olof. Your behaviour towards me is often hurtful and damaging. Why do you enjoy tormenting me?'

'That's not true. It's not like that. You're with me always. Always, you're inside me.'

Ester held the handset out in front of her, as though seeing the apparatus would help her understand. She heard Olof shout, 'Hello.' The conversation stood out as one of their most absurd, which was no small statement, and it seemed even more so when he said:

'You're always on my mind.'

'I don't understand what you're saying, Olof. Then why do you act the way you do?'

'I have to pay the cabbie. I'll call you in a minute.'

Ester lay in bed and thought about Olof paying, getting out and shutting the door behind him, feeling the moist but not-too-crisp January air on his cheeks as he hurried over the dark road, gleaming with the streetlights' silver streaks. He probably didn't want to call when he was in the building, it added to his guilt, so he'd do it out on the street, outside his front door.

She held the phone and awaited the call. It didn't come. After ten minutes, he sent a text. 'I'll call you tomorrow. Hugs.'

These dazzling mid-January mornings. It had snowed again. Since the beginning of December the ground had been covered in snow. When she woke up, she saw that two identical texts had come in during the night. They'd arrived within minutes of each other, as though Olof wanted to make sure the message would reach her.

They read: 'You r sexy,' nothing more. It was the first time he'd written anything that could link him to an active relationship with Ester Nilsson. An unremarkable formulation and not an unexpected thing to say to one's mistress, but the content wasn't open to interpretation or denial. The duplicate messages had been sent at one in the morning. Olof's and Ester's conversation had ended at ten thirty. When he came home, he must have sat up drinking alone. Was he remorseful? Did he have a guilty conscience? Was he hoping that Ester was awake too and with one reply would neutralize the debt, as always? The wife must have been sleeping in the next room when he reached for his phone and wrote his message, writing to stop Ester from doing anything nasty, a diffuse premonition, to save the current state of affairs and his self-image, and he said what lovers say to their mistresses, according to the cultural guidelines (better known as clichés) which had rewired his poor synapses.

On any other of the one thousand or more mornings that had gone by, this text would have delighted her. But now his inability to rise above baseness made her rueful. Still she waited the whole day for him to call as promised.

The hours passed. Late in the afternoon, a text message arrived. 'I don't understand your sour display yesterday and your whining. I thought we had a nice walk, a good rehearsal and a pleasant dinner. You should write a hand-book on how to make Ester Nilsson happy so that one can be clear on the instructions. All those rules and prohibi-tions aren't exactly simple. Later.'

She read the text several times. Then she called Elin and Elin said:

'Enough already. Isn't it time to take the tap out of the keg?'

She knew Elin was right. And she had to act in the next few hours while the adrenalin was still high, and hesitation – for the first time – was hesitating.

They talked the matter over and made a plan. Ester promptly ended the call to do what needed to be done. It had to happen tonight while there was still a clear connec-tion to the weekend's events, so that Olof could see the part he'd played and not blame Ester or dismiss her as unpre-dictable and crazy. Women and madness were so closely linked – where madness was all that compromised life's usual rhythms.

Ester Nilsson looked up Ebba Silfversköld's number and called her. She would have preferred to write but Elin thought that it was fairer to call. The wife should have the chance to ask follow-up questions. Ester certainly had no desire to speak with Olof's wife and couldn't predict how a conversation like this would end or where it could lead.

The wife didn't pick up.

Ester set the phone aside, closed her eyes. She shouldn't take this as a sign. It had to be done tonight, otherwise the misery would never end. She waited two minutes and called again. No answer. She composed a text. When she was about to send the message, her finger slipped and it didn't send. Ester's heartbeat pulsed throughout her body. She had been given one last chance to change her mind and stay with the old, to continue as before.

She thought it through again. If she didn't flip the board over, she wouldn't have it in her to put a stop to it by discreetly slipping away, that was clear. The slightest enticement or response from Olof pulled her back in, every time. She could make the cut and even tell him about it, but in a few weeks or months she'd try again, putting out feelers, exploring the level of interest, finding an innocent reason to contact him, forgetting the negatives and only remembering the delights, and regardless of what it was like before, determine that it was better than the void he left behind.

The only path to freedom was to force Olof to take a stand by getting the wife involved. She sent the message. This time she didn't slip.

> Hi Ebba. I don't know if you know, but I don't think you do. Olof and I have been having a relationship for over three years, taking longer and shorter breaks. The last time we were together was on Sunday a week ago. I love him but the situation is difficult and undignified for the three of us. I'm sorry it turned out this way. / Ester Nilsson

Exhausted, she slumped in the armchair; the wife's phone was beeping, she was picking it up, reading the message, rereading, reading it a third time slack-jawed, calling Olof in shock, enraged but not yet invaded by the despair that was to come, that was to begin its slow hollowing out and would never quite disappear.

As for Ester, she called Elin and asked if she could spend the evening at her place.

'Now things can finally start happening,' said Elin.

'I'm scared to death of what's next, of what I've done.'

'I get that. But there's nothing you can do right now. Come over as soon as you can. I'm cooking.'

'I want wheat . . . and sugar.'

'And for that very reason, you're not getting any. It's chicken stir fry with spring onions and ginger tonight. You're going to have real food. You don't need to comfort yourself any more. You've set yourself free and that's excellent! Now, hurry over!'

The warmth in her friend's words cheered her up, but the freedom Elin had described sounded gruesome. She was on her way to the subway towards Alvik where Elin lived with husband and child when a text from Olof arrived. Forty minutes had passed. The message was brief and read in its entirety: 'PIG!!!'

Ebba's call had probably reached him on the train to Gävle, where he was returning before the start of the working week. Because he was surrounded by people he couldn't express his denial as brutally as he wished – the company of strangers called for a measure of consideration.

Ester had reached Thorildsplan by the time the next instalment of Olof and the wife's conversation was transmitted. Now the wife was writing, not as brief a message but still sententious, and dripping with sarcasm besides:

'Would've been quite a tight schedule on Sunday . . . but sure!'

Ester saw that Olof's strategy, after three or thirty years, was flat-out denial. And the wife was trying to trust him. Clearly he was thinking that if only he could refute one fact, namely that of their carnal encounter a week ago, he could cast doubt over the whole story.

Ester replied to the wife's message in the spirit of objectivity from which she had decided never to stray.

'After rehearsal on Sunday. Between seven thirty and

twenty to. After which I gave him a lift home to Bonde-gatan. He should have walked in the door at exactly five to eight.'

At Elin's, over food and wine, they examined the matter methodically and from various angles.

'This was bound to happen,' Elin said. 'You've been on hold for too long. If you still want him, which I hope you soon won't, you have to find out what happens to your love when it's exposed to truth and light.'

'He won't want to see me after this. It's over.'

Elin looked into the darkness outside and seemed to be wondering whether or not she should speak her mind.

'It would be best if it was over inside you, too.'

'Yes. That would be good.'

'Unfortunately, Ester, Olof might be getting a kick out of the sneaking itself.'

'I know.'

'So, you've got what you want. Except it means you and Olof can't see each other again, and now you have to con-tend with the part of your relationship that won't fade. You might be doomed to never being together. You have to find out whether or not that is true.'

'There are indications that this might be the case. But I don't understand.'

'The only way for an unfree person to be free is to keep their true self hidden.'

'Maybe I should go far, far away for six months and throw away my phone.'

'But you'd still know his number by heart.'

'Yeah. Landline and mobile. But what if I get rid of my phone?'

'Then you'll buy a new one when the fancy strikes. Or borrow someone else's.'

'Indeed.'

'Going far, far away doesn't help, we've known that for ever.'

'Nothing helps.'

'Actually, doing what you did today helps.'

Another text arrived from Ebba. She had changed tack but was still on the offensive. Ester read aloud: '"You speak of indignity and yet you do this. Hoping for catastrophe. How dignified is that?"'

Elin shook her head.

Another five minutes went by before Olof called.

'Should I answer it?'

'If you want a scolding.'

The ringing faded away, no message was left.

'We'll see how time treats those two,' Elin said.

Ester felt how hope grabbed hold of those statements against her will, filling every space inside her. Perhaps it was but the hope for redress. Another half-hour passed; Olof called again. It was eleven o'clock. Many were the lonely nights over the past years when Ester would have done anything to make him reach out with the eagerness he had shown in these past hours.

'Well, now it suits him to get in touch,' Elin said.

'Do you think he's angry?'

'We can be sure of it.'

If Ester had been alone, she would have answered. The wish to hear what he was thinking and to appeal for understanding would have been too strong.

'Isn't there any other alternative to him being angry?'

'No.'

'Do you think he hates me?'

'He does right now.'

'This feels awful.'

'It will pass.'

'Or not,' said Ester.

'Or not,' said Elin.

'We just don't know how it will turn out. I took a gamble,' Ester reeled off as if she were reading from a book.

'A necessary gamble.'

'I can't stand not having any control over the outcome.'

'Who knows how anything will ever turn out? The only difference is that now you've taken the initiative you've torn it from his hands. For the first time since you two started, you're the one calling the shots.'

'It's going to be a frightful winter and spring,' Ester said.

'Time is your friend. Whatever the outcome, time is your friend.'

'I'm so tired of time. So tired of waiting.'

'But you've also been in the upper stratosphere of emotion, you've had moments of unsurpassed joy and intensity. How many of us have ever had that kind of experience, do you think?'

'Most people.'

'No, no way. Time is on your side however it goes with Olof.'

Under a celestial sparkle, Ester arrived home late at night and turned on her computer out of habit. There were two emails from Olof, each written right after the unanswered phone calls. The first was brief: 'You're pleased with yourself, aren't you, having destroyed my life. You are in fact the most disgusting person I've ever met.'

The other was longer and less coherent. It was about how much he loved his wife and that Ester had to be out of her mind to think that he'd ever been interested in her. It began with him saying that 'now' he'd 'read up on *stalking* and *stalkers*' (This evening? Ester wondered, ever faithful to people's will to truth) and had 'spoken to his friends about it'. And so he'd come to understand that this was the condition from which she suffered.

So she was his stalker. She'd anticipated a lot, but her

imagination hadn't stretched to a fantasy this bizarre. Olof as Ester's innocent victim – an honourable, hard-working husband who'd spent years being stalked by a madwoman, a crazy poet. This was the story he'd settled on. The email contained many more epithets. Ester wasn't only a stalker but also 'psychotic, psychopathic and a crazy cunt'.

She read it and read it again with an almost bemused distance. This was more dishonesty and charlatanry than she thought was possible to muster for even such a profoundly divided person.

The world around her seemed to be asleep. The darkness outside was mighty. How often had she sat in this chair by this computer in a darkness this dense seeking statistics on how common divorce was in married couples where one partner was unfaithful and how long it usually took. She had sought probabilities and empirical evidence in which she could lay her unhappiness to rest.

Now she was a block of ice. What Olof had written was too wretched for it to cause her much pain. But in spite of the serious allegations and uxoriousness, his tone was now askew. In the middle of this catastrophe, it was as though he didn't feel what he was writing, but was figuring out which feelings he should be feeling. Here and there a coaxing turn crept in with the spite, as though he was incapable of not enticing and intimating as he pushed her away. In the middle of a tirade, he exclaimed: 'I thought you were a humanist!' and 'I would never have thought this of you.'

Ester read the email one more time and noted that the

word 'crazy' was redundant after the previous three words (psychotic, psychopath, and stalker), but for a change Olof apparently wanted to delimitate. Maybe he liked the alliteration of 'crazy cunt'. If nothing else, this was a tried and tested epithet for women against whom one needed to invoke antipathy, and perhaps the email wasn't for her, but was a receipt of his innocence, to be shown to anyone who needed convincing.

One month passed. More messages of the same character arrived from Olof and the wife. They consisted of psychological diagnoses, denials and belittlement. Then it quietened down.

Ester considered disavowal as a phenomenon. If disavowal weren't so human and common then it wouldn't constitute one of the pillars of the earliest Christian myths, she thought. This made Olof's actions less grotesque. She wanted to avoid passing judgement on him, she who wanted to share her life with a man who was capable of such a thing. As long as confession was impossible, for reasons that were unknown to her, he was forced into disavowal, and with disavowal it had to follow that Ester was nuts. No other alternatives were offered. This had a logical consistency. What was hard to understand was why the association with Ester was so shameful, and how a marriage he'd handled so carelessly could be so important. But this was nothing other than her eternal question loop.

She'd heard that there'd been a few rounds of Olof's wife leaving him and coming back. One frozen night in February six weeks after the incident Ester was at the pub with some dear friends after a reading of Charles Rezni-koff's poetry at a small publishing house in a basement on Linnégatan. The pub happened to be the one on Kommendörsgatan where she and her ex-lover Hugo Rask had briefly been regulars a long time ago. The party of four had just been given their menus when Olof's ringtone began to play, the one she'd assigned to him and him alone and that accompanied his name and number. She still hadn't got around to deleting it. Surprised, overexcited and curious as to what he could possibly want, she excused herself and went out on the snowy pavement to answer. The location meant nothing to her any more other than as the fading memory of a street corner that used to make her pulse race. Olof Sten, on the other hand, still meant far too much to her. She answered by stating her full name and waited for him to announce his errand.

'Why'd you do it?!' he screamed.

The question surprised her, the answer should have been obvious, but it also elated her, for it implied that he didn't believe any of the things he'd accused her of being. It was important to her that she and Olof preserve the truth in their hearts, that the disavowal was not inside him. With each passing day, it had felt all the more humiliating.

'There a few ways to answer that question,' she said. 'Various levels of answers. Which level are you interested in?'

Olof wasn't interested in Ester's levels, and even less in re-encountering her sophisms.

'Why'd you do it?!' he repeated using the same mono-tone scream.

'Because I'd had enough. And all of my previous meth-ods proved to be useless.'

'I've been very clear about never wanting to make a life with you. I was a victim of my carnal desires.'

'The only thing you've been clear about and a victim of is your ambiguity.'

'Well, yes, because you've nagged me so much.'

'So you've given up on the idea that I'm your stalker?'

Throughout the conversation, she'd been pacing and had carved a path in the slush.

'You and I have never had a relationship,' Olof screamed.

Could it be, Ester wondered, could a person's language centre exclusively be composed of ready-made phrases from the collective factory that was society and history? Olof chose phrases that were a decent fit for the situation, but seemed to have no emotional connection with their meanings. That's why it could sound the same each time, but grate with the mood and occasion.

'If we never had a relationship, and you never wanted to be with me, and I'm your deranged stalker, does that mean that I raped you each of those times we slept together?'

Olof deliberated in silence.

'Yes. I would say that.'

'You would say that.'

'I would. It must be so.'

The pub cast its cosy glow on the passers-by. From

inside, Ester's friends were giving her wondering looks. She signalled to them that everything was OK.

'And what does that make you, Olof? Year after year, you asked a lunatic who was stalking you to come to your home and travel around Sweden to see you, all to have the pleasure of being raped by her. Regular as clockwork you visited the madwoman who was harassing you at her home, savoured her dinners, conversation and caresses, eagerly undressed in front of her and let your body be embraced. After the dinners and conversations, you were raped and stayed until morning when you were raped anew only to ask for a lift home from the very same lunatic. And when you, shortly after Midsummer each year, managed to free yourself from this psychotic rapist you made sure your "intellectual fellowship", as you called it, continued. You called her in the middle of the night sometimes just to have a chat about this or that, and you kept praising her company. You scheduled dates, directed her plays, fixed and arranged and carried on. Olof, I don't think you should wait. You have a duty to put yourself at the disposal of researchers, not just in psychology, but in sexology, sociology and gender studies, too! There must be very few people who have praised sexual congress in rape as you have, and few who have expressed such a degree of appreciation for time spent with a crazy person, their stalker besides. It must be unique the world over.'

Olof listened, said nothing, did not hang up. Ester got the impression he was enjoying this, as he had always

enjoyed it when Ester schooled him. Like an obedient
dog, tone and steadfastness meant everything, the words
hardly mattered. Perhaps this explained all that seemed
unresolved between them. Ester Nilsson with her precise
relationship to language had fallen in love with a man for
whom words were only variations of sounds; whereas she
strove for the precise verbal representation of each event,
Olof used sound pictures and compound words that he'd
learned fitted together. In spite of all this, she still had that
feeling about cogs.

'There's one thing I've been wondering,' she said, 'and
that I'm curious to know if your wife asked you about
when you lied to her and disgraced me. Why didn't you
call the police if you, for several years, had a stalker on
your heels? Is it because you wanted to direct the lunatic's
plays first? Just one more production, you thought, then
I'll call the police and tell them I'm being stalked by
the playwright I'm collaborating with.'

Olof muttered, neither troubled nor ill at ease, but
interested and half-tickled.

'Doesn't Ebba wonder why you never, during all these
years, told her about your difficult situation?'

'She knows I'm scared to death of you. That's why I
didn't say anything.'

'You're what?'

'Scared to death.'

'Scared to death? I would be too if I were dishing up

your lousy lies. Scared to death of people thinking I have a stunted brain.'

'You've destroyed my life.'

His tone was probing, as if he were testing the thought. He said his lines with greater ease. The longer the conversation, the more it sounded like he was partaking in a simple seminar where different stances were being assumed for the sake of argument. No, not a seminar, it was role play, of course.

'Olof, why did you call me tonight?'

'To tell you I want nothing to do with you.'

Ester burst into laughter, in the true sense of the phrase, for her laughter was like those thousand splinters of unbreakable glass, which breaks nonetheless when put under certain strain.

'You know, it is exactly this habit of yours to call me to say that you don't want anything to do with me when that was made clear a long time ago, that makes it tempting to believe that it is contact you want. You call me to say that you don't want to talk on the phone with me. You sleep with me to show your indifference to my body. You eat dinner with me so you can tell me you're not really hungry.'

'Ebba left me.'

'She'll come back.'

'I doubt it.'

'Take it easy, Ebba won't be able to live without you for very long. If she could, she would have left your meagre, mendacious company just as I'd have given up on your meagre, mendacious company had I been able to. Sit tight, Olof, your wife will return to you. People get stuck with each other.'

'Only you would want to live in your world of truth, Ester Nilsson. Have you considered the tyranny of absolute transparency?'

'Yes, Olof Sten, I've thought about that much more than you. But a little of it can be good, an ounce in any case. Constant lies and manipulation are tyrannical, too.'

Ester prepared to hang up. She was exhausted. Most of all she wanted to go home, but she couldn't just leave her friends. She could see they'd already eaten most of their meals. Then Olof said, as if nothing of what had happened had happened, as if nothing that had been said during this conversation had been said, as if the halves of his brain didn't correspond and had no idea of what the other part was doing or saying.

'The rehearsals of your play are going well. A test audience came in yesterday and it went like a house on fire. The premiere will go ahead as planned. And I . . . (an artificial pause) . . . hope that you . . . (another pause, more hesitant) . . . won't . . . show up for it.'

Down to the slightest modulation, it had sounded like he wanted to say that he hoped she *would* come, but stopped at the last second and added a 'won't' because that was what the scene and his life required.

And Ester wished he'd asked her to come. Her amputated hope was having phantom pains even though she knew it was irrational. Nourished by old memories (ignoring others), against her will and contrary to counsel, it was extrapolating future prognoses using a unique bliss algorithm.

'Of course I won't come,' she said, hung up and walked into the hot pub, chilled to the marrow because she'd left her coat inside. She was shaken and didn't feel hungry, but ordered spaghetti vongole. Her party, perusing the dessert menu, asked if everything was all right. Ester said it was just her brother, calling with some minor emergency from abroad.

The premiere of Ester Nilsson's play *Disunited Trinity, Nicaea 325* took place one rainy Friday in March at the same little theatre on Västmannagatan where *Cog* was staged the year before. Fatima was Ester's scout, sent to observe the performance, the atmosphere, the status of the married couple and report back. Ester was waiting for her on Odenplan. They took the subway to crêperie Fyra Knop, situated on one of Götgatsbacken's cross-streets, where they each had a savoury galette and a sweet crêpe. They went there sometimes during the dark months when the stores of company, hearty food and rigorous problem-solving needed to be replenished. After they'd placed their orders, Fatima looked at Ester's face, hungry for news and observations, and said:

'You're going to be disappointed in me, but I'm not sure if Ebba was there. I mean, I'm not sure it was her that I saw.'

'What do you mean "unsure"?'

'I saw her in profile and have only seen her in a photo before. On the homepage of the Borlänge general hospital. But I think it was her.'

'Were they sitting together?'

'No.'

'No?'

'No.'

'That doesn't have to mean they're separated. Olof probably wanted to sit on his own so he could concentrate on the performance.'

'He didn't seem to be concentrating that hard. Actually he seemed quite absent. And Ebba laughed the loudest and most of all.'

'Ebba laughed?'

'Heartily. If that was her.'

'At my dialogue?'

'It was one of the gayest laughs I've ever heard.'

'Forced gaiety?'

'That's how I took it, yes.'

'Did she laugh at the lines or with them?'

'I can't say. Her laughter was just too loud. It sounded like she might break into tears at any moment. But that could be post-facto rationalization because I happen to know she has more reason to cry than to laugh.'

'And Olof?'

'He laughed once. And chuckled twice.'

'How did he look?'

Fatima hesitated, looked at Ester and then at the buckwheat pancake with chèvre the waitress had placed in front of her.

'Run down. Really awful. Ten years older than at last

year's premiere. Unshaven and dirty, wearing a wrinkled flannel shirt, saggy jeans and a pair of clunky yellow boots that aren't at all suitable for a premiere. Last year he wore a blazer and a starched shirt, I want to say, nice leather shoes, looked freshly washed and clean-shaven. This time he looked wan and like he didn't have any self-respect.'

They ate their galettes and talked about consistency and flavour combinations while Ester mulled over Fatima's observations.

The restaurant, inspired by Brittany, was built like a ship's cabin. They sat at the back where there was no phone reception, so after about an hour when Ester went to the toilet, she saw that she had two voicemails even though the phone hadn't rung. She knew who'd called and wanted nothing more than to rush out of the restaurant and call him. She sat back down. When they were out on the street, she listened to the messages. They were both the same. Movement could be heard, a breath, a person who seemed to be hesitating before speaking and then thought better of it. Ebba and Olof must have gone to the premiere as a married couple to keep up appearances, but after his wife took off, he'd called Ester. Or they'd fought tooth and nail when the perfidious air went out of them because the premiere was over and the facade could finally fall.

She fretted over having missed his call.

'He'll call back if it's important,' said Fatima.

Ester didn't think so, but held her tongue. Certain things were important in the moment and so you called, only for insight and dread to catch up with you later. Sensory states came and went. You could call on a whim and there was no guarantee that the whim would return. But an entire life could be changed by one phone call made on such a whim at the exact right, or wrong, moment.

Ester wanted to go home to Sankt Göransgatan, be on her own and call Olof, but Fatima made it clear that doing so would be insensible and disloyal. Ester stopped and tried to cool her thoughts. She was convinced that Olof wouldn't call again, just as she'd been convinced for the duration of her romantic life that she had to do all the work for anything to happen.

But with Olof Sten she no longer had to worry, the time of him being out of touch was behind them. Now he kept trying until he reached her. They had their sights on a bar on Österlånggatan and had made it to Järntorget when his ringtone sounded. Ester answered with all the warmth she couldn't manage to dispel, that lingered in her core, as in a volcano. Olof delivered his first harangue. It was like running towards someone and throwing yourself into their arms only to find that their clothes are made of razor blades.

'You told the ensemble that you and I were in a relationship!' he shouted.

'Because you slandered me to them. Of course I'm going to assert my humanity when you attack it. But that was two months ago. Why are you dredging up this ancient history, tonight of all nights?'

'You're spreading lies about us having had a relationship!'

'But we have had a relationship. Why can't you understand that? Are you still trying to convince yourself otherwise?'

'You're a fucking psychopath.'

'And you're out of your fucking mind.'

She hung up and put her phone in her bag. Shakily, she walked with Fatima to the bar they'd decided to go to. Fatima was filled with horror and disbelief. They spent the night talking about what had happened. They parted at one. Ester took the subway home. As the doors shut behind her, a text arrived from Olof. It said, 'Good premiere.'

Ester thought there might actually be something wrong with Olof's brain, that he really did have a screw loose. Maybe he was missing something essential that made him incapable of understanding the inherent trajectory of events and their moral essence. Might there even be a nameable syndrome for people who can't see their role in a course of events? A sense of self so fragile it was inappropriate to talk about personal responsibility, because it presupposed the existence of a person?

Ester typed a reply but felt spent and indifferent. She wrote it out of courtesy and a sort of unflagging consideration:

'Glad to hear you're pleased, but you don't have to work yourself up to contact me. In spite of everything, we can still be civilized.'

Twenty minutes later she was home, brushing her teeth and on her way to bed when the reply came: 'You've destroyed my life. We have nothing to say to each other.'

It registered on the seismograph of her memory, but only in passing. Before she fell asleep she deleted Olof's number and all of his texts from the past three and a half years, the ones that when they'd arrived had been the most precious of pearls.

March went by and then disappeared, the melting snow thudding from the roofs. April arrived with its crisp air and bracing nights. Ester Nilsson felt mute. Sometimes a day would pass without her thinking about Olof, but for the most part she continued to brood over why and how. The analysis had gone on for so long that there were no more pieces to be added to the puzzle and the pieces she had didn't fit together. Upon examination, she found that it had become an automated thought process. She understood what there was to understand, but wouldn't accept that a person could operate that way, there must be an error, one final missing piece.

In April it came to her attention via a number of channels that Olof had decided on a new and more specific version of events. He'd gone beyond total disavowal and was now saying that he'd succumbed to Ester one single time after a long period of manipulative entanglement and clinginess on her part. Using her cunning, she'd poured alcohol down his throat and seduced him. One single time, one measly time, that was all.

This new version was in line with Olof's programme for

dealings between the sexes and their discrete characteristics. His little mistake slipped right in friction-free, fitted into the programme and turned him into a man. Because a man has urges that require his full stoic and rational powers to shut down, and a woman has her age-old ability to trick men into impregnating her while being irrationally unreliable, once was as good as never. Faithful wives accepted the order of things, and could therefore forgive one slip, but not two.

This is how he explained his troubles to those who knew or sensed that the ground beneath his feet had shaken.

For that reason, Olof Sten also called Zoran, the actor who had played his son in *Death of a Salesman* and who he knew was Ester's friend. Olof wanted to tell Zoran what 'really' went on, regardless of what he'd heard from Ester Nilsson who, in case Zoran didn't know, was extremely unstable and not exactly known for her normal or healthy history with men, and was surrounded by embarrassing rumours. Regarding Olof, Ester had made up everything Zoran had heard. She had been living in her twisted dreamworld, always knowing where Olof was performing and where he was touring, and pretended to be there with him. In case Zoran had heard details about specific places, this explained it. Moreover, Ebba and Olof 'were in agreement' that Ester was 'psychotic'.

When Zoran called Ester to apprise her and ask what happened, he sounded shaken and scared. But she also heard that a hint of doubt had crept in and nestled inside him.

At the time, Ester was in Kalmar for a lecture and a reading. When Zoran called, she was out walking but had to find a bench and sit, it got too heavy to breathe. She asked several times: is that what Olof said? Had he called Zoran expressly to tell him this?

What she heard brought with it a special type of inner chill, a chill that would linger like frostbite, a place that could never be warmed again. She hadn't known this about people. Olof having written and said things out of panic and fear just as she'd detonated the bomb in January was more understandable than this elaborate lie he was dishing up months later. This suggested grievous recklessness.

That no calumny was too harsh or no tactic too heinous when it came to saving your own skin and position and to staving off shame stunned Ester.

Before they hung up, she grilled him one last time about the details and the words Olof used to tell his story and how his voice had sounded.

When the shock had subsided she got up from the bench and walked to the centre of town. It was a blustery day and thick dark grey clouds hung over the Öland Bridge where seagulls sailed in the winds and the eiders were flocking north. To avoid the coming rain, she went into an anti-quarian bookseller's on Kaggensgatan right by the hotel. The bell jingled pleasantly whereupon the proprietor, a mid-dle-aged man with an absent-minded, placid countenance, nodded in greeting and went back to his accounts at the far end of the cosy disarray.

Ester spent an hour browsing. It did her well, for ages antiquarian bookshops had been her place of meditation. She paid and went her way with the unabridged edition of *The Count of Monte Cristo*. She hadn't read it since childhood, and then in its abridged form. She looked forward to getting to the hotel and delving in. Hunched against a stubborn rain, she hurried away.

The month of May came and went with its fragrances and ever-surprising beauty, light late at night and pastures in bloom. The lilacs arrived with the splendour of those who know not to hope for tomorrow, but live nonetheless. Ester had trouble sleeping on account of the light.

Midsummer rolled around this year, too. Three days after Midsummer's Eve she was at home working. Soon she would eat lunch and then work a little more, and then take her long walk through the city. To keep sane, she stuck to routines and habits.

Inside, she was a desert devoid of sun – a stinging emptiness where once her feelings for Olof and the venture of their relationship had been. It wasn't unlike when she dedicated herself to orienteering in her youth or to learning how to think and make the world intelligible. The risk of failure had been inherent to each of these ventures.

And once again, Olof called her three days after Midsummer, but in all likelihood, with a different motive. But what was it? Did he want to rekindle the flame inside her?

They hadn't been in touch since the phone call after the theatre premiere in early March. After Zoran's call, Ester had written a brief email to Olof and his wife in which she had strongly urged them to stop spreading nonsense and slander.

Ester was on the landline with Lotta when the call came. She recognized Olof's number and felt afraid. If one goes without water for long enough, a person might even quench their thirst with a poisoned drink, and she didn't trust herself, not even now.

'What should I do?' she gasped, throat tight.

'Answer and see what he wants,' said Lotta.

'Will you stay on the line? I need a witness.'

'I will.'

Her 'hello' was subdued.

'Hi Ester. It's Olof.'

It was the embarrassed, gingerly accommodating Olof on the line, he who believed work needed to be done to compensate for and rebuild what had been destroyed, who knew the account had not only been drained but closed and the bank had gone bankrupt, but who, deep down, knew another account could always be opened.

'Why did you harass Ebba?' he asked with an amicable curiosity that belied the question's content.

'What?'

'Hurting Ebba in this way . . .'

Ester waited for an explanation for his call and the introduction.

'Writing to tell her that we were in a relationship and all

the rest. During the winter. And then again a month or so ago.'

As so often before, his statements were mostly noise, what he was saying was obviously not the content of the words, and by the softness in his voice Ester could tell that he was not averse to beginning anew, in the same way, an endless *danse macabre*, the whole performance again from the top in a senseless encore, where she'd beg and he'd pretend to resist.

From the conversation, it could also be discerned that the awfulness from the past winter, the blow to his marriage, had registered but hadn't been incorporated into his psyche and being. It was more like reading a bulletin about a natural disaster; you're moved but only for a moment, and after a while you have to actively think about it in order to feel anything at all.

Or perhaps it would be more correct to say that Olof seemed to have been touched by his own disaster like a character in a play is moved by the text's calamities and forgets them as soon as the curtain drops?

'Was there something you wanted to tell me or was it just this old chestnut?'

'Ebba was really sad.'

Ester noticed her stale, aching breaths, noticed them flowing in and out, in and out before taking a deep breath. Remembering that Lotta was listening, she readied herself and said:

'Why do you keep calling me?'

She could sense the stunned pause that he hadn't managed to stifle with blitheness.

'To ask you to stop harassing my wife.'

'No, that's not why you're calling and you know it, like you know that I've never harassed your wife. And you should really think hard, not least for your beloved wife's sake, about why you keep calling me, what it is that you can't be without, what fire inside you refuses to die and why. And think about who destroyed whose life over the past years. Then do as I do, put us behind you and stop contacting me. Stop contacting me!'

Yet another silence followed, this time not stunned but full of shame for being found out. Ester sensed how it was rolling through him in sticky swells, wave after wave. For the last time, she felt his mind as clearly as if it were her own. What was moving through him wasn't performed; it was authentic. The curtain had fallen on his play.

Olof Sten hung up without a word.

Epilogue

Two years passed in Ester Nilsson's life. Her ravaged trust hadn't healed. There were certain words and sentences she couldn't bear to hear, and she had averted her gaze and walked the other way the few times she felt a flutter in her chest. Hers was an existence of active renunciation and forced asceticism. It was like a dead person's ECG. She would eventually invite intoxication and play into her life again, but it was still too soon.

She continued decoding existence, the existence she so long ago had decided to understand, but it went more slowly now that she wasn't spurred on by love's narcotic enthusiasm. With each passing week, she understood a little more of some intellectual problem that needed to be clarified. She had placed the Olof Sten conundrum in the file that contained the Hugo Rask conundrum, a special archive for unsolved puzzles.

She sold the car. She published a suite of demi-sec verses entitled *Mistress Elegies 1–49 and The Duties of Marriage 50–99*, which were received by the public with certain interest.

One afternoon in late summer, Ester was reading on the Mosebacke terrace when, out of the corner of her eye, she thought she recognized someone approaching in the distance. It was how he held his large head, jutting slightly forward, the defined, heavy face and short neck that made her remember him, but not where she'd met him, as well as the baggy clothing covering his unshapely body. Altogether it made the man's contours indistinct. With increasingly assured steps, he strode towards Ester's table and when he reached her, she remembered who he was. It was that friend of Olof's who'd sat with them at the premiere party that March evening when Olof and she had resumed their carnal encounters, the year before everything crashed. Göran Berggren. The scenographer without a project. Ester hadn't forgotten the knowing look he'd given Olof, a congenital gaze that said one was not enough but the result of being too greedy was zero – and such solitude was an abyss. 'Handle it with care,' the look had said. 'Whatever you're doing, handle it with care.'

Göran Berggren asked Ester if she remembered him.

'The scenographer,' she said and offered her hand in greeting.

'May I sit?' he asked and sat down without waiting for her reply. 'So here you are, reading.'

She put her book down. Admonition quivered in those words.

'Must be nice.'

Ester waited. What he wanted to say was deep inside him, but one thing was clear, he wasn't here to make small talk.

'Olof isn't having a good time.'

Ester held his gaze until he looked away.

'He's not doing particularly well.'

Göran Berggren seemed to want Ester to fill in the blanks and spill, but against all habits, she managed to quietly await the continuation.

'The last time I ran into him, it was at the off-licence. He'd started buying box wine.'

'Maybe he wanted to put the wine in a lovely meat stew on a Friday night surrounded by good friends,' said Ester.

She remembered one such dinner that he and Ebba had around St Lucy's Day, when he'd bought beef over the counter in Söderhallarna and had seemed giddy with the joy of being twice desired and burdened by none.

'It's not looking like there'll be any lovely stews over at theirs,' said Göran Berggren.

'Ah.'

'Surely you understand what it's like for them now.'

As is the way with insinuation, his half-lyrical, aggressive confidences couldn't be countered with questions or clarifications, so Ester held her tongue. Göran Berggren made himself comfortable and picked up the book she had been reading as if it was public property, eyed the jacket copy, put it on the table, whereupon Ester put it in her bag.

Then Göran Berggren said that Olof had looked him up a while ago. He'd wanted to confide in someone about him and Ebba and about how Ester Nilsson pursued him and the harm it had caused him, how deeply he regretted giving in to her that one single time.

Mosebacke was full of people milling about, a number of them tourists from far away admiring the view. Ester rested her eyes on them.

'Did you believe him?' she asked. 'You, who saw us together.'

Göran Berggren's eyes darted, and he shrugged.

'He has his reasons. What is he supposed to say? But something else Olof said was even stranger, and that's what I wanted to ask you about, with your writing on the human psyche and all, granted it's way over most people's heads, but still.'

'What did he say?'

'He talked about his relationship with Ebba; he said he'd realized it was like two ... well, accounts. Two accounts. Did he ever say that to you? And Ebba had learned to control him and their marriage using these accounts, because somehow she always knew her balance and credit down to the last öre. She always kept him short, he said, and never shelled out unless she had to, to keep from losing him or going into the red.'

'He said that?'

Göran nodded and observed Ester as if he were conducting research.

'He used the words "balance" and "credit". I reacted to it because those are such sad words to use when describing a relationship, but so typical for our time. Not even love can escape money nowadays.'

Ester looked out at the water. The waves continued their carefree clucking. It was getting too cold to be sitting outside.

'And between the two of them there was constant balancing. When Olof wanted to come close, Ebba pushed him away and when he pulled back, "sad and crushed by her hardness" as he said, then she met him halfway, was thoughtful, intimate. Each time it happened he thought it was permanent, but nothing ever changed at the core, they were always balancing on edge, because that's the only way she could live, swinging between two extremes, that's how she gained her power and her lust for life, and all Olof wanted was to be standing on solid ground.'

Ester hoped the prickling in her skin wasn't visible. To be sure, she put her hands to her cheeks.

'He said it was like trying to catch his own shadow. When he took a step forward the shadow stepped back and when he stepped back, it followed. Only after being together for years did he notice this, and then it was too late. I've never heard Olof talk or think like that before. Do you recognize this about him?'

She noted that Göran Berggren was assuming that she and Olof had been extremely close and knew each other well.

'And when you betrayed Olof and did what you did . . . well you can imagine what it's been like for him since. After this, Ebba will never have an empty account again. It's filled to the brim for ever. She can treat him any which way she likes, ask anything of him. It goes without saying that Olof can never fill up his own account. Anything he amasses goes straight to her.'

When Ester finally spoke, her voice was raspy and she had to clear her throat.

'But that's when Olof feels best,' she said, 'when the lead is short and he gets clear commands, inside and out. It's to his advantage when he lacks means. Olof can't handle assets, they make him cruel and he wants the world to remove his potential for cruelty, because he doesn't like how he enjoys it. So it probably did him good to have his account emptied for ever and to lose his tiny window of freedom and space with Ebba. I'd even say that's what he was after. He used the people available to achieve it. Using his agency to force castigation, to do away with everything and become a slave, never again having to make a decision using his own judgement or feeling. Nothing frightened him as much as his abuse of freedom. Thank you, Göran. You've helped me find the last piece of the puzzle.'

Göran Berggren gave Ester Nilsson a curious look; it appeared that he found her exposition as unseemly as the growing relief with which it was expressed. He said:

'I'll have you know, Olof and Ebba have never got over what you did. Her using it against him is human. Her hardness is just paralysed despair. You knowingly introduced a poison to their relationship that will never stop seeping.

LENA ANDERSSON

Olof isn't one to complain, but everyone can see he's been a wreck since then.'

'What I did? What are you thinking about exactly?'

'You ruined their marriage. That just isn't done, meddling in people's lives. You don't do that. Sending messages and whatnot. What people don't know can't hurt them.'

Göran Berggren stood up, nodded, and went his way.

The sun was sharp, the light harsh. Ester Nilsson was left alone.